SHOT THROUGH
THE HEART

IRON VALLEY SERIES

TAMARA GIRARDI

 WISE WOLF BOOKS LAS VEGAS

WISE WOLF
BOOKS

This is a work of fiction. All of the characters, organizations, publications, and events portrayed in this novel are either products of the author's imagination or are used fictitiously.

For information, address Wolfpack Publishing,
9850 S. Maryland Parkway, Suite A-5 #323, Las Vegas, Nevada 89183

wisewolfbooks.com

Cover design by Wise Wolf Books

ISBN 978-1-953944-34-4 (paperback)
978-1-953944-35-1 (hardcover)
978-1-953944-33-7 (ebook)
LCCN: 2022948205

PRAISE FOR GRIDIRON GIRL

"A fast-paced, character-driven novel about a girl going her own way." — *Kirkus Reviews*

"*Gridiron Girl* is an engaging story about an elite athlete and her journey to step away from her role as the captain of a state bound volleyball team to pursue her true passion and earn the spot as the football team's starting quarterback. Julia's timely story of sports, family, determination, and romance will inspire readers to stay true to themselves, especially those who have ever considered redefining themselves."
—Kimberly Gabriel, award-winning author of *Every Stolen Breath*

"*Gridiron Girl* is an uplifting read packed with tons of girl power, delightful banter, and a whole lot of heart! I can't get enough of Julia's strength and her take-no-prisoners attitude! Definitely a must read!"
—Molly E. Lee, author of *Ember of Night*

"Inspiring and entertaining, Tamara Girardi's *Gridiron Girl* expertly balances sporty-action, depth, and humor as she speeds us through the challenges and rewards of a teen who rises above expectations to accomplish a dream."
—Nova McBee, author of the *Calculated series*

"*Gridiron Girl* is the book my football-obsessed heart has been craving. Give me a girl who knows how to go after her dreams even when the world is set against her, mix that with all of the epic sports-movie feels while also showing young women that they can do anything they set their mind to, and top it all off with phenomenal writing and edge-of-your-seat action, and you've got a story destined to become a young adult classic. Every teen girl needs to read this book."
—Chelsea Bobulski, author of the *All I Want for Christmas* series

"*Gridiron Girl* lives and breathes football with the same intensity as its star athlete. A compelling book about drive and bravery and believing in yourself."

—Stephanie J. Scott, author of *All Last Summer*

"Julia's got as much grit as she has heart, both of which she'll need to navigate obstacles on and off the field. A well-written debut novel. Tamara Girardi is a literary talent to watch."

—Tina Ferraro, author of *Top Ten Uses for an Unworn Prom Dress, How to Hook a Hottie,* and *The ABC's of Kissing Boys*

"*Gridiron Girl* delivers on so many levels, and features a fierce, clear-eyed heroine who isn't afraid to fight for what she wants, both on the field and off. I loved it!"

—Kes Trester, author of *A Dangerous Year*

"Girardi has crafted an uplifting, powerful story about a girl who refuses to give up!"

—Simone Elkeles, NY Times bestselling author of *Perfect Chemistry*

SHOT THROUGH THE HEART

IRON VALLEY SERIES

To my grandparents —
the late Anne and Clarence Farneth,
who adopted me when I was lost in a cloud of grief.

CHAPTER 1

WHEN JOSH BRIGHTON'S FINGERTIPS INTERTWINED
with mine and spun me down the sidewalk for our regular Friday
night date, his smile didn't look quite whole.

"Everything okay?"

He kissed the back of my hand. "Definitely."

"Where are we going?" I asked, burying my suspicion.

He opened the passenger door. "It's a surprise."

With prom a few months away, I only wanted one surprise. I
checked my hair and makeup in the visor mirror while he drove, so
I'd be ready for the cameras that would film his inevitable promposal.

"I hope you don't mind getting your clothes a little dirty," he said
with a sideways grin.

I loved that grin. The way the edges of his short, curly brown hair
poked out from under his hat. His dark brown eyes and the muscles
in his shoulders from hours of lifting at the field house. The way he
moved on the football field, catching passes as one of Iron Valley's
top receivers.

And him.

I loved him.

My friends' boyfriends had already asked them to prom. Even my
younger sister, Melanie, a sophomore who'd started the year wanting

nothing more than to hide away in her bedroom or play volleyball in our backyard had a prom date. Josh and I had been together for almost a year. It was expected he would ask me, but every day that passed made me question if there was something going on between us I didn't know about.

Josh swerved off the road into a parking lot.

I grabbed the handle above the passenger window to steady myself. "What are you doing?"

He shifted the car to park and leaned across the console. "This." His lips brushed mine. His kiss was soft, but his lips were confident. I wrapped my arms around his neck and shifted my body closer to him. Our kiss deepened as we pulled at each other—my fingers in his hair, his hand gripping my hip. A horn blared from the road, and we jumped apart, laughing.

"What was that for?" I asked.

"Sometimes, you have to do things because you want to. Is that okay?"

"Definitely." I kissed his cheek because I wanted to. When nobody jumped out from behind the bushes with posters, my hopes for the epic moment deflated, and Josh merged back into traffic.

"I got my roommate request form today," I said, trying to brighten my own mood. Josh and I had both planned to attend Mon Valley College in the fall. The campus was an hour away from our hometown, Iron Valley. He'd play receiver on their football team, and I'd compete in their new archery program. "Did you fill out yours yet?"

"No."

"It feels so high pressure," I said. "If I say I like to go to bed early, are they going to give me someone who never goes out at all? Or if I like to have fun, will I get a roommate who isn't serious about school?"

"Be as honest as you can," Josh suggested.

"I wish Kate was going there." My best friend had decided to spread her wings and go to school in New York City. At least it would be a cool place to visit. I chattered about school while Josh interjected his thoughts here and there until he parked in the gravel lot of Pittsburgh's largest indoor paintball course.

"Paintball?" I asked, totally not believing it. Two competitive souls like ours had maintained our relationship with a single rule—no competition. I'd shot compound bow for years, dabbling in a little crossbow and recurve bow shooting, too. When it came to catching, Josh had me beat, but shooting? I destroyed him every time.

The last time we'd gone paintballing, I'd left with my clothes and gear nearly spotless. Josh had looked like a spin art project gone wrong.

"Your gear's in the trunk," Josh explained. "Melanie may have helped me out with that."

Sneaky little sister.

"Are we playing on a team or against each other?"

He groaned. "Against each other."

"You're serious?"

"I'm giving you a night to remember."

I snorted. He was pulling out all the stops for the big ask. "You know I'm going to crush you."

"I'm willing to take that chance." He pointed to the entrance of the repurposed factory where his two younger siblings stood with his mom, all shivering in the winter chill. "I brought backup."

"What is this? Boys versus girls?"

"No." He grinned. "It's the Brighton family versus you."

"What!"

He laughed and climbed out of the car, but he wasn't joking. His brother, a sophomore named Mason, and his eleven-year-old sister, Alexis, suited up to serve as his backup, while I readied myself to take them all down.

"I don't want to shoot your little sister," I argued.

"But you're fine shooting me?" Mason said, tightening his chest protector.

"Eh." I nudged his hip with my own.

Mason did his best to glare at me. "Ruthless."

"You have no idea," Josh warned his little brother. "Don't turn your back. And if you think you're far enough away from her to be safe, think again."

I smiled sweetly at him. "Thanks for the compliment."

Team Brighton entered the shooting zone through the east-facing portal, while I headed west. We'd meet back up in the course in a few minutes. Probably with me devouring them until I ran out of paintballs.

Actually…I ran back inside the lobby. "Are there any rules on the number of balls you can take into the course?" I asked the guy at the counter.

"Nope."

"Excellent. Can I get another bag? You can put them on my boyfriend's tab."

He passed them to me, and I hooked them onto my belt. Josh Brighton was so dead.

The shooting zone was what most would expect from an old factory. Wide open. Dated. Metal stairs here and there turned into outlooks. Cushioned obstacles and wooden panels for taking cover. And of course, bright colored splatters of painted against the otherwise grey walls and ceilings.

The first Brighton I found amidst the obstacles was Alexis. She'd found a good spot with a wall to her back and a seven-foot, triangular cushion for cover in front of her. I couldn't bring myself to shoot her. Not to mention, taking a shot would mean giving up my position, leaving me vulnerable to Mason and Josh. Instead, I climbed the stairs to a crow's nest that would ensure my victory. Toe by toe. Back to the wall. Not making a sound.

Lucky for me because Mason was already perched in the nest, looking down at the course with no idea I was behind him.

Too easy.

I aimed for his thigh, hoping the shot wouldn't hurt too badly, but when the bright yellow ball splattered against his camo, he still yelped and grabbed his leg.

"C'mon, Elle. Point blank range?"

"Sorry. Couldn't exactly go back down the stairs without taking you out."

He pressed the safety on his gun, slipped the barrel cover on, and raised his arm, signaling he'd been hit. "My brother's in The Tower. Make him pay for dragging me out here."

"Done," I said with a smile.

My turn to perch in the nest, I slid a triangular mat behind me to protect my back from the same fate Mason had faced. Careful not to reveal myself, I watched the elevated lookout across the field affectionately known as The Tower. It was a circular stand, elevated above the field. When a player was inside, they had complete protection from all angles, unless they poked their heads out for a better view of the field. Opponents could charge The Tower, but at a significant loss. I had no intention of charging. I'd wait for Josh to demonstrate his impatience. After a few seconds, slight movement from the left of it caught my attention. I counted. Twenty seconds later, Josh tipped his head to the side to search for me. I counted again. About 18 seconds later, his mask reappeared. I aimed, taking the distance into consideration. Slightly above him should be perfect. When his face disappeared, I counted again.

One, two, three…eighteen…nineteen…twenty. Fire!

Josh peeked at the exact moment the paintballs flew his way, splattering on his face mask. Mason cheered from the staging area.

"Elle!" Josh shouted. "My face! Seriously?"

"It was the only part of your body exposed." I stood, obnoxiously waving as he left the course and felt a thump against my side. A splatter of pink paint covered the camouflage of my jacket. Alexis cheered from the ground below. She'd moved to a new position that had given her a good shot at me, and without me noticing.

"Alexis!" I shouted. "Good girl!"

She victory-danced while her brothers lifted her onto their shoulders. We reset, and the game went on until all of our paintballs were gone, and we'd left our marks of fresh splatter on the course and our gear. Alexis had bested me a few times, mostly because I didn't have the heart to take her out first, but Josh had never gotten the better of me.

Throughout the game, I expected he'd pop the question with a series of paintball shots to the wall to spell it out. Nope. Maybe I was off, and he didn't plan to ask me at all. But if not, why?

***

ALEXIS AND MASON TEASED JOSH THE WHOLE WAY back to his house. When we pulled in the driveway, I unbuckled to go inside, but Josh stopped me.

"Let's go grab something to eat. I'll walk them in and tell my mom, okay?"

"Sure," I said, settling back into the seat.

While they were gone, I scrolled through all the social media apps on my phone, but closed them after two reels of promposals popped up. I shook my head. This was ridiculous. Why was I waiting for him to ask me anyway? I took to the internet and searched promposal ideas. Before the weekend was out, if he didn't ask me, I'd do the asking. I grinned at the thought of taking control of the situation.

Josh's phone buzzed in the console. After a minute, he still hadn't come back, and it buzzed again. The screen read a text from his best friend, Neil.

Neil: You home? I want to swing by and say goodbye.

Still no sight of Josh, I headed for the house, bringing his phone with me. Maybe he'd forgotten Neil was leaving and would want to stay home after all and hang with him. That would give me time to plan the perfect promposal. I slipped through the screen door and heard Josh assure Mrs. Brighton in the entry hall he was fine, and he'd be back in an hour tops.

The door slammed behind me, and they both turned.

"Hey," I said, lifting his phone. "Neil messaged you about coming to say goodbye. Hi, Mrs. Brighton."

Mrs. Brighton pressed her hand against the frayed neckline of her old t-shirt. "I'm so glad you finally told her, Joshua."

In that second, my world came into focus. The look of terror on Josh's face. His mother's gasp when she'd realized her mistake—that her son hadn't told me anything. And the boxes. All of the boxes. In the living room, the dining room, the kitchen. Even the landing at the top of the stairs.

"Josh?"

"I'll leave you two alone," his mom said.

"Let's go outside and talk." Josh took my hand and walked the stiff robot that had commandeered my body back outside.

"Are you...moving?"

"I didn't want you to find out like this."

He'd asked me to stay in the car. On purpose.

An unstoppable heat spread through my core. "Did you want me to find out at all?"

He ran his fingers through his hair, his silence answering my question.

"Is this because your father lost his job? You don't have to be embarrassed about wherever you're moving. I don't care about any of that."

"I know."

If he knew that, then what? "Tell me the truth."

He took a deep breath. "My uncle has some work for my dad, so we have to move there."

My head told my mouth not to ask, but whether I vocalized the question or not, the answer wouldn't change. "Where exactly?"

"Philadelphia."

My breath caught in my throat.

"Elle, I'm sorry."

I brushed his arm away, and let the word Philadelphia play in my mind until I couldn't stand the thought of the city and its Liberty Bell. Or its Rocky steps. I had no brotherly love for the place that was taking Josh five hours away from me.

"When," I croaked.

Josh lowered his head. "Tomorrow."

"What?" The word escaped my lips like a shocked gasp.

"I wanted to tell you so many times, but I couldn't. It happened fast. It hasn't been long."

"Long enough to pack every belonging in your house."

"Technically not everything. My parents aren't listing the house yet. We're…"

I glared at him.

"Not the point. Sorry. I don't know what to say."

Right. Because there weren't any words in the English language—in any language—that could rationalize the fact he was moving to the other side of the state in fewer than twenty-four hours and still hadn't told his girlfriend.

"That's what tonight was? Giving me a night to remember as some grand goodbye?"

He squeezed my hands, and even through my numbness at hearing the news he would be leaving, sparks and tingles managed to wake up every part of my body. I bit my lip to keep from crying.

"Goodbye is too final," Josh said. "I'll live there for a few months. We'll talk all the time, and I'll be back for prom and graduation. We'll see each other. And then we'll graduate and go to Mon Valley together like we planned. Our lives will still be everything we want them to be, Elle."

Not seeing him in school every day. Not being able to touch him or kiss him. That didn't sound like the life I'd wanted. But we were talking about a few months. We could make it work. Josh and I had both dated other people in high school, enough to know that together, we were better. He pushed me to train for archery on the days I didn't want to. I encouraged him to get in the weight room for football. We loved each other's families, spending lazy weekend afternoons picnicking in the park, playing volleyball with my athletic sister, Melanie, and looking at the stars with my scientist sister, Lily. If it weren't for his insistence, I'd be leaving for college in a few months not nearly as close with my sisters as I was now.

We'd studied together. We'd laughed together.

We'd done everything together.

"Do you promise?" I asked.

My mistake was dismissing the twitch on Josh's face before he swallowed and said, "I promise."

CHAPTER 2

FOUR MONTHS LATER

THE LATE SPRING SUNSHINE ROASTED THE ROW OF AR-chers crowding the field. Fresh off my shift assisting with archery lessons for beginners, I squeezed into a middle spot and took my stance, perpendicular to the range targets. After hours of lessons and given what was on the schedule for the evening, my fingers itched to shoot. Sliding an arrow from my quiver, I rested it on my bow and gently pushed with my left hand. With every simple act of shooting—drawing the bow, positioning the string against my nose and the kisser button at the corner of my mouth, lining up the peep through my sight, and finally releasing the arrow—the disappointment of the day dissolved.

To dissolve a massive amount of disappointment, you needed a massive amount of shooting.

Archery was a sport of repetition. I could trust the motions. The same stance, the same draw, the same anchor points, the same alignment on the sights, the same release. To compete, you kept it simple. You practiced repeating the same moves. Over and over.

Life was not that simple or that easy to control.

I shot as the sun faded behind clouds that threatened rain. I shot as the other shooters cleared the range. I shot when I was the only archer, standing amidst the quiet of the grass and the trees, alone with my thoughts and my memories.

Josh's laugh. The way he'd played volleyball in the yard with my sister, Melanie, while I'd finish getting ready for our dates. The awe on his face when he'd watched my shooting competitions. His intensity when I'd taught him to shoot at this very club, on the indoor range. A smile crossed my lips at that memory.

"So you just pull back the string and fire, right?" he'd said.

"Not even close."

"What then?"

"First, we need to know if you're right or left eye dominant." I'd tested him, and thankfully, he was a right-handed shooter. Easier teaching that way.

"You want to nock the arrow on the string until you hear a click. Then, rest the arrow here with the different colored fletching pointing upward."

He'd squinted at the arrow's fletchings. "They're all green."

"Yes, but one of them has a stripe. See that?"

He'd looked closer. "Got it."

And on it went. His first shot had hit the corner of the target. I'd have been furious with a shot like that, but he'd shouted and kissed me. Deeply.

"Are we really alone here?" he'd whispered, running his fingers along the bare skin of my arms and making my body tingle every-where else.

"We are, but we're here to shoot. And you should not make out while shooting. It could be dangerous."

Josh had rested the bow on a hook. "Better?"

I'd pinched my lip between my teeth and nodded. Staying focused when Josh looked at me like that had challenged me more than an outdoor championship with 3D targets the same color as the trees in the background.

"Safety is the top priority in archery. You can never be too careful."

"I'm all about safety," he'd teased.

I suppressed the memory and brought my thoughts back to the present. On the outdoor range of my archery club, all alone, I raised my bow for another shot, ignoring the miles between Josh and me and the pressure building in my chest, like it had every time I thought of him.

When I released the arrow and it hit the inner gold ring, earning me a hypothetical ten points, someone clapped from behind me.

"Well-done, Miss Elle," said JoAnn, an impressive shooter in her own right. She'd taught me when I was a kid and had kept her eye on me ever since, even bringing me on as an assistant in her shooting lessons, so I could earn the extra cash I needed to plan a visit to Philadelphia and pay for new shooting equipment and textbooks in the fall.

"Thanks. Training for the local summer circuit."

"You can win a lot of money on those regional competitions."

"I'm banking on it," I said.

"You competing this weekend?"

"Yep, and I better crush it. The registration fee was a hundred bucks, and Captain Archery will be there looking for new shooters to sponsor. One of them will be me."

"This all sounds great, Elle," she said, tucking her short, gray hair behind her ear. "But isn't today the prom?"

I pulled another arrow from my quiver, nocked it, and aimed. Another ten. "Yep."

"And you're not going?"

"I am. Eventually."

"How does your date feel about you being late?"

My date, Neil—Josh's best friend who'd taken me out of pity when Josh had broken his promise and couldn't return for prom after all. "He'll be fine."

"Elle," she admonished. "You don't really believe that."

"I'm a pity date."

"A girl who looks like you is never anyone's pity date."

My next shot scored an eight. JoAnn crossed her arms, her disapproval lingering in the humid air. I hit a seven.

"Fine. I'll go."

"Not on my account, surely."

I rolled my eyes at her. She'd known exactly what she'd been doing.

"There's something else, Elle."

"Okay," I said, clued in to her ominous tone.

"Most of my families have paused their lessons for the next few weeks. Graduations, vacations—everyone is too busy. I don't think I'll need you to assist until at least July."

July? That was more than six weeks away.

"JoAnn, I need to work."

"I know. That's why I'm telling you this before all the good summer jobs are scooped up. You'll find something."

"Not something that keeps me on the range." The lessons didn't pay much, but assisting with them meant I spent my days at the archery club, prepping for competitions that could earn me cash. I wanted to be shooting, not clearing tables of dirty dishes, taking drive-through orders, or stocking shelves.

"There will be time for you to shoot around your work schedule."

A work schedule could prevent me from visiting Josh in Philadelphia when school ended. I did not want a work schedule.

"It will work out," JoAnn assured me. I'd learned not to trust assurances that relied on things beyond my control.

I retrieved my arrows and packed up while my phone buzzed for, I don't know, the twentieth time. I dug it from my pocket to find a stack of notifications from my best friend, Kate. They amounted to: where are you, when are you coming, they're not going to hold your appointment, to all caps: ELLE CORWIN!

I'd missed my hair and makeup appointment. Technically, I'd told Kate to cancel it since I didn't want to spend the money on someone else doing my hair, nails and makeup for a dance I didn't even want to attend. My phone buzzed again.

Josh: You all ready for the big dance?

An unexpected breeze blew across the range. I pressed the phone to my chest, closed my eyes, and let the air rush around me. Josh was on the other end of the connection. I envied the wind, how it could travel across the state, brushing through my world and then Josh's. The phone buzzed again, reminding me of Josh's text. Not that I could forget.

Me: I'll be home soon. Video call so you can see for yourself?

***

MY PHYSICAL APPEARANCE WHEN I PLOWED INTO MY kitchen after hours of shooting could easily be summed up in my youngest sister, Lily's reaction: she dropped her pencil into her Pre-Algebra book and her bottom lip to the floor. "You look tragic."

"Melanie's already dressed," my mom said with wide eyes. "Oh, Elle. You have to go to prom."

"I'm going," I said. "I need a minute."

"She needs more than a minute," Lily muttered. "She needs a beauty team from one of those makeover shows."

Nice, Lil.

I met Melanie, and her bestie, Chandra, on the stairs. They took in my cargo shorts, tank top, ponytail, and sunburned shoulders while I shielded my view from the millions of sparkles on their dresses. Looking into Melanie's eyes felt like a tilt of the planet. At the beginning of the year, I'd insisted she lose her athletic clothes and dress for parties and dates with style and flair. I'd taught her how to straighten her hair and extend her repertoire beyond a ponytail.

By the looks of the elegant stunner in front of me, I'd obviously excelled at it.

"Get upstairs," Melanie demanded.

"Josh is going to call."

"Until he does, we're getting you ready." She pinched her nose. "After you shower."

"Hey. It's hot out there. I was soaked with sweat."

"I believe it," Chandra said.

"Josh—"

"I'll take your phone and chat with him until you get out. If you hurry, you can be done in two minutes," Melanie said.

"And if we all move our butts," Chandra added, "you can show him what he's missing by being dressed, styled, and hot. Not..." She studied me from head to toe. "This."

"Fine," I grumbled.

Seconds later in the bathroom, I stepped under the stream before the heat from the water tank had made its way to the shower head. I rushed through my routine and slammed the water off.

I dried and dressed in shorts and a tank. Brushed my hair. Smoothed lotion on my skin while Melanie and Chandra each pointed hair dryers at my head.

"Why isn't he calling?"

"Stay still," Chandra warned. "You don't want to suck your long locks in the back end of the hairdryer."

I watched my phone while the girls styled my hair and applied my makeup. "Thanks for helping me."

Melanie squeezed my hand. I urged my lips into an awkward smile my sister wouldn't buy. She'd seen Josh and me together. She'd loved him, too. She'd kept a sisterly eye on me every day since his family had moved.

Now, she watched me dress for a prom he wouldn't attend. Despite his promise, a month earlier he'd called to say it wasn't going to happen. He had to work to save up for college. Out of pity, Josh's best friend Neil had asked me to be his date.

At least we still had Mon Valley on the horizon. We'd be back in the same zip code in a couple short months.

My mom's choked voice brought me back to the disappointing moment. "You look so..." She tried not to cry.

And failed.

"We'll be downstairs," Melanie said, she and Chandra fluttering away in a cloud of sparkle.

Between gaspy sobs, Mom managed, "I have something for you." She draped a diamond bracelet over my wrist and fumbled with the clasp.

"Mom! You wore this at your wedding. I can't..."

"You can. I know it's tough for you without Josh, but I want you to have fun tonight. Prom is something you'll always remember." She squeezed my hands in hers, and I let my mother's touch work its magic like it had in elementary school when someone had called me a stupid head or ate the last of my favorite sprinkle cookies at lunch. Problems that had seemed so huge at the time, but now felt so small.

I wasn't sure living life without Josh would ever feel small. Good thing we'd be on the same college campus in a few short months. Then we could share all the breezes we wanted.

"Tomorrow, we'll figure out tomorrow. Okay?"

The hope in my mom's smile nudged the word from my mouth, "Okay."

My phone rang downstairs, but before I could rush for it, my mom grabbed me by the shoulders.

"Elle, it's not a crime to make a man wait. Take a deep breath." I inhaled and held for the motherly advice that always followed that command. "You are a beautiful young woman. He's lucky to be in your life. Don't forget that."

"Thanks, Mom."

Her eyes glistened as she jerked her head toward the door. I grabbed my silver purse and heels on the way out, thudded down the stairs, rather unladylike, and sprinted to Melanie. "Do you have my phone?"

She reached into her bag. "Yeah. Sorry."

I tapped the screen. I had a missed call and follow-up text from Kate, telling me she'd be here in a minute.

"Elle!" Lily shouted. "Josh texted me."

Everyone in the room froze.

"Josh texted you?" Melanie asked.

"Why?" Chandra added.

"He wanted to know if Elle got his letter."

I glanced sideways at Melanie and Chandra. "I checked the mailbox today. It was empty. Did anyone else bring it in?"

The front door slammed. Chandra stood in front of it with an Express Mail package in her hands.

"I don't know why he didn't send an email," Lily said. "That must have cost fifteen bucks."

Josh had always said sending letters the old-fashioned way was romantic. We'd sent letters and cards since he moved. Lots of them. Despite talking every day, there was something about opening the mailbox and finding an envelope with my name in his handwriting. The anticipation of opening it, and being able to treasure what I found inside—usually a personal note and some quote or song lyric that made him think of me—utter perfection. The letters didn't detail the monotony of our lives. We shared that in real time. Instead, they became a treasure trove that connected us across the distance we had to face. I flipped the cardboard envelope over and over in my hands. Same handwriting. Same names. Yet different somehow.

"You should open it," Melanie said.

Kate's voice in the front yard told me I didn't have the time. She'd arrived with her date, my date, and the limo, but I couldn't go to prom without reading Josh's letter.

"I need a minute."

"We'll stall them," Chandra said. Melanie nodded, and they headed outside.

I turned over the package in my hands. Only one way to find out what was in it.

CHAPTER 3

I CLOSED THE DOOR TO THE COMPUTER ROOM AND ripped open the package to find a small, letter-sized envelope. Josh's familiar handwriting was sloppier than usual.

Dear Elle,

I can't believe it's time for prom already. I'm sorry I can't be there with you, more than you realize. It's crazy being so far away from the friends I've known since Kindergarten, but sometimes things don't work out like you planned.

I couldn't bear to have this conversation over the phone, or worse, video. And you deserved better than an email or a text. I made sure this letter was delivered to you today, not to upset you before prom, but to give you an opportunity to start fresh tonight without an attachment to me.

I can't explain it. I want you to know that I'll always care about you, but there comes a time when you have to end everything, even if it's good. So that's what I'm, doing. I'm, ending our relationship. It's time for me to start fresh here and for you to do the same there. I know this summer will

be a great one for you before you head off to college. You'll
be the most gorgeous girl on campus. The smartest, too.
    Take care,
    Josh

Take care? I read the letter again, baffled. Take care? After nearly a year—A YEAR!—of dating, that was his way to say goodbye to me?

He wanted to be here with me, but he broke up with me.

In a letter.

A letter!

It was time to start fresh without any connection whatsoever, but I was going to be the most gorgeous girl on campus?

I read it again. An uncomfortable lump formed in my throat. There was one way to get rid of it.

"No." I tried to swallow and commanded my phone to call Josh. My muscles relaxed when it rang, but after two chimes, it went to voicemail. I called again, and it went straight to voicemail.

Did he block me? I pressed my fingertips into my temples.

In our last conversation, had he been too quiet? No. But he'd sounded tired. What could have happened? What had I done wrong? We'd laughed and flirted and talked about how awesome it would be if he were here for prom.

How could he do this?

"Elle? Where are you?" Kate called from the kitchen. I hid the letter in a pile of my mom's papers. The room moved, a surprise to me considering I stood still.

"Elle, are you okay?" Kate asked.

"Fine," I mumbled. My legs succumbed to the pressure, and the hardwood came closer. Before I landed, Neil scooped me into his arms with ease.

"Okay, let's sit you down," he said as he carried me to the couch.

"Elle? Oh. My. God," Kate said.

"Have you eaten anything today?" Neil asked.

I'd been out in the heat, shooting all afternoon. I drank some water, but not a lot. I shook my head.

"I'll grab you something, and you'll be fine." Neil left the room, on a mission. He had an objective, a usefulness. A plan. I'd had a plan, too. Prom with Josh. College with Josh. Life with Josh—all of it dissolved by a letter.

"That was so romantic," Kate said, drawing out a sigh. "The way he scooped you right out of the air! If it wasn't for Josh…" But I didn't hear the rest. The lump in my throat won, and my makeup ran down my face with the tears.

"You have to stop. You're melting!" Kate shoved a Kleenex in my face, but it was too late. The gates had opened, and I had no choice but to wait for the pressure to subside.

***

PROM PASSED IN A BLUR OF BLARING MUSIC, FLASHing lights, and pretending to be in the moment of joy and elation everyone else in the room seemed to be immersed in until four o'clock in the morning. After sleeping the next day away, I woke up Saturday afternoon, still exhausted. I opened my eyes to a tiara on the nightstand. I'd been voted Prom Queen. Square Weaver had been voted King—hilarious considering he'd dated my sister, Melanie, at the beginning of the year. He'd made some self-deprecating jokes while we'd spun around the floor in our royal dance, forcing me to break a smile.

And then I'd remembered the letter, and my smile had faded.

I wanted to hate myself for letting Josh's decision control my emotions. I didn't want to be that girl. No guy had ever had enough of my heart to crush it, not until Josh. I urged myself to be that strong, independent girl who didn't let a guy ruin her prom.

My mom always said, "Sometimes being strong is admitting when you're an absolute wreck." I guess that never really made sense until now.

"Incoming, your highness," Melanie said and pushed her way through my bedroom door carrying a tray of eggs, bacon and my mom's signature fried potatoes.

"You made me breakfast?" I asked.

"Mom did. I brought it to you."

Mel and I had definitely gotten closer my senior year, with us both realizing I'd be leaving for college soon, but something felt suspect. "Why?"

"You're the Queen. You can't be in the kitchen eating with the staff." Melanie turned the tiara over in her hands. "Totally not surprised by this, but also kind of surprised."

"That makes no sense," I said between bites.

"You're like the hero of my life or whatever," Melanie said, blushing. "I guess it's kind of cool that everyone in the school sees that about you, too."

She was definitely up to something. I dropped my fork with a clank. "You read the letter."

"Sorry," Melanie said, and pointed to the envelope next to me on the bed. "I didn't mean to invade your privacy. I was looking for a field trip form I asked mom to sign last week, and I found this."

"But you read it, knowing it was mine?"

"Um…"

"Melanie!"

"I was worried about you."

"So you know then."

She nodded. "You mad?"

I faded into the comfort of my pillow. "I'm relieved. Now I have someone to talk to."

Melanie moved the tray of food to my desk and climbed under the covers, holding me against her chest. "I'm sorry Elle. Did you see this coming at all?"

"Not even a little."

We sighed, letting the quiet settle.

"Does Neil know?" Mel asked after a few minutes.

"I don't think so." I paused before deciding to tell her what I'd spent the better part of prom debating. "I'm not sure I'm going to tell anyone."

She looked confused. "How will that work?"

"I just, you know, don't tell anyone. Josh deleted his online profiles. He's not taking my calls. Neil said he barely speaks to him anymore, either. It seems like he wants to stay out of touch with everyone."

"What makes you think it's a good idea to act like you're still dating him?"

Anger bubbled inside me again. "So my friends don't treat me differently. So I can live the last three weeks of my high school career without all the questions and chatter over us…"

Breaking up. I couldn't even say it aloud.

"Are you sure you're not doing this because you think Josh is going to change his mind?"

"I'm going to make him."

"What's that now?"

"I have enough money saved for a trip to Philly but not enough for textbooks and the new equipment I need to shoot in the fall. All I have to do is find a job, save up, and then ask mom and dad if I can take the car for a weekend to see Josh."

"Why don't you call him?"

"He won't answer," I admitted.

"So you think the best plan is to show up at his house?"

"It might not be the best, but it's the only plan I have right now. Something's not right. I know Josh. I think if we could see each other and talk about things, then…"

Melanie sighed. "Sometimes people change. Look at Harris and me. We changed and grew together."

"Are you saying that Josh and I grew apart?"

"I don't know," she said quietly. "Maybe."

I could admit, at least to myself, that the situation looked bleak, but I had to trust my heart. My heart told me things weren't entirely over with Josh Brighton. I set aside breakfast and dressed in my shorts and shooting jersey.

"I forgot you had a shoot."

"Not any shoot. This is the first shoot of the outdoor season." I shoved an extra jersey, my rain gear and shoes into my bag while we talked. I checked my arrows, fresh with new fletching, and marked them. "Not only do I have to get on the podium for the prize money, I also have to catch the eye of sponsors." No way would my parents let me spend money on a trip to see Josh if I still had hundreds of dollars to raise to pay for equipment, and if I didn't want to be tied to a job every spare moment while I was at school, I needed a sponsor.

Melanie nudged me into the seat in front of my vanity and brushed my hair. "You've been working toward this your whole life. All you have to do is focus."

Focus. Right.

I tucked the letter from Josh into my drawer while my sister braided my hair.

***

MY WHOLE FAMILY TRUDGED TO MY SHOOT. MY MOM schlepped the chairs while my dad carried a tent to keep us in the shade. I packed my bow complete with my old wrist-strap release that desperately needed replaced and heavier-tipped arrows to combat the potential weather changes that could occur in outdoor shoots. Every time I looked back at my family from the shooting line, I zeroed in on the empty space next to them, the space where Josh had always stood.

I imagined him in Philadelphia with this family on a Saturday afternoon. Maybe they'd gone to play basketball at the park or went hiking. He'd be with his brother, Mason, no doubt.

Or a girl.

My arrow slipped off my rest.

The timer for my shot ticked down. I'd have to pull it together to shoot the five arrows for that end. Typical ends consisted of three arrows, but some of the local shoots liked to mix things up. For me, that meant more shooting on a day I probably shouldn't have been anywhere near a range. I shook my thoughts away and positioned the arrow again, pulling the string back to full draw, releasing in time, and landing only a seven for my efforts. It was the first shot of the first end. I followed it with four eights and one seven—maybe my worst shooting ever.

"You got this, Elle," my dad called.

I couldn't bring myself to look at them, or more specifically the empty space next to them. The second end didn't go much better. I wasn't tracking the rest of the shooters, but instinctively I knew if I didn't score mostly nines and tens in the last end, I'd fall short of advancing let alone stepping on the podium.

I rubbed my temples. What distance were we even at? How much time did we have? I sipped the blue sports drink that always gave me luck and retrieved my arrows from the target, keeping my head down on the way back to the shooting line. Melanie had been right. I needed to focus. That was all. I could pull myself out of this.

In position, I calmed my breathing and nocked my arrow. I thought of JoAnn and all of my training. With my arrow pulled back, I locked in on the target. My pin bounced over the yellow center of the target more than usual. I struggled to still the bow, but the pin moved up, down, left and right. I released and gasped when the arrow struck the nine ring.

In position for my next shot, I tried to let the pin float, trusting that my mind was playing tricks on me more than my equipment. I scored another nine and then two tens.

"That's it, Elle," Dad called.

I made the mistake of turning around to nod to him before remembering why I didn't want to do that.

Focus, Elle. Not on your boyfriend dumping you or him spending time with another girl or the plan you needed to put together to find a way to get him back.

The shot clock ticked. I nocked my arrow and took a deep breath. When I looked through the sight, I saw Josh's face. Not on the target. In my head.

Stop!

Josh didn't belong in my head when I was shooting. He belonged in Philadelphia with his family and who knows who else.

The pin bounced all over the place. The clock ticked. The pin. The clock. No deep breath was going to calm the rising and falling of my chest. When the pin moved over the yellow center of the target, I released the string.

Except, I didn't. The arrow hadn't gone anywhere.

Release!

I pulled at the trigger again and again, and finally, the arrow flew, scoring me four points. I fell to a squatting position and buried my face in my hands.

CHAPTER 4

MY PARENTS TRIED TO TALK TO ME ON THE WAY HOME.
Target panic, they said.

"Everyone gets it, honey."

"It was bound to happen eventually."

"Some guys at the club swear a new release helps."

"And shooting. You'll want to keep shooting, not keeping score, just working on your technique."

"It will all work out."

I stared out the window, the hills of Pennsylvania rolling by. I hadn't only lost a competition that weekend. I'd lost my boyfriend, my hundred-dollar registration fee, my chance at scoring a sponsor who would give me a free hand-held release—or at least one at cost.

I had more tournaments coming up with more registration fees and travel expenses. And the cost of visiting Josh and school. I closed my eyes and listened to the hum of the tires over the road, urging myself not to cry. Only a year earlier, I'd been training for the Junior Olympic Archery Development Program—or JOAD—nationals, which I'd placed in and attracted the attention of college scouts. I'd been on the verge of hanging out with Josh. I'd been on the apex of life.

Life had defeated me since then.

"Elle?" Melanie whispered. "Are you okay?"

I grunted.

"How worried should we be?" Lily asked.

That remained to be seen.

***

I NEEDED A JOB THAT WOULD PAY ME ENOUGH TO COV-er registration fees and travel, and if I couldn't kick my newly acquired target panic, one that would pay for the equipment I needed to maintain my college scholarship in the fall.

Archery lessons had been the perfect income, even if it wasn't as consistent as I'd have liked. When I couldn't find anything online, I excused myself from class Monday morning to visit the guidance counselor.

She ushered me into her office while chatting over her shoulder to one of the secretaries, giving me the esteemed opportunity of enjoying her ever-changing motivational wall art.

"Carpe diem."

"Don't waste your effort envying someone else's life. Make your life what you want it to be."

And a quote she must have seen as a clever twist on a classic, "Nobody can make you feel anything without your consent."

If only life could be fixed by a motivational quote hanging on a pretty wall.

Mrs. Michaels closed the door with care, barely making a sound.

"Welcome, welcome! So glad you could come by, Elle. I hear congratulations are in order, our Prom Queen."

"Thanks," I said, grateful she didn't curtsy like the rest of the school had been doing all morning.

Mrs. Michaels shuffled some papers on her desk until she located a file with my name on it. "What can I do for you?"

"I need a summer job. One that's flexible with my archery competition schedule but also pays enough to save money for equipment, books, and spending money at college." And a trip to Philadelphia to see my ex-boyfriend who should still be my boyfriend. "I looked online, but when I didn't find anything, I thought maybe you might have heard about something local. Maybe?"

Mrs. Michaels rested her reading glasses on the edge of her nose and scanned her computer screen. "And what skills do you have for the position?"

"I don't have a resume or anything. I could make one. No problem." There were enough templates online to whip something up.

"As long as you don't go to the internet and copy one of the millions of templates," she said.

Oh.

"You want the resume to be unique to you, Elle. Of course, most of the jobs you're qualified for, you won't need a resume. Are you thinking food service? Retail?"

"Neither," I said. "I've spent some time filing for my dad's law firm, but I'd like to avoid being stuck in an office all summer."

"So no restaurants, stores, or offices?" She raised an eyebrow at me.

I cringed at the thought that pretty much ruled out most everything. "Do you have anything archery related in your search?"

Mrs. Michaels glanced at me over the rim of her glasses. "Archery, dear?"

"Yeah," I said slowly. "I've taught private archery lessons."

"That's something," she answered, tapping onto her keyboard.

Everything felt like a rush, like my heart rate still hadn't slowed down since my target panic incident. Every moment I sat here in Pittsburgh, Josh could be meeting someone else, or worse building a relationship with that someone else. I'd have to get to work fast, save money fast, and convince my parents to let me visit him.

Fast.

That meant scoring a sponsor before they found someone else to sign with on the summer circuit. I had one more competition before graduation, so that seemed like the best option. Of course, I had to go to class and work in addition to my training.

I glanced at the calendar. The clock was ticking.

"Look at that," Mrs. Michaels said. "The universe always gives you what you need."

Sounded like the perfect addition to her wall of motivational quotes.

"We have an invitation from one of our own students for a summer camp looking for counselors," she went on. "You'd be outside, and archery is listed as one of the activities."

A million questions flooded my mind. How far away was the camp? Would I have to stay there? How much would I make? Could I shoot on my own time and take some weekends off for my competitions? The questions kept coming, but I pushed them aside. For now. At least it was a lead.

"Can you print that, please?"

***

TWO SOPHOMORES ACROSS THE HALL FROM MY locker kissed like they were on the set of a soap opera instead of standing outside of the girls' bathroom notorious for after class smoking breaks. Not exactly a romantic destination.

I thought of Josh and the way his fingers had cradled the back of my neck, how his thumbs would graze my cheeks when he was about to kiss me. How his lips had appeared chiseled in marble by the great Michelangelo but were somehow so soft. I wanted to tell them to live it up.

I read the job description Mrs. Michaels had printed for me. I'd be teaching archery at a summer camp for kids, but there were counselor positions, too. The contact was Drew Peters, a junior I knew only a little. He played football, so I'd heard his name announced on Friday nights. He'd also been voted Prom Prince. I don't think he and I had ever talked, though.

I texted the number on the paper, asking if we could meet to talk about the job.

He replied, "Sure."

Before I could type, "When and where?", he appeared in front of me wearing a hoody, jeans, and a very messy hairstyle.

"Are you my mom or my mother-in-law?"

"Huh?"

"Stupid conversation starter, I guess. I'm Prom Prince. You're the Queen. I was wondering how this royal family is structured."

"Right. I, uh, never thought about it, I guess."

He smiled in an awkward acceptance of the situation and then changed the subject. "So you're interested in the counselor position?"

"Yep. I shoot archery."

"Oh perfect. We really need someone there. I help staff the counselor positions. I've been working at the camp a few summers now."

"That's cool."

"Yeah, I guess," he said with a laugh. "I make some cash and get to spend my summers outside."

"That's exactly what I'm hoping for. Are those flyers for the camp?"

He offered me one at the same time I reached for it, and we fumbled the handoff, knocking the papers out of his hands. We bent to retrieve them. "I'm sorry."

"It's fine." He recovered and more effectively passed me the flyer.

The words "Good Grief" were bold and centered on the page. "A grief camp? I didn't realize."

"It's more fun than it sounds, and I thought with Josh gone for the summer you may be interested—"

"You know Josh?" I asked, but of course he did. Everyone knew Josh. "I mean, like, you're friends?"

"Our families are. And we played football together. He's a good guy."

Sure. He dumped his girlfriend by Express mail.

"What are your other options?" Drew asked.

"Huh?"

"For summer jobs?"

"Oh. Filing at my dad's law office."

"Filing papers? For eight hours a day in the summer?" He shook his head. "What else?"

"According to Mrs. Michaels, food service," I said, walking down the hall slowly, so Drew could dodge oncoming traffic and keep up.

"Hairnets and queens don't really mix."

"You know prom's over. I'm not a queen anymore."

"You are until a new queen is crowned next year. I'll be milking my prince status until then."

If all the curtsying from the day told me anything, he'd probably benefit a time or two.

He held the door leading to the stairwell open for me. "You can get paid for getting a tan at summer camp."

"It sounds perfect, but I need to know about pay and time off and stuff. I kind of need a job now, so I'm wary of waiting a few weeks to get started."

"We're starting next week, actually. The school is excusing anyone in good standing who wants to participate. They're calling it an educational trip."

"Really?" Instead of sitting in the holding pattern that is the last few weeks of high school, I'd be out in the sun, training, and making money to visit Josh even sooner. "This sounds too good to be true."

"It's pretty awesome. I won't lie."

There had to be a flaw somewhere. "I have some travel scheduled for summer." And to drive to Philadelphia to convince my ex-boyfriend he made a mistake.

"Perfect. We can work that all out with scheduling."

"Okay," I said.

"Okay." He smiled. "There's a meeting today after school. I'll answer all your questions. Bring some friends, too. We're really hurting for counselors this year."

CHAPTER 5

AT 2:30, I HEADED TO THE HEALTH CLASSROOM WHERE Drew was holding the information meeting. Students packed the room, sitting at the desks and also along the window. Neil and Kate waved to me from the back corner. Even after months of Josh being away, seeing the two of them without him made my breath catch in my throat. If he were still here, we could have worked the summer camp together. My mind fantasized about the possibilities around the fire, daytime sports and games, and late-night swims. I swallowed hard. None of that would happen. He was gone, and worse than that, he didn't want to spend his summer with me.

"How sold are you two on this counselor idea?" I asked them.

"Thinking it over, Queen Bee," Neil said. Kate didn't bother to answer. She was too busy tapping her phone screen, paying attention to nobody until the door closed behind Drew.

He handed some flyers to the first students in each row and asked them to pass them back. He had changed his clothes since that morning and stood tall with confidence. He was wearing a tight white tee and workout shorts. The shirt hugged generous muscles. Kate's mouth hung open, and her fingers paused mid-text.

"When did that happen?"

"When did what happen?" Neil asked nonchalantly as he studied the flyer.

"That!" Kate pointed to Drew. "He was like a little kid yesterday."

Neil grinned sideways at me. "Kids grow up, Kate. Drew's been in the weight room like every day for a year."

Drew stepped behind the podium and leaned on it, his eyes scanning the room. He summarized the camp—for kids struggling with grief. Each camper would come for two weeks. There were a total of five two-week sessions. The camp was all about dealing with grief and building self-esteem through sports, activities, and unfailing support from the counselors—from us. The first session would be meant primarily for home-schooled students and last the two weeks before graduation. In other words, I'd be done with high school.

Forever.

Application, please?

After his pitch, Drew opened the meeting to questions.

"So wait," said a guy who definitely did not raise his hand and was slumped over a desk in the back corner of the room. "Is this all about, like, touchy feely stuff? 'Cause shrinks aren't my thing."

"It's a survival camp," Drew responded. "The need for spiritual, physical, emotional, and mental well-being is considered part of the survival goal."

"So, touchy-feely," the guy said.

"There is some peer group therapy, but those sessions are supervised by licensed clinicians. Some camp counselors participate and some don't. If you're uncomfortable with that, as you said, like, this might not be your thing."

"What would we be doing there?" Kate asked.

"You could be a counselor for a specific cabin of kids, which means they are your responsibility each morning and night. You could work a particular sport or activity. That involves some teaching and mentoring. Or you could do both, which comes with a boost in pay."

"Can we sign up now?" I asked.

Drew walked down the closest aisle of desks and handed me an application. "That would be great." He held the pile of applications high in the air. "Anyone else?"

Kate wiped the drool from her chin, and raised her hand. Neil smiled at me and followed suit.

The questions continued, but the answers didn't matter. Bottom line, the camp was willing to pay me to shoot and hang out on the archery range. Done and done.

Next task: keep my secret about the breakup until graduation.

***

IN MY EAGERNESS TO ESCAPE THE PRYING EYES OF high school and find the perfect summer job, I'd overlooked a few details. Starting with my sisters.

"You're leaving for the whole summer?" Melanie spat.

"Not the whole summer. I'll be back for graduation and maybe have a few breaks here and there."

"So the whole summer," Lily summarized, hands on hips. "It's our last summer together before you leave for college, and the Corwin sisters are changed forever."

"We'll have fun, too," I promised, and hated myself for making empty promises like Josh had. "I mean we'll try."

"I thought that we'd gotten this sister thing figured out, but now I see you're as selfish as I always thought you were."

Lily scrunched her little face at Melanie's words, but she didn't outright disagree with her.

"You know what? I'm done with this," I said. "You think you're being here for me? You have a crappy way of showing it."

My mom intercepted me the second I left the room. "You okay?"

"Ready to pack."

"Before you do, your dad and I want to talk to you."

The interrogation continued.

"How are you going to shoot?" my dad asked.

My first reaction was to say that didn't matter since I hadn't picked up my bow since my target panic incident. Realistically, I had to get back on the range. Not everything in life was realistic.

"I'm helping with their archery program. I'll be able to shoot any time."

"Aren't you going to miss your friends? This is your last summer, honey."

"Kate and Neil are working as counselors, too."

Questions about how much I'd make, if I could afford books in the fall, if my shooting would suffer, if I could make our family vacation and on and on.

"Elle, this is crap," Melanie finally said after I'd battled the onslaught. "You can't make a decision like this."

"Why not, exactly?" I said, feeling my face heating. "It's my life. My life that I haven't been living because I've been moping around about Josh for months in case you haven't noticed. My life that is now shattered because, guess what, he doesn't want me anymore. My life. You get that?"

"Okay, maybe we should calm—"

"Shut it, Lil," Melanie and I said.

"You're going to spend the summer looking at the stars with your perfect boyfriend who lives right next door, so don't tell me I can't deal with my own breakup how I want to deal with it."

"Except you're dealing with it by shutting the rest of us out," Mel shouted.

"Melanie," Mom warned.

"Forget it," my sister went on, ignoring my mom's warning. "Nothing to see here. Just Elle planning her life without the rest of us. Looking out for number one. Some things never change."

Lily shook her head, and my sisters stomped out of my room. Mom looked at me with questioning eyes.

"I have to pack," I said not louder than a whisper.

But I didn't. I plucked the photos off my bedroom mirror one by one. Josh and me at the Medina pool party the summer before. That might have been our first picture as a couple. I smiled at how nervous he'd been to ask me out, which made no sense.

"I didn't think you knew I existed," he'd told me months later when we laughed about how badly his hands had been shaking.

"You're Josh Brighton," I'd said. "Everyone knows you exist."

"Yeah, but you ran in different circles, spent evenings and weekends shooting instead of at school sports and stuff. You were like this unicorn. Totally gorgeous. Totally mysterious."

"Shut up."

He'd tickled my lower back with his fingertips. "I'm serious."

"And now?" I'd asked, shivering from his touch.

"Now, we're together, and the only thing I'm nervous about is you figuring out you're too good for me."

"Seriously shut up this time."

And then he'd kissed me.

The photos on my mirror stood as evidence those perfect moments had existed. I hadn't imagined or fabricated them. I'd lived them.

I opened my email. Nothing from Josh. No reply to my embarrassing number of emails to him that weekend. He'd closed his social media accounts. I tugged my Josh box out from under the bed and sifted through the letters he'd sent. I found one filled with promises. I took a picture of it to keep for myself and slid it into an envelope with a note that read, "I haven't forgotten. I don't believe you have either." Maybe it was bold. Maybe it was stupid, but I couldn't sit here and cry without trying something. I wrote his address on the envelope, stamped it, and set it on the table next to my door.

In the morning, I'd drop it in the mailbox, and then we'd see.

CHAPTER 6

"WOW. YOUR CABIN IS...NICE," NATE SAID AS SHE
pushed through the flimsy, wooden screen door of Cabin 12 at Camp
Good Grief.

"Thanks for trying to lie."

"Sorry," she said. "And you can't even bail because you spent too
much time convincing your parents this is what you wanted. Can't
give them the satisfaction."

True on all accounts. I'd convinced my parents I could raise
enough money for everything I needed that fall. I hadn't mentioned
the Philadelphia trip. Yet.

"If you don't," my dad had said, "you'll be spending weekends
working at the law firm to make up the difference."

If I spent the entire summer working at the camp and managed
to win some prize money, I'd squeeze enough into my bank account
to be safe from that fate. Working weekends in the fall would mean
leaving Josh behind on campus. I had every intention of convincing
him that breaking up wasn't the answer when I visited him in a few
weeks, but my backup plan was spending time together at college.

One way or another, Josh Brighton and Melanie Corwin would
be a couple again.

Except.

Josh still hadn't answered my calls, texts, or emails. The letter should have arrived at his place days earlier, and no response. My anger hadn't settled from it. In fact, thinking about him warmed my body all over, and not in a good way. The thought had crossed my mind more than once that all the effort I'd been putting in wasn't worth it. That he wasn't worth it.

I looked around the cabin. I'd changed my whole world, and Josh couldn't even answer the phone.

My parents had ended our conversation about camp satisfyingly slurping their pasta primavera, but my sisters had glared at me over their untouched plates. Neither of them had even said goodbye when Kate had picked me up.

No matter what I did, life tugged me five steps backward for every step I managed to claw forward. Like bringing a pile of board games to be counselor of the year for my campers but having nowhere to store them.

"Your cabin's even worse than mine." Kate wandered around, poking her head into the corners and the bathroom. "Where are your closets and shelves?"

"I was wondering the same thing. Wait. Are you telling me you have shelves in your cabin?"

"I have a walk-in closet. The shelves are wooden and dusty, but it's still a closet."

The perks of the universe followed my best friend around.

"And I'm assuming you left some room in the closet for your campers, right, Kate?" Drew said from the porch. He politely knocked on the wooden screen door, and I waved him in. "Bad news, Elle. You have the, um," he looked around the single room and said, "crappiest cabin."

I sighed, not surprised my luck had followed me the two-hour drive from home. "Of course I do."

"What's up with that?" Kate protested. "You'd think we had an in with the place. Guess you don't carry as much clout as we thought, huh, Drew?"

"I have enough clout to tell you you're late for the swim counselors and lifeguards meeting."

Drew was being playful, but Kate groaned. "When you're late, they always volunteer you for the awful jobs."

"Better run, then," Drew teased. Kate blew a kiss at me and let the door clatter on her way out.

"I've never seen Kate bow so quickly to authority."

He reclined on the bed next to mine.

"Make yourself at home," I teased.

"Sorry. I was up most of the night getting everything ready for today. Do you mind if I sit?"

"Sure," I said. "I was only joking."

"I wasn't—not about Kate. Wait until you see the head lifeguard. I have a suspicion Santino's her type. Besides the cabin, everything good so far?"

I shrugged. "I guess. I haven't seen or done much."

"Anyone give you a hard time about giving up your entire summer to come to camp?"

I squinted at him.

"I may have heard your sister complaining to Harris in the cafeteria," Drew admitted.

"Yeah. Melanie's not happy with me."

"Do you want to talk about it?"

I studied Drew. We barely knew each other, but something about him disarmed me. Maybe it was all this time he spent at a grief camp, but he exuded this persona of being easy to talk to.

"I can't blame her on the one hand," I began. "We weren't always close. She was the type to stay home and be alone. I was the type to go hang out with friends, but this year, we've gotten better."

"She's sad to see you go to college. It's sweet."

"She thinks that I'm here because Josh—" I froze. I'd almost admitted to Drew that Josh had broken up with me. He was way too easy to talk to.

"I get it," he said. "It's hard with Josh away and everything."

I nodded, willing to let his assumption ride, and busied myself organizing the few toiletries in the small bathroom in the cabin.

"You know you can bow out of camp after training if you feel you're better off at home with your family. Maybe I'm being selfish, but I hope you don't do that."

"I can't do that to you and Robert." Them or my bank account.

"You're short on counselors already, right?"

He nodded.

"Wait. What if Melanie could come here and help with volleyball or something? She did make varsity as a sophomore. She's incredible."

"I've seen her play," Drew said with a laugh.

"You have?"

"Don't sound so surprised. The volleyball team is the pride of Iron Valley, and yes, that would be great if she wants to come for a session or something."

"Thank you. I'll ask her." I smiled at the thought of Melanie being at camp with me while I focused on sorting through my clothes and deciding how to stuff them in the suitcase I'd shoved under my bed. By the time they were put away, Drew had fallen asleep. His light brown hair defied gravity, messily swooped up and to the right, and his sharp features and lips relaxed. After watching him a few seconds too long, I shook my head, awaking from my stupor.

My Josh box was still on the bed. I sat next to it and lifted the lid. The express letter was on the top, but I buried it beneath the other letters he'd sent me. I sifted through movie stubs and photos, thinking of all the time I spent with this one guy, how much I'd invested, and how he'd carelessly cut me out of his life.

And yet I was still building my world around him.

The letter on the top of the pile was written on a thick piece of stationary. Josh's handwriting inside scrawled song lyrics about distance in relationships and that magical moment when you see the person you've been thinking about every day.

I pressed the page between my palms and closed my eyes.

A breeze rushed through the open window. The cabins weren't equipped with central heat. I hoped the weather warmed up before the campers arrived. But not too much. No central air either. Drew shivered and rolled onto his side, toward me. The wind showed no sign of slowing down. I unfolded the blanket at the bottom of my bed and covered Drew with it as a spider crawled towards my foot. Instinctively, I jumped onto Drew. He woke up and thrashed under the blanket I'd tucked him into, nearly pushing me onto the floor—where the spider was.

"No, Drew. Please, there's a spider."

"What?" He stopped thrashing.

Awkward.

After checking the floor, I tiptoed off the bed and hustled to the bathroom for a tissue, or more like a pile of ten tissues to prevent any chances of the spider connecting with my skin. With the flashlight from my phone spanning the dusty, hardwood floor, I searched for the little critter with no luck.

"What happened?" Drew asked.

"You fell asleep, and I put the blanket on you, and then, the spider…" But where was it?

I kicked at my suitcase. "It's gone."

"Hey," Drew said. "If you're up for it, I'd like to show you something."

I searched the floor one last time. "Sure."

He led me through the rickety cabin door. The fresh air was cool for May.

"Have you been to the main lodge yet?"

"Kate parked out front, but we headed straight for our cabins."

"That's what I thought." With an excited smile, Drew chatted about the camp, pointing out cabins, activity spots, fire pits, and the water of the small lake in the distance. He opened the door to the main lodge as if he were welcoming me to a castle.

"Thanks," I said, a small smile spreading across my lips.

"You haven't even seen the surprise."

"You're looking out for me. After I woke you up from your nap. Sorry about that."

"Don't worry about it."

It didn't take more than a couple steps into the lodge for me to gasp. Massive, colorful, elaborate quilts hung from the wall opposite the door. They extended to the left and the right, and from what I could see all down the hallways.

"Every camper designs a quilt square for the person they've lost," Drew explained. "They bring mementos—photos and personal items—and the last few days of camp, they build the square to honor their loved one. Even more than that, to celebrate the beautiful life they lived."

"How many are there?"

"I honestly couldn't tell you. They line the walls of the entire building."

"They're beautiful."

I stepped closer, running my fingers over the soft fabric that protected the memories of a person long lost, but very clearly not forgotten. Hearts, stick figures, silhouettes, musical instruments, sports memorabilia, flowers, police badges, and military honors decorated the squares. Sesame Street characters on colorful felt stopped me. A boy, Zander, honored on one of the quilts had died at the age of three years old. My breath caught. I'd lost Josh—at least for now—but he was still alive and healthy.

"I don't know if I can do this," I mumbled.

"Do what?"

"Be here. Support these kids."

"Of course you can. You're going to be amazing."

"I'm a mess. I…" I pointed to Zander's square as if that would answer everything.

Drew rested his hands on my shoulders. "I won't lie. The camper's experiences and stories might bring you to tears. That's not a bad thing, Elle."

"Feels like it to me."

"It won't after you spend a summer here. Trust me. Tears are the norm, and the kids will see that you care about them. We're not here to distract them from their grief. We're here to walk with them in their journeys. The clinicians help with the deep stuff. Part of the counselor role is to keep them active and engaged. Remind them what it feels like to live life and be happy. To smile and have fun."

I'd spent the last few months hiding on the archery range since Josh had left, and I couldn't even bring myself to do that since the last shoot. I might need my own reminder.

"When I'm having a tough day, reading some of the quilt squares lessens the load a bit. Not because I think my problems aren't important. The quilts make me feel…" He quietly struggled for an explanation. "Less alone. Life can always get worse. And it can always get better."

With my phone in my hands, I wanted to check my email one

more time to see if Josh had finally replied. That would make things better.

"Speaking of getting better, I came to your cabin today to tell you we ordered armoires that should arrive soon. They'll be installed in your cabin right away."

I could get my suitcase off the spider's playground also known as the floor. "Thanks, Drew."

He nodded.

"If you don't mind," I finally said, "I'm going to hang out here a bit longer. Read some more squares."

"Sure thing. I have a few things to catch up on. Is it okay if I leave you here, or would you rather I stay?"

I thought about the strength Zander's family had to come to this camp, work through their grief, and create such a beautiful tribute to him on that quilt.

"Go ahead," I said. "I'll be good on my own."

CHAPTER 7

THE BELL SIGNALING THE FIRST EVENING OF COUNSEL-
or training sounded as Kate and I cleared our dinner trays in the
cafeteria. We shuffled through the halls of the main lodge with the
dozens of other counselors until we reached a wide, open room lined
with floor-to-ceiling windows. The walls, floors, and rafters were
wooden with rustic chandeliers hanging low to provide light. A circle
of chairs occupied the center of the room, where Robert, the camp's
director, Drew, and a few other counselors sat. Drew's eyes met mine,
and he tapped the seat next to him.

"How you doing?" he asked.

"The quilts helped. Thank you."

Robert started the meeting with a general greeting and some news
that sent grumbles through the room. "You may have already noticed
the unreliable cell phone reception in the area. I consider this an asset.
Both you and the campers will be forced to disconnect from outside
influences such as email, text messaging, and web sites like MyFace."

Kate leaned toward me and Drew. "Did he say MyFace?"

"Aah, here come my lovely assistants," Robert said as a boy and
a girl entered the room with stacks of binders bigger than them.
"Meet my kids, Stephanie and Steven. They will be distributing the
counselor handbook."

Stephanie smiled shyly at Kate as she handed her a massive tome.

"This is like a Bible," Kate said, eliciting a few snickers from the counselors sitting closest to us.

"Exactly right, Miss…?"

"I'm Kate."

"Kate. Thank you," Robert said and turned to the group. "Consider this your Bible for the duration of your leadership time with us. Tonight, when you return to your cabins, please read the first fifty pages…" The shouting in my mind overpowered Robert's voice. Fifty pages! I thought school was out for summer. "We take this very seriously, and so should you. A child who is struggling with the loss of a loved one needs our support. And that's what we're here to give them. They have to live in a new world that they didn't ask for. Nobody can tell them exactly how to do that, but we can be there in a peer support system as they help each other in their grief. Hopefully they'll find some joy here, too, whether that be sports, games, crafts, sciences, or exploring the outdoors. They'll work with licensed clinicians in group sessions here in the main lodge throughout their stay. Our goal is to help them see how they can continue living life, in a new way, without the person they've lost."

Robert's words broke through the strong facade I'd secured around me, right to my core. Figuring out how to live in a new world I hadn't asked for? Finding joy in life? Continue living without the person I'd lost?

I swallowed again and again and forced my emotions to stay hidden, deep inside. When I realized I'd projected the pain of the campers onto myself when they had literally lost the lives of people they'd loved—over a boy breaking up with me? My sister's accusation of being selfish rang all too true.

"I lost my grandfather when I was young," Robert continued. "He and my grandmother had had an epic romance and a long, healthy marriage, so of course, she was devastated. She taught me one of the most important lessons of my life. She'd always say, 'Grief is the price we pay for love.' It's true, and it's a beautiful sentiment. Yes, grief is challenging, devastating and debilitating, even, but in reality, it comes about because we have had the extreme privilege of loving someone so deeply."

And now the tears rolled down my cheeks. No stopping them.

"We want to help our campers understand that and even celebrate the life of the one they've lost. You may have noticed the quilts around the building. That is one way we celebrate life, but there will be many others. Grief is a natural process of building a new existence after a major life change. It's important that you all understand how we approach grief here, which is what my friend Kate aptly called the Bible is for. Please read it closely tonight. We will discuss it more throughout our training week together, but trust me when I say it will prepare you to work through the difficult situations you may find yourself in as a counselor here at Camp Good Grief. That said, I will expect you all to set a quality example for your campers, and that starts with the camp motto." Robert held up the "Bible" and swiveled from side to side, displaying the cover for everyone in the circle to see. He read the motto aloud. "'We laugh together. We cry together.' Be prepared to do both in the coming weeks."

I'd already done the crying. I hoped laughing would come in time.

***

BACK IN MY CABIN, WHICH I'D CHECKED FOR SPIDERS, I curled up in my bed to discover the handbook was more of a page-turner than I'd expected. The introduction detailed a narrative from Robert about his experience with grief. He recalled his family members traveling from around the country to be with him when his mother died from breast cancer. He and his siblings and cousins had shared stories from their childhood and laughed for days. But when he'd sat next to the casket in the funeral home, and tears had glistened his cheeks, one of his aunts had insisted everyone leave the room and "Give him a minute." She'd meant to be helpful, but Robert had felt pressured to regain control, to wash away the tears and rejoin his family. In other words, when he had been crying, he'd had to be alone.

And he hadn't wanted to be alone.

Thus, the motto: We laugh together. We cry together.

The irony wasn't lost on me. Without realizing it, I'd spent months grieving Josh moving away. I'd hidden my emotions behind shooting and friends, probably not very well. I'd thought I'd make a good counselor—that I would be fun and silly with the girls. I'd even packed board games and random play makeup and jewelry for rainy days. My remedies had been superficial. If I was going to help these girls, I'd first have to figure out a way to help myself.

Take the first point of grief for instance—shock. The training manual used the word "fog" to describe the experience. I'd used the word to describe how I'd felt in the last few months. Even if I forced myself, I couldn't conjure clear memories from the last few months, or worse the last week. I'd allowed the fog to settle around me and to rob me of the last few months of my high school experience.

Worse, the way to move past the shock, apparently, was to acknowledge my reality. I'd never acknowledged Josh being gone. I'd only waited for him to come back. For prom. For graduation. For college. And then when he broke up with me, I hadn't told anyone. I still acted like we were together, like he was my present, not my past.

Robert's grief Bible described my entire existence in a way that made me question the reasons I'd come to camp—to save enough to go to Philly and convince Josh to get back together. Instead, I wondered if I were there for a different reason, a more important one. What had Mrs. Michael's said when I was in her office? Something about how the universe gives you exactly what you need?

Maybe whether you realize it or not.

Under the night light clipped to my headboard, I flipped to page fifty-one of the handbook and continued reading.

***

"RULE #1," ROBERT LECTURED IN OUR MORNING SES-
sion the following day, "Never compare losses."

My diligence from the night before paid off. The rules were in my head. I could recite them with ease. Rule #2: Healing might come from time, actions, or both. Rule #3: Every person reacts differently to grief. Rule #4: People should not be judged based on their unique reactions to grief. Rule #5: Never tell someone how to grieve. Rules the counselors were expected to follow when interacting with the campers. The handbook covered more than the rules. It offered examples of questions kids and teens tended to ask while they were grieving, questions that broke my heart. Are they coming back? Were they mad at me? Who else is going to die? Who am I without them? I wouldn't have the answers if a camper asked me any of those questions, but I could do what Robert suggested—I could learn to listen with patience and understand that validating the camper's need to ask was more important than providing an answer.

Kate and I partnered and simulated asking questions and responding in a way that didn't necessarily answer but gave validation to the camper.

"The fact that a camper even speaks to you about these questions and thoughts they're having demonstrates trust in you. That's a powerful thing," Robert said. "You can't take them out of their grief, but you can be there with them as they navigate it."

Because of the intense content during training, Robert had incorporated lighter tasks throughout the morning like silly scavenger hunts and relay races. And when it came to how to respond to grief, he set the example. As he lectured, he shed the occasional tear, letting it fall down his cheeks, and to the floor before keeping right on, talking about the campers he'd known over the years—how they'd grieved, what they'd survived, how their lives had been changed by understanding that healing was a complicated process that differed for everyone.

"Speaking of actions," Robert said as many of the counselors were looking at the time on the clock above him, "it's almost time for lunch, but we still have some planning to do."

Drew took the podium. "I know you're all hungry. I'll make this quick. If you've been assigned a cabin, that's considered your base pay contribution to the camp. However, we don't have enough coverage for all of the activities and sports, so any cabin counselors who are interested in helping with one can earn a bonus in pay. I have a list of options here if anyone's interested in taking a look."

Kate shoved her pen and notebook into her purse. "I have a cabin and am helping with lifeguarding duty four days a week, so I'm good."

I squeezed my way into the crowd that had formed around Drew. When the group of counselors dwindled, he flipped through the papers on his clipboard.

"How did it go?" I asked.

"That was surprisingly helpful. We filled a lot of slots. I'll need to be strategic about shifting people around and covering camper groups, but yeah." He sighed. "I think we still have a couple options for water games, like races in the kayaks and stuff, sand volleyball, and…" Flip. Flip. Flip. "I have you down for archery. Is that right?"

"Perfect. Do you use recurve bows or compound? Probably not compound?"

Drew stared at me.

"There are different kinds of bows, but I would expect probably recurve." I slid Robert's laptop across the table and searched online for an image of a recurve bow.

"I think that's what we have. Look, you clearly have more expertise than me on this. The campers usually like archery and are terrible at it if I'm being honest. We have a teacher from the local archery club that does some kids' programming who's volunteered to help out a couple days a week, but they hoped someone could assist. This seems like the perfect fit."

"Excellent," I said.

"I'll schedule it for two days a week. On those days, we'll find an assistant counselor to help with your cabin campers. Sound good?"

"Perfect, but I have one more request."

He stopped writing and glanced up at me.

"Would I be able to shoot there myself on the other days? Maybe even some evenings? I'm supposed to be training for a few summer competitions. I put the dates for those on my application, too."

"Yeah. I remember. We shouldn't have too much trouble getting coverage. Maybe I should look for a more permanent assistant counselor for you. If we have one, that will free up your time to train and provide some consistency for your campers, too. I can walk you down to the archery fields after dinner if you want to see the facility."

"That would be great. Thanks." I needed to log some serious hours training to get ready for my first summer circuit competition.

Drew made a note on his clipboard and tucked it into the box of papers nearby. "Want to walk to lunch?"

"Sure."

We headed for the cafeteria through the hallways lined with quilts, and for the first time since I'd arrived at Camp Good Grief, I felt like when the campers arrived, I might actually be able to help them.

Especially if they liked archery.

CHAPTER 8

WHEN HATE DROPPED ME OFF FOR OUR POST-TRAIN-ing, weekend break, I ran into the house, greeted my mom since my sisters were still in school and my dad was at work, and made an excuse of wanting to shower to lock myself in my room to read the mail I'd missed. My head was telling me to let it go, but I had to know if Josh had sent something—a card or letter groveling for how stupid he'd been. But the mail on my desk was from Mon Valley College, and it wasn't even anything important. I collapsed on my bed, spent, but refusing to cry.

Two weeks since Josh had dumped me. Fourteen days. The break-up looked permanent.

Too permanent.

I sank deeper into my pillow.

Then there was the training about grief and how to process it. I could ask questions like, "Why did he break up with me?" and "What had I done wrong?" and "Will he ever want me back?" Overcoming grief, according to Robert, meant accepting the reality of your new situation. I had no intention of accepting a reality without Josh.

Instead, I planned to change it.

***

LILY DUG HER HAND INTO THE BOWL OF POPCORN WHEN my sisters and I assembled later that evening for movie night. "Have you heard from Alexis? She hasn't emailed in a while, and I wanted to tell her hi."

Alexis was one year older than Lily. With Josh and me spending so much time together and babysitting our little sisters sometimes, too, Lily and Alexis had quickly become buddies.

"Not any time soon, Lil."

Lily squeezed me into the biggest hug she could manage considering her size. "It's really over then, huh? I thought for sure you guys would, like, make it to happily ever after Disney princess style."

I hugged her back. "There's still time."

"We need s'mores," Melanie said.

"I'll get them." Lily ran to the kitchen. She'd always been our snack wrangler, and her absence gave me a perfect opportunity to pitch my idea to Melanie.

"I know you're mad at me about working at the camp this summer, but I want you to come with me."

She scoffed.

"Not the whole summer. I know you have volleyball camps and travel league, but I looked at the calendar, and Lily will be away for science camp the same two weeks you have off. I thought you could come and help coach volleyball for that session. It would look great on your college applications, and Harris could even come and show off some of his favorite, less dangerous, experiments for the science enthusiasts."

"You've given this a lot of thought," Melanie said, a genuine smile on her face.

"I have. I should have thought about what it would be like to leave you and Lily. I'm sorry."

"That's good. As much as I hate for you to be gone or to even admit that," she sighed. "I'm happy for you, Elle."

I blew her a kiss. "Thank you. And...it's fun. They're in need of assistant counselors who help with activities. You'd be teaching girls to play volleyball. It's perfect for you."

She snuggled next to me. "I'll think about it."

For now, that would have to be good enough for me.

***

MY PARENTS DROVE ME BACK TO CAMP IN EXCHANGE for a tour also known as a thinly-veiled attempt to check up on me. Sweet—although I'd never tell them that.

Walking through the main lodge, I showed them Zander's quilt square. My mom squeezed me and cried. "You're doing something special here for these kids, sweetie."

My dad gave a nod that said he was proud of me, too.

With only about an hour to spare before they had to head home, we found our way to the archery range. I unlocked the small shed that held all of the equipment, and my parents each chose a recurve bow and three arrows.

"Wow, Elle," Dad said. "This is perfect for you."

The same giddiness I felt at the beginning of shooting competitions bubbled inside me. "I know. I spent the last week shooting recurve. I'm thinking about setting a goal to try some competitions this winter or next summer."

"It's a new challenge for sure," Dad agreed. "But what about your compound?"

I pulled my ponytail over my head to cover my face.

"Elle?"

"I haven't shot it."

"For how long?"

"Since…you know." Shooting the recurve had kept me on the range, but at some point, I'd have to pick up my compound bow again.

He and my mom exchanged glances.

"You have another shoot to prep for. You're ranked for it, Elle. You have to be ready."

"I will be. I have a plan." Which amounted to being ready for it. Not very intricate.

"Up for a little game?" Dad asked, pretending he didn't see right through me. "Like old times?"

"With recurve?"

He laughed. "It will make it more difficult for sure."

"What's the game?"

"Color match."

I pressed my hands over my heart, and my parents laughed. Color match was the first game we played when I'd learned to shoot. I had been a tiny little person chasing the colors he hit on the target. He hit yellow, I'd have to hit yellow. Since my arrow had mostly struck the red, he strategically never aimed for it. Whoever lost the round got a letter in ARROW, and the first person to spell the word lost.

"I'm going to win you know," I teased.

He threw his head back in laughter. "Not happening."

"I'll watch from here," my mom said, sitting on a blanket she'd found in the shed.

My dad and I lined up, ready with our arrows. He offered me the first shot, and my arrow struck the outer blue ring. He raised an eyebrow at me. Not the best shot, but also not my go-to bow. With a compound bow, once you pulled the string, the draw weight lessened, giving a mechanical advantage. With recurve, the shooter had to hold the weight at full draw.

Dad nocked his arrow and pulled the bow string.

He let the string slip through his fingers and missed the target completely. "What!"

My mom and I laughed.

"Letter 'A' is it?"

"Enjoy it now," he teased. "This is the only lead you'll have."

He was wrong again. We worked our way through the game with him only besting me on one round and joined my mom on the blanket with water bottles.

"This place suits you," she said.

"Thanks. It's weird though."

"How's that?"

"I've always spent my summers away from archery. I'd shoot now and then, but being here is so immersive. If I wake up early, I come shoot. If our afternoon sessions finish quickly, I shoot. I shoot more here than I ever did at home."

"It's paying off," Dad said. "Your shots were impressive. Definitely enter a few recurve competitions this winter."

I leaned against him. "Thanks, Dad."

He kissed my forehead. "I'll walk back and get the car. You two catch up."

I scowled at my mom. "That was obvious."

"He knows I want to talk to you," my mom said.

"About?"

"Josh."

I sighed.

"Have you come to terms with the breakup yet, honey?"

"Define 'come to terms.'"

She raised an eyebrow at me.

"I was going to talk to you and dad about visiting him, so we can hash things out face to face."

"Visit him? Drive to Philadelphia alone?"

"Mom, I'm eighteen."

"Doesn't make it any safer than when you were seventeen."

"I can't accept that this is what he wants, or maybe that this is what he would want if we were in the same place," I said, talking fast, hoping my mom didn't interrupt my logic. "If we see each other, then maybe he'll know. And if he knows, I might know, too. I want to know. I don't want to wonder anymore."

"Elle, what if he does know? Have you given that any consideration?"

Had I? Probably not. "Mom, I…" Tears trickled from my eyes.

"Oh, honey." She pulled me closer and held me until my father pulled the car down the gravel drive that led to the range.

"I know it's not easy, Elle. But with some distance, these things always sort themselves out."

In other words, she didn't want me driving to Philly to see him. I'd change her mind. My dad climbed out of the car holding a sparkly blue gift bag. My mom grinned.

"What's this?" I asked.

"A little something to show how proud we are of you," Mom said.

"There's the smile I like to see." Dad handed me the bag.

I sat on one of the hay bales near the shooting line and moved aside the tissue paper to find a new trigger release for my bow.

"Get it warmed up for the next shoot," Dad said.

I hugged them both. "Thank you. I love you."

"Try it," Dad suggested.

"You had this planned all along, didn't you?"

He crossed his arms. "Maybe."

My parents reiterated the internet, sharing every strategy for overcoming target panic while I readied my bow.

"I got it," I finally said to them. "Let's see how it goes."

I bounced on my toes and strapped the release to my wrist. The material sat differently on my hand, signaling it would take some getting used to.

"It's going to work," Dad said. "You got this, Elle."

I repeated his words in my head while I readied my compound bow, nocked an arrow, and pulled back to full draw, inhaling a deep breath. With the target in my sight, I remembered the heaviness of my breath and twitching of my arm when I had been at full draw, and the bow wouldn't release. I closed my eyes to reset my brain and reopened them with the pin in the same spot over the target. My dad repeated his mantra. I pulled the trigger. The string slipped through the opening propelling the arrow to the target with ease.

I fell onto the closest hay bale and lowered my head into my hands.

I did it.

"Not that we're worrying about the score right now," Dad said, "but that was a ten, honey."

"Thanks, Dad."

"Keep shooting," he said, giving me one last hug. "Be safe."

"Have fun," Mom said.

The dust from their tires cleared, and I checked the time on my watch. With an hour until we had to report to dinner, I shot a few more arrows with my new release, vowing to become comfortable with it by my next shoot. Following my dad's advice not to focus on the score, instead I worked on my form.

I sorted a few shelves of the archery shed and thought about what my mom had said. It had aligned with the grief training from Robert. I'd accept my new world and the fact Josh wouldn't be in it, and then I could transition into this new identity.

The thing was—I didn't want to transition to an identity that didn't include Josh. I wanted to win enough prize money to cover my expenses and a trip to his front door. I lifted by compound bow off its peg and headed back outside.

CHAPTER 9

THE RELEASE WORKED EVERY TIME AS IF MY TARGET
panic had never happened, which made me fear it more. On the
camp's range, alone, with nothing at stake, so what if I could hit the
target. I had to be able to hit the target in a high stakes, tense competition in two weeks. I had to earn prize money, especially to make up
for the major loss I'd had in my last shoot, and the only way to attract
sponsors was to step on the podium at the end of it all.

Suddenly, the range didn't feel low stakes anymore.

The sound of wheels on the dusty gravel took my attention away
from the targets. A golf cart appeared from behind the trees with Drew
in the driver's seat. He parked next to the shed and headed my way.

He pointed to my bow. "What is that?"

"A compound bow."

"Oh. I can see why you were asking. That looks wildly different
from the ones we use."

"It comes with more gadgets and tools," I said. "It's what I use
for competitions."

"Can I see?"

Having an audience definitely raised the stakes. I took a deep
breath. "Sure."

I felt Drew's gaze on me through the process. When I triggered the release, the arrow wobbled its way to the nine ring.

"Impressive. What distance is that?"

"Forty yards. I'll have to shoot that plus from fifty and sixty yards in two weeks."

Drew came closer and studied the components of the bow. "You sound nervous."

I gestured toward the target, and he walked with me to retrieve my arrows. "I am. A little. I sort of tanked my last shoot."

"Tanked how? Like got low scores?"

"I had something called target panic."

"What's that?"

I pulled my arrows from the depths of the target. "Some psychological thing. I'm not sure anyone really knows how to explain it, and it can be, like, any form of panic while you're shooting. For me, my brain kept telling my hand to release the arrow, but I felt stuck."

He shielded his eyes from the sun. "Sorry."

"Thanks." The sincerity of his apology for something he'd had no control over made me swallow a lump in my throat. "We should pack up and head back."

Drew picked up a few stray arrows and the sparkly blue bag from my parents' gift. "How important was the shoot?"

"I'm afraid it set the tone for the rest of the summer circuit. More than ever, I have to be ready for the next one and have a drastically different outcome."

"Sounds like a lot of pressure," Drew said while I detached my sight and stabilizer and put the pieces back in my case. "It must have been good to see Josh this weekend then."

Confused, I set him straight. "I didn't see Josh this weekend."

"Oh." Drew fumbled with the recurve bows he was hanging on pegs.

I stopped breathing. "You saw Josh?"

"Not him," he said. "I was driving by on the way to the store for my mom—we have a camp nearby. I was in a rush. I said hey to Alexis and his parents. I thought Josh was inside. Were you there?"

Josh had been in Pittsburgh? All weekend. While I'd made popcorn and s'mores with Lily and Melanie. And rushed home to search for a letter from him. And told my mother that if we were in the same place, we'd be able to work things out.

We'd been in the same place. I just didn't know it.

The anger inside of me had been building since prom, but I'd suppressed it. I'd wanted Josh back. But why?

"I should never let a guy treat me like that," I mumbled, my muscles quivering.

"I'm sorry?"

"Josh and I." I urged my mouth to form the words. "We aren't together."

And exhale.

There.

It was out.

No more secret.

Drew's head jerked in surprise. "Since when?"

"Prom. He dumped me by Express Mail."

"Wow."

"Yep. I didn't even know he was in town this weekend."

"Wow."

"Exactly." Feeling the urge to shoot again, I loaded my arrows and headed back to the range. "We weren't married or anything. I get that. Really. I do. But nearly a year of my life, and all I get is a letter by Express Mail saying it's over."

"At least he sent it Express," Drew joked.

I laughed. Not like it was funny, but just because.

The range was quiet for a couple minutes before Drew asked, "Why didn't you tell anyone?"

"Who says I didn't?"

"The fact that the entire school didn't know before the first dance."

Thirty yards from the targets, I took my stance and prepped my bow, hoping shooting would ease the emotions flooding my body in that moment like it always had. "Very true. I guess I didn't know what to say."

He crossed his arms and waited in silence for me to say more. When I didn't, he supplied the obvious. "And you wanted to get back together."

I tilted my head from one side to another, emphatically considering his point and then focused on my shot, hitting a ten right in the center of the bullseye. "That, too."

"Impressive. Can I tell you something?"

"Your tone implies you're going to tell me anyway," I said, reloading.

"It sounds like you have some unresolved grief."

I groaned.

If Drew was anywhere near that perceptive with kids, it was clear why he was the head counselor.

I paused before my next shot. "I guess I felt like I was vapor without Josh."

"Not true. I knew who you were way before you started dating Josh."

"Liar. No way I would have been voted Prom Queen—not that I'd desperately wanted it or anything—without having been with Josh."

"Fine. Your relationship made you both high profile at school, but not because of Josh. People like you because you're a nice person, Elle. That doesn't always happen in high school or in life, period. People who knew Josh got to know you, but they liked you for you, not because you were with him."

"Thanks," I said quietly, but he scowled at me. "What?"

"You don't believe me. Okay. I'll prove it. Freshman year, my locker was right across from yours outside the French classroom in the new hallway."

He was right. It had been my sophomore year, but I didn't remember Drew.

"Stunned into silence?" he teased.

"My locker was near yours. Big deal. That doesn't mean anything."

"Does the fact that I had the hugest crush on you?"

I aimed, doing my best to calm my heart rate. "You're saying that to make me feel better. I've been through the training, too, you know, Drew. You can't use that counselor psychology on me."

I waited for his response. But he didn't offer one, not verbally. I looked away from the target to find his eyes locked on my face, and his lip tremble into a tiny smirk.

He was telling the truth.

I nearly melted to the grass.

Forcing myself to look away, I took the shot I'd prepped for and landed a seven.

"You okay?" Drew asked.

I nocked another arrow. "Fine." Except I shot another seven. I lowered my bow to its stand. "You're sweet to reveal an old crush in an attempt to boost my confidence."

"You're welcome," he said with a regal bow.

"I'm going to forget about Josh for a while." If you can, a voice whispered, but I told it not to challenge me. Like I'd crushed my father's challenge on the range and I'd rebounded from my target panic, or at least was in the process of rebounding, I'd crush a challenge about Josh, too. "I want to get out of my own head and grief, if that's what it is, and think about someone—something else instead."

"That sounds noble," he said.

To me, it felt finally less selfish than I'd been for months.

***

AS PROMISED, DREW FOUND ME AN ASSISTANT COUN-selor—Lake. Despite being younger than me, she towered over me like Melanie did. I guess at my height, that wasn't hard, but I could easily see campers thinking she was the cabin counselor, and I was the assistant. She showed up that evening and promptly filled one of the armoires with her things. Drew might need to order more of those. When my alarm buzzed at 6 a.m. the next morning, Lake's bed was made, and she quietly scrubbed the bathroom with disinfectant.

I could get used to an assistant counselor.

"Morning," she called and continued cleaning.

I dressed and prepped for the day in the bedroom mirror, my goal of thinking of others at the forefront of my thoughts. I did *not* spend the morning thinking about Josh being in Pittsburgh and not even reaching out to me.

Not even a little.

"I'll head over to the main lodge and greet campers as they arrive. Then I'll send them over here for you to help them get settled."

"Sounds good."

Good. I smiled at the mirror. Today was going to be great.

My first camper was 15-year old Izzy Bleu. I recognized her immediately from the photo in her file. Clearly athletic, she moved easily despite wearing two heavy-looking duffle bags. When she got to the registration table, she dropped them one by one, the sounds assuring me of their weight.

"Izzy, right?" I said. "Welcome to Camp Good Grief. Here's your welcome packet."

She took the folder and nodded a greeting.

Behind her, parents and campers rushed in different directions. I studied the parents, waiting for one to stand by Izzy. I expected her father. According to her file, she'd lived with a grandmother most of her life, but when she'd passed recently, Izzy's father had taken her back in. I couldn't imagine being shuffled around so much. Despite my family's many flaws, my parents had always created a safe and solid home for me and my sisters. Feeling pleased with myself for following Robert's rules of studying camper files before they arrived, I asked, "Is your father going to be joining us this morning for orientation?"

She snorted. "No. Just me."

"Right. Sorry. That's fine," I said, curious if her reaction was the kind of thing I should focus in on as a counselor or step back and give her some space with. "The assistant counselor, Lake, will be there to greet you and help with anything you need."

"Great," Izzy said and picked up the bags again.

I stepped around the table to help her. "I can carry one if you'd like."

"I got it," she called over her shoulder.

Independent. Like her file had said. Yet, the file hadn't given more details about her father. Clearly, not everything I needed to know about the girls was in the files. Which kind of freaked me out.

"Hi," said a tiny voice from behind me. Ann Stall. My youngest camper at age 14. She'd be 15 in two weeks, so technically, she was with the 15-16 age group.

"Ann!"

Her eyes widened.

"I'm sorry," I said, realizing I'd made yet another bad first impression. "I'm your counselor, Elle. I saw your picture."

"Oh. Hi." Ann's face had a soft perfection to it that reminded me of my grandmother's porcelain doll collection. Her cheeks were rosy. Her hair was blonde and fine, and her eyes were oval with the longest eyelashes ever. All of this, and I was pretty sure she didn't have a drop of makeup on.

"Ann. There you are!" A woman with the same delicate features appeared behind her daughter. "I got lost. So many kids running around. Hi," she said to me and extended her hand. "I'm Rose Stall. Nice to meet you."

"Hi. I'm Elle."

"Elle. Lovely. And are you Ann's counselor? You'll be staying in the same cabin with her?"

I smiled. Mrs. Stall obviously did the talking in the family. "Yes. And I have an assistant counselor who will be around to help. We will take good care of your daughter."

Mrs. Stall was doing her best to appear convinced.

"Mom, it's fine."

Mrs. Stall shifted her purse on her shoulder and studied the other counselors checking in their own campers. "There are family events this morning, right?"

"Yes." I handed her the folder with the parents' information and offered Ann her welcome packet, too. "You can drop your bags at the cabin." I drew an "X" on Cabin 12 on the map and pointed up the hill. "Can I help with your bags?"

"No, thank you," Ann said and walked toward the parking lot.

"Elle, I asked if Ann could give us a minute alone," Mrs. Stall said.

She stared at me with those big ovals as if I planned to devour her daughter.

"I'm really worried about her. She's been quiet since the accident. I want to help her, but I don't know if she needs space or me or time or what."

Ann's father and twin brother had been in a car accident—their SUV had been hit head on. The driver of the other car had been too distracted by her cell phone and didn't realize she had crossed into oncoming traffic. Mr. Stall and Ann's twin brother Andrew had been killed instantly.

"Do you think it will help her? Being here?" Mrs. Stall asked with her perfect face that was attempting to hide an interior that was far from perfect. I suspect I could probably sense her turmoil even if I was as far away as the archery range on the other side of camp.

"I promise to do my very best," I said and hoped that would be enough. "But really, my role is to help Ann stay on schedule with her activities and have fun. The licensed therapists are the ones who work more directly with the girls about what they're experiencing in life."

Mrs. Stall twisted her wedding ring around and around her ring finger.

"They're here today, too. You should talk to them about any concerns you have before you go. It might help you, too."

She lowered her head and struggled to hide the emotions that usually made people uncomfortable. "Mrs. Stall, Robert cries openly in front of us and encourages everyone to do the same. If you want privacy, that's fine, but please don't feel like you have to compose yourself for my sake."

She laughed and cried at the same time. "You're really kind, Elle. I think Ann will be fine with you. Thank you."

I breathed in her confidence and hoped more than anything that would be true.

CHAPTER 10

AFTER THE MORNING FAMILY SESSIONS, CABIN 12 GOT together on the hillside overlooking the lake to play a few ice breaker games. We learned names and other tidbits like month of birth, favorite color, and preferred sport. Izzy liked to invoke the cabin's rule of passing at any time. She introduced herself by name, but other than that, she'd said, "Pass," every time the spotlight fell on her. Robert had a rule that no matter what the task, a camper could simply pass and not be required to participate.

Ann, on the other hand, smiled at everyone and said all the right things. In the quiet moments, she slid closer to Izzy and got her talking, and even smiling. Savannah, an athletic brunette, loved basketball and other sports, too. Her dad, who had been her first basketball coach had passed away the summer before. Savannah connected immediately with Bridget, another basketball player. Bridget had lost her dad in the last year, too. Jordan was the last of the five girls in our cabin, here because of the death of her first cousin. She couldn't wait to tinker with experiments in the science lab. She would have gotten along perfectly with Harris and Lily.

The girls elected to call themselves the Lionesses, which sounded great to me. We made signs to hang inside and outside of the cabin. Ann designed an impressive logo of a lioness staring intently, but also somewhat wickedly, right at you. The girls loved it. Even Izzy nodded her approval, and I promised to make color copies in Robert's office as soon as I could.

Around camp, the girls were quick to make friends with Neil's cabin especially. Fifteen- and sixteen-year-old boys and girls—why would we expect any different. From Red Rover games that gave them the chance to wrap their arms around each other to the anticipation of hide and seek, the campers flirted and had fun.

"Guess that's what it's all about," Neil had joked.

In all the silliness and chatter, Izzy isolated herself. She wasn't contrary. In fact, she went along with all the ideas the other girls suggested, but she didn't seem to want to be directly involved.

"You think she's all right?" Lake asked.

"People adjust to situations differently," I said, proud of my studies during training. "She might like a little solitude, which is totally fine."

"If you say so."

"I do," I insisted. "But we should keep an eye on her."

We marched around camp stopping for instructions on water safety, where to find the sports equipment, the appropriate etiquette for getting food and clearing trays in the cafeteria. The introduction to camp crash course finished in time for the evening campfire where hot dogs and sticks were distributed as the main course, and s'mores followed for dessert.

The day before, the girls assigned to Cabin 12 had been photographs and words on a page, tucked into a file folder. Now, their laughter, facial expressions, and interests were real to me. Ann would spend most of her time in the art room. Savannah and Bridget had their sunscreen and water bottles ready for days of basketball, and Jordan's eyes lit up at the sight of the STEM room in the main lodge. Izzy—well, nobody was quite sure about Izzy. She had passed on everything so far.

"Izzy, are you sure you don't want to—" Lake had started, but Izzy said, "Pass," before she could finish.

I smiled at Lake and gave it a go. "Izzy, what activities are you looking forward to at camp?"

"Sleeping."

I groaned, but instead of scolding her like she probably expected, I said, "I love sleeping, too. There are these hammocks by the lake in the shade. I slept there every chance I could during training."

She looked at me sideways.

"And if you dig in the shed near the pool, there's a massive float. More like a boat, and you can sleep in that all afternoon."

"You want me to sleep?"

"You said you wanted to sleep."

She looked away from me and said, "That's actually kind of cool."

I hid my smile. Win for the counselor.

***

WHEN THE CAMPFIRE BECAME THE PRIMARY SOURCE of light, I leaned back against a tree trunk and watched my girls, the Lionesses, and Kate's girls, the Rock Stars, share graham crackers and help each other squeeze toasted marshmallows onto melting chocolate. Campers and counselors from the other cabins milled around, too.

It was in that quiet moment that I violated the first rule of Camp Good Grief—never compare losses. It was like saying don't compare ice cream flavors or film adaptations of your favorite books. Or anything really. While I'd promised not to compare the losses of my campers, I couldn't help but feel ashamed for letting something like a high school breakup get to me like it had.

Ann was sweet and delicate. Yet, she was living with the loss of her father and her twin brother. I couldn't imagine something happening to my dad or one of my sisters. When I felt the pressure building, the lump forming in my throat, I finally felt free to let the tears fall. The girls. Feeling their pain. Trying to help them and wondering if there was anything I could realistically do.

From across the fire, Drew made eye contact with me and tilted his head to the side. He mouthed the words, "You okay?"

I shrugged. He must have seen that as an invitation because he circled the campfire and sat next to me. "I'm going to have to cry with you. Camp motto."

I wiped my tears away. "I'm sorry."

"Don't apologize. The first day is the second most tearful day," he said, handing me a tissue. "There are travel packs of tissues in a basket at the registration desk."

"I'd missed that," I said, dabbing my eyes. "What day is the most tearful?"

"The day everyone leaves," Drew said as if it had been obvious, and I guess it was. "Your campers look like they're in good hands with Lake and Kate. Want to walk it off?"

Solar panel lights illuminated the path around the lake.

"Sure," I said. "Thanks."

We fell into a rhythm, walking side-by-side until we'd made a lap around the lake. Neither of us said anything, and somehow that helped more than talking. There was something warm and comfortable about Drew. Maybe it was all the summers he'd spent training with Robert. Being around him felt like coming home.

"I feel like being here, working with these kids is like the experience of grief," he finally said. "It's not always the same. Sometimes it's easier than other times. Sometimes, campers stay with you, become part of you. Most of the them, really."

The campfire was ahead, and I could see the campers sitting around it. The laughter carried through the night air, and it made me smile.

"Did you shoot today?"

"A little. I was able to sneak away for about an hour."

"How did it go?"

"Good. I'm still in the first stage of overcoming target panic. I'm working on my motion and the smoothness of it. My parents got me a new release."

"That was nice."

"Yeah, but I have to get comfortable with it. After that, I'll pay closer attention to my scores and then finally practice the exact shooting distances and number of arrows for the shoot."

"I don't mean to sound ignorant, but what is your goal with summer shoots? You have a scholarship to college to shoot, right?"

I explained the expense of equipment, the new equipment I needed, and how the prize money can offer me the freedom to shoot more and work less.

"What would a sponsor do for you?"

"Give me equipment at cost, or even better, free."

"Nice."

We walked a little farther before Drew switched to a new subject of questioning.

"How have you been, you know, with Josh?"

"You mean without Josh." Gravel crunched under our feet. "I kinda hate him."

"I'm sorry."

"He was pretty much perfect, and I was crazy about him. But then he dumped me."

"Maybe he had a good reason," Drew suggested.

I went hands on hips and glared at him. "What is that supposed to mean?"

"Or not. Sorry. I guess I don't want you to hate him."

"I don't want to hate him either, but it's working out that way at least for now. Anger's part of the process, right?"

Drew nodded.

The night sky was clear, and the reddish hue of Mars caught my eye. I dropped to the ground, lying on my back, watching the vastness of the universe.

"What are you doing?"

"Appreciating the stars."

Drew joined me. "No light pollution up here."

"Do you see that M-looking constellation?"

"Cassiopeia."

I gasped. "How did you know?"

"It's near Perseus and Andromeda." He pointed, too, but I didn't have to follow the edge of his finger to know where those constellations were. Too many nights stargazing with Josh, Melanie, and her boyfriend, Harris. "How can you not love Perseus? He was clever enough to defeat Medusa without getting turned to stone."

I loved Perseus. Although possessing Medusa's skills in high school would be incredible. "It would be cool to be able to turn people to stone."

"But your hair would be made of snakes."

"True," I conceded.

"You could be Andromeda and be saved from an evil sea monster."

"Are there any stories in Greek mythology where the woman saves herself? Or better yet, her man?"

"Uh. Sorry," Drew said. "Not sure when this became a feminist conversation. I'm not really a scholar on mythology."

"Just astronomy."

"Yep. How did you get interested in the stars?" Drew asked.

Josh, I thought. Instead, I said, "My next-door neighbor, Harris. He would get his telescope out for us over the years, and we picked up a lot. When apps came out that mapped out the night sky, that helped."

"Harris is a good guy. Has he been dating Melanie long?"

"Since the beginning of the year. They were completely unexpected yet totally obvious at the same time."

Drew laughed. "Maybe that's how it should be."

"I don't know," I said. "When I figure out relationships, maybe I'll have the answer to that."

"If you figure out relationships, that alone should be enough of a victory."

I couldn't help but think about how terrible I had been at figuring out my relationship with Josh. Even after he moved away and broke all of his promises, I still thought we were good. Harsher reality? He broke up with me, and I still thought we'd work it out.

Worse yet? He'd come home for the weekend, not made any effort to see me, and deep down, part of me—hell, all of me—watched my phone every second of the day as if he was about to call and admit he'd been an idiot for breaking up with me.

I was as far from figuring out relationships than a person could be.

If only there was an app for relationships like there was for the night sky.

"What makes you such an expert on the stars?" I asked Drew.

"Remember when I said that my family has a camp near Josh's?"

"Oh." Of course it came back to Josh. Everything did. Josh had known more than what the star and sky apps listed. He'd told the stories of love and power and heroism.

"It's like anything else," he would say. "Some people know all the players on professional sports teams or like to go bird watching.

I happen to know the constellations in the sky."

His eyes would twinkle when he'd tease, "You know it's sexy."

That, I did not want to think about. I stood so quickly that dizziness threatened to knock me back down. "I'm ready to head back."

We made our way toward the campfire in the distance. The shifting shadows around it served as some sort of salvation. I'd be able to suppress any thoughts of Josh and enjoy the girls' company. I'd focus on my purpose in being here, on helping them.

And on helping myself.

CHAPTER 11

DREW DIDN'T MENTION JOSH'S NAME AGAIN. THE LION-esses fell into a groove of breakfast, group therapy sessions, lunch, activities, dinner, and then campfires and s'mores. Our archery groups were small, but that made it easier to teach them. Diane, the youth instructor from the local shooting range, stayed longer on most days to help me train through my episode of target panic. My first summer competition was on the day we had off between sessions one and two, and luckily, it was about twenty minutes away from camp. Sitting in on the morning therapy sessions and shooting in the afternoons, not to mention the scenery of camp—I spent less time sneaking glimpses into my Josh box and more time standing in the breeze, my head tilted back, breathing fresh air.

In my limited experience, those moments of euphoria tended to be dashed.

"Elle, I think we should talk," Lake said near the end of our two-week session while the Lionesses and the Rock Stars were loading their trays for dinner. "I'm worried about Izzy. She's quieter than before."

"I was afraid of that, too," I said. I'd hoped that as the days passed, she would become more comfortable and open up, but the reverse had happened. "I haven't even seen her talk to Ann in the last day. Where is she?"

"She was using the phone in Robert's office last I saw her, but then she never came to dinner. I know you're supposed to train after dinner, but can you try to talk to her first? She seems to like you more than me."

I wasn't sure I agreed with that. Izzy hadn't exactly taken to anyone at camp. She tolerated Ann because it was difficult not to with Ann's endless patience and kindness.

"I'll find her," I promised.

I left Lake with the other Lionesses and wandered the halls of the main lodge toward Robert's office. Izzy's voice carried down the hall. I moved toward it more quickly, eager to check on her, but stopped as soon as I registered the words. "Can I stay with you when I leave here? My dad's traveling for a while." Silence. "Sure. I get it. Parents, right?" Silence. "No problem. Thanks."

I hovered in the hallway, guilt creeping over me for eavesdropping, but not enough to stop. After a few seconds, Izzy's voice floated through the open doorway again.

"Hey, it's Izzy." Silence. "Yeah, you, too. So, um, I was wondering if I could stay with you this weekend for a few days while my dad's out of town." Silence. "Great. Shoot me a text or whatever and let me know if they're cool with it." Silence. "Yeah, thanks."

Robert appeared down the other end of the hall and called, "Hey, Elle. What do you need?"

I closed my eyes and sighed. Izzy popped her head out of Robert's office and glared at me. "Are you eavesdropping on my phone time?"

"No," I lied. "I wanted to see if you were ready for dinner."

"Pass."

"Izzy, you can't pass on dinner. You have to eat."

"No. We can pass on anything. So, pass."

Robert reached his office by then and asked if everything was okay. Neither of us answered. By the sound of it, everything definitely was not. My instincts told me Izzy's father wasn't traveling, that instead, he'd left her. The right words to say to something like that eluded me. If I was right, Izzy didn't have anywhere to go when she left camp, but if I told Robert that now, especially in front of her, she'd never trust me. If I knew anything in that moment, Izzy desperately needed someone to trust.

Robert looked back and forth between us. "Izzy, is something going on?"

Izzy studied me, and I did my best to look nonchalant.

"You were listening," she yelled at me, pointing her finger in my face. "You don't think I know when a grownup is lying."

"Izzy, that's enough," Robert said, standing between us.

"I want a new counselor. Elle's terrible. She should be fired."

What? No. I didn't deserve that. Anger flooded my body, urging me to blurt what I'd heard on the phone and that Izzy was only trying to cover up her own emotions by targeting me. Instead, my heart broke for her even more, and I kept my mouth shut.

Robert didn't even look my way. He half smiled at Izzy with nothing but love and patience. "Izzy, it's okay to feel whatever you feel, but it's not okay to say things like that about people when you're angry."

"She invaded my privacy."

Robert nodded. "You think Elle invaded your privacy by hearing some of your phone call?"

Izzy crossed her arms. "Yes!"

"Yet when I asked if everything was okay, she didn't answer me. She let you decide what to tell and what not to tell."

He'd picked up on that.

"If she did hear your conversation, and I'm not sure if she did, she in fact respected your privacy anyway."

Izzy snuck a sideways glance at me but didn't say anything.

"I hear you haven't had dinner. Why don't you join my family and me, and we can chat more?"

"Pass," Izzy said.

Robert smiled at me. "Let's all walk back to the cabin then. I understand it's your evening to train, Elle. Better get that in before the rain comes."

"It is. Izzy, would you want to come shoot with me?"

She didn't even glance my way. "Pass."

Good thing I liked a challenge.

***

BY THE TIME I MADE THE HIKE TO THE RANGE, DARK clouds cut through the horizon. I loaded my quiver and did my best to focus for the competition that was now two days away, but Izzy's voice played in my mind. The scared undertones. The way she'd tried to sound nonchalant. My gut told me she had nowhere to go. Respecting her privacy or not, I couldn't let her leave camp without telling Robert. What if her father didn't even come to pick her up?

Thunder roared. The first drops speckled my face. I ran to the shed to store my bow and headed back to the target for my arrows, but the skies opened before I reached them. By the time I got back to the shed for cover, I was soaked through. Rain blew sideways so thickly that the view from the doorway was a blur of green trees and grass in the distance. I found a few pieces of cardboard and piled them onto the wooden floor to wait out the storm. As soon as I got comfortable, a thump against the side of the shed made me scream.

Groaning followed the thump.

I tiptoed to the entrance and found Drew in a pile of mud against the side of the shed. "What are you doing?"

"I was running to the shed for cover, but I slipped. You heard the thump I'm assuming."

"I think Robert heard it back in his office."

"Funny," Drew said, but his lip had curved into a smile.

"Let me help you." I tried to pull him upright.

"No. You're going to get soaked."

"I'm already soaked," I said. "Come on."

I helped him to my pile of cardboard boxes, and we sloshed to the floor with a splat, water leaking out from under us.

"It's raining out there," Drew said so seriously we both laughed.

"What are you doing down here?"

"I thought I could get here before the storm and give you a ride back, but I had to bail out of the golf cart on the way. It's stuck in mud."

"Robert will be thrilled," I teased.

He ran his hands through his thick hair. He could have been wringing out a towel.

"Here," I said, grabbing a roll of paper towels from the shelf. When I reached down to hand them to Drew, I slipped and landed in his lap. He groaned again.

"I'm so sorry," I said.

"It's okay. I've maxed out on injuries today."

I apologized again, but he waved it away and called Robert on the walkie talkie to let him know we were stuck there for a while.

"Since we're going to be here for a while, how's the counselor gig going?" he asked.

"Okay, I guess."

"Convincing."

"I may have overheard Izzy's conversations on the phone today, and I'm concerned about her." I explained the situation to Drew.

"You're right to be concerned. Let's talk to Robert. He can connect her to support through the authorities where she lives."

"Like an orphanage?"

"Foster care, probably," Drew said. "But maybe she has other relatives she can stay with."

"I have a feeling if she had other relatives, she wouldn't be with her dad. I read her file, and a child psychologist from her school recommended—practically insisted—she come to the camp."

Rain pattered on the roof. I closed my eyes, urging the natural sound to soothe the tenseness that had taken over my muscles. After a few minutes, I felt lighter.

"You good?" Drew asked.

"Getting there. I can't believe you've been doing this for years."

He propped his hands against the floor and leaned back. "I guess you could say I've had a unique understanding of emotions, grief, even death for a long time."

"Sounds like there's a story there."

He licked his lips and took a deep breath. "I was a two-time cancer survivor by the time I was ten."

"Oh." I couldn't think of anything more sophisticated to say. Sorry wouldn't cut it. Congratulations didn't feel right either.

"When I was three, and then again at eight," he continued. "The first time, I didn't know what was happening except it wasn't fun and my parents cried a lot. At eight, I was pretty convinced I was going to die."

"I, um… Wow."

He shrugged. "When I talk about it, people usually get all tongue-tied."

"Sorry to be predictable."

"The thing is I've done everything I wanted in life. Almost. I got to play sports, build meaningful relationships, spend time with my family, grow up. When you're living as a cancer survivor, you always have that possibility that it could come back. It's like that song about living like you were dying. In a way, we're all dying, but people like me are more aware of it."

I sucked in a breath. "That's deep."

"Perfect conversation for when you're stuck in a shed in the middle of a storm?"

I laughed. "Pretty much."

"It helps me connect to the campers. Every counselor has their thing. For you, maybe it's Josh."

I checked on the storm outside, but the sky was dark in all directions. We were definitely stuck.

"If you don't want to talk about him…" Drew's voice faded.

"It's awkward. You're his friend. And honestly, I don't know what to say."

"Why?"

"Enough time has passed that it's not so fresh, but not enough time has passed to give me any sense of what I'm taking away from the whole thing."

"That makes sense."

Even more since I'd said it aloud. Talking to Drew made me sort through things that had previously felt like knotted balls of yarn in my head.

"I'm trying to focus on the girls," I said, "but I feel way in over my head. Even if it were a regular summer camp, supervising teenage girls would be a lot, but these girls are really struggling. Some more obviously than others, and I don't want to make it worse for them."

Drew leaned on the side of the door frame opposite me. "You won't. I can see how much you care about them, and that's what they need to see and feel and know right now."

"I can't fix anything for them."

"Nobody can," Drew countered. "They have to find a way to envision a new life without the person they lost. For some, the change is bigger than for others."

Maybe that was the thing with Josh and me. I'd already been living without him for months. If I'd been seeing him daily, then the breakup may have shocked my system a bit more.

"You're pretty smart. You know that?"

Drew blushed. "Thanks."

The rain had turned the dirt path into a mini stream, and the skies showed no signs of forgiveness.

"You think at some point we'll have to make a run for it?" I asked.

"Maybe when the lightning stops."

"Fair point. What do we do until then?" I glanced at Drew and swear I felt a spark of flirtation in his gaze. His lips curved into a smirk, and he licked his lips and broke eye contact with me. I didn't dare push and ask what he'd been thinking about. The heat creeping up my neck told me I probably didn't want to know.

Drew cleared his throat. "We could sing camp songs. Or play word games. Those really pass the time."

"Word games?"

"You learn all sorts of games when you have to entertain children between sessions summer after summer." He explained a few of the games and let me pick. Within minutes, we were laughing so hard, we couldn't stand. We retreated to the cardboard rug. Besides a few overly long glances, he'd held all flirtations in check.

I couldn't tell if I was relieved or disappointed.

"Looks like it's finally letting up out there," Drew said. "We can attempt to dig the golf cart out of the mud and if it doesn't go, I'll come back for it tomorrow with the tractor."

"Sounds good to me," I said.

We made sure everything was in its place in the shed and locked the door.

"Thanks for keeping me company."

"My pleasure," he said. His glance definitely held on too long. And a little longer. I took a deep breath, but I couldn't look away either. "You ready?" he whispered.

I'd lived long enough to know that life brought you moments where you and another person were in a bubble of some kind. In a moment of time when the circumstances created this vibe that might never be captured again. The vibe freed your inhibitions, letting you say things you might never say outside the bubble. Maybe it was the realization that Drew and I had had one of those moments while the rain had pummeled our little shed and the grassy world surrounding it, but I felt the urge to ask him one last question.

"You said earlier that you've had the opportunity to do nearly everything you wanted to do in life."

"Yeah," he said.

"What haven't you done yet that you still want to?"

His cheeks flushed, confirming I'd been on to something to ask. "You're going to think it's stupid."

"Promise I won't," I said.

He took a deep breath and left me in suspense a few seconds before finally closing his eyes and answering. "I want to fall in love."

CHAPTER 12

THE GOLF CART WASN'T GOING ANYWHERE. DREW
walked me back to Cabin 12 with both of us strategically avoiding
any personal topics after his declaration about wanting to fall in love.
I didn't blame him for wanting it. Falling in love with Josh had been
all the clichés people say—magical, mind-blowing, heart-stopping,
life-changing. What was crazy about falling in love was although the
clichés applied, it also felt like nobody had ever fallen in love quite
like you before. Like it couldn't be. Like our love was somehow
more or better or extra or something. Like all those other couples in
love had nothing on us. That our love story was unique and couldn't
be matched.

"Elle! Thank God." Lake appeared from the shadows of a nearby
cabin, gasping for breath.

"What's wrong?" Drew asked in his professional, head counselor
tone.

"Izzy's gone."

I grabbed Lake's arm and pulled her back in the direction of our
cabin. "Gone, how?"

"I don't know. She was with us all evening. Reserved and quiet as
usual. She was sitting on a chair, watching the rain out the window.
Did you talk to her like you said you would?"

"Sort of. She was on the phone, looking for somewhere to stay. Wait. Drew, do you think she ran away to avoid getting put in foster care?"

He shrugged. "Maybe. It's hard to say what she's thinking. Lake, when did you see her last?"

"Everyone was brushing their teeth. About thirty minutes ago."

Drew stopped us before we entered the cabin. "Do the other girls know?"

"They know she's not here," Lake said.

"Does Izzy have any areas of camp where she seems most comfortable?" Drew asked.

Lake shrugged. "The fire pit, maybe."

"I told her to check out the hammocks earlier," I suggested. "But she's passed on every activity, so it's hard to say."

"Every one?" Drew asked.

"Yep," Lake and I said in unison.

"Lake, stay in the cabin. Elle and I will find her."

Lake gave a weak wave and headed back inside. Drew had a lot more experience than me. I deferred to him. "Is there some sort of protocol for this?"

"Not exactly. But when anyone is missing, the first place we're told to look is the pool. Or in our case, the pool and the lake."

An image of a lifeless Izzy floating in the pool sent acid up my throat.

"Probably she's not there, but it's best to check."

I nodded. "I'll take the pool. After I check it, I'll meet you at the lake."

"Done. I'll radio Robert on the way."

We both took off, sprinting toward our destinations. The pool was down the hill and to the right of the recreation lodge. Drew had to continue straight down the hill to the lake. My shoes sank into the soft ground. I splashed through puddles and slipped more than once, but I didn't slow down. Lights illuminated the pool and the chained fence surrounding it. From the border, I couldn't make out anything out of the ordinary, but I had to be sure. I pressed my toe into an opening in the fence and climbed. Toe after toe, I pulled myself up, my heart racing from the run and for the fear that I might see the very thing I desperately didn't want to be true. When I was high enough to see every inch of the surface and all the way to the bottom with absolute clarity, I rested my cheek against the cool steel and caught my breath.

No Izzy.

In the distance, the moonlight shone on the lake. It wouldn't be as easy to search as the pool. Without another thought, I dropped to the ground, sliding in the mud. Ignoring an uncomfortable pull in my ankle, I slid down the hill as if skiing but without the skis. I ran toward the image of Drew on the dock, pointing a flashlight in all directions.

"Anything?" I called.

"Not yet."

"What's going on?" Neil yelled from the hillside.

I waved him down and briefed him. He dove into the water swam to the dock at the center of the lake. He climbed onto it and scanned the water around him. Drew directed the flashlight to help him search. He gave me a flashlight, and I ran the path along the lake, searching the water.

When the three of us were wet, muddy, and out of breath, we agreed—Izzy was not in the lake.

"She could be in the woods," I suggested.

"Or back at the cabin by now," Drew offered.

"You don't think Lake would come and tell us?"

"She doesn't know where we are."

Good point.

Neil handed his flashlight back to Drew. "I'll go by the cabin and see if she came back."

Drew gave him his radio. "Give her this, and tell her to call Robert if Izzy shows up. Elle and I will search the rec and main lodges. At least we can mark those off the list if we're going on a formal search around the grounds."

"Neil, ask someone to do a round of all the cabins in case she got caught up visiting someone and stayed because of the rain." Not that I believed that for a second. Izzy had barely talked to the girls in our own cabin. Venturing out for friendship didn't seem like her way.

We all agreed and set off.

"The rec lodge is closer," I said. "Start there?"

"Sure. There's a security system that should be triggered at this time of day. We can check the main areas, but the classrooms should be locked. If she was locked inside, it would have triggered the system."

"Could the system have been shut down by the storm?"

He groaned. "Possibly. We'll check every room."

Drew had a key to the front door of the lodge. We knocked on every door and flashed the light through the glass. I hate to say, but being in the old building late at night without lights and people amplified the camp's horror movie vibe. When the wooden floorboards creaked, I jumped into Drew.

"You okay?"

"Embarrassingly, no."

"I get it. It's creepy." He held out his hand, and I slipped my fingers into it.

"Thanks." I did my best to ignore the spark of energy tingling where our skin touched, and released him. "You know what? I'm good. Let's find Izzy."

We picked up the pace and searched every room and stairwell. All the doors had been locked, and the security system appeared intact.

"Do you know anything about her?" Drew asked. "Anything we could use?"

"She really only talks to Ann," I said.

Robert caught up with us then and gave us each a radio. We updated him on our search.

"I'll talk to Ann," Robert said. "Can one of you check the main lodge?"

"I got it," I said.

Drew offered to search the other outdoor areas like the baseball dugouts and picnic pavilions.

"Radio if you find her," Robert said, and we all agreed.

In seconds, I was at the main lodge. Since the kitchen entrance was usually open because of deliveries and for people to grab snacks, I headed down to that basement door.

Inside, a custodian mopped the floor with ear buds in. I did my best to warn him of my presence before I scared him into a heart attack, and we had two issues on our hands. Unconcerned, he waved and got back to work. With more lights on, I didn't have to rely on my flashlight nearly as much, but the quiet building still creeped me out. I searched the rooms and called out for Izzy in each one. As I was about to go up the stairs, I swore I heard something down the hall.

Doing an epic, and I mean epic, job of ignoring all of the scenes from horror movies flashing in my mind, I tiptoed toward the noise. Hell, why had Drew and I separated? That was like the absolutely biggest faux pas in horror. Breathe, breathe. The last door at the end of the hall read "Laundry." A crash inside made me jump.

Please don't be a rat. Or a bear. Definitely not a bear.

I took a deep breath and mustered all of the bravery I never knew I had to push the door open. Of course, it creaked the entire way because why the hell not?

The flashlight beam revealed white washer after white washer until something on the floor reflected the light. I fumbled for the light switch.

Click.

"Dammit!" Izzy shielded her face with her hands. "Shit."

"Language," I said, maintaining my calm until my eyes and my heart rate adjusted. Izzy was slumped on top of one of the washers, her hair ruffled and matted. Her face was smeared with the black of her mascara. Liquid spread from the broken glass beneath her, and the room reeked of the distinct scent of my parents' liquor cabinet.

Her language might have been right on after all.

"Izzy, tell me you're not drunk."

She peered between her fingers, which were still protecting her eyes from the sudden light. "Otay. I not junk."

It was official.

Worst.

Counselor.

Ever.

CHAPTER 13

AFTER THE CUSTODIAN RADIOED ROBERT AND CLEANED
up the mess of broken glass and alcohol, I left Izzy with the higher
ups. I got as far as the swing on the front porch of the main lodge
before I put my head in my hands and lamented my absolute failure.

One of my campers had gotten drunk. My first session. I didn't
even know if that was the first time she'd been drinking. Or where
the alcohol had come from. Or whether I could have done something
to anticipate this or stop it or anything.

"This seat taken?" Drew asked, and I groaned. "I can leave you
alone if you want."

I scooted over on the swing, not even looking at him.

"It's not that bad, Elle."

"You're joking, right?"

"No. I mean. It's a grief camp. We've seen some things."

"I'm supposed to look out for her," I said. "For her basic safety.
Nothing about her drunk, alone, in a dark laundry room, with broken
glass around her demonstrates safety."

"No matter how much we want to, we can't take responsibility
for everyone, and we definitely can't take responsibility for their
decisions."

I rubbed my face, unwilling to unpack that statement or how its life lessons could be applied.

"Elle, look at me." Drew peeled my hands away from my eyes.

His expression was soft and kind, as usual, but something new—he hadn't let go of my hands. I didn't release his either.

"She'll be okay," he said.

"Will she? She's clearly hurting. And she doesn't participate in anything. I want to help her."

"That's because you're a good person."

I rolled my eyes. "A good person whose camper gets drunk while she's off in a shed with—"

Drew straightened. "Oh. Guilt. I get it."

Guilt and other stuff. Like the tug I felt urging me to be close to Drew when he was around.

"Let's be real," he said. "You were on approved training time. A storm came in that made it dangerous for you to head back, and the whole time, your campers were safe with your assistant counselor."

"Were they? And I'm not blaming Lake. There's a reason she's supposed to be my assistant. Maybe I'm putting too much on her plate."

"You're not putting it on her. Robert and I are because we believe she's capable. What you're feeling right now is natural. When someone we care about does something they shouldn't, we internalize all the ways we went wrong and sent them down that path."

"You're psychoanalyzing me?" A fact that only moderately annoyed me.

"I'm trying to help you."

"Sure you're not internalizing something about how I'm feeling?"

He laughed. "You're impossible."

"I want to help her."

Drew ran his thumb along mine, the gentleness of the gesture making my breath catch. I closed my eyes and leaned against his shoulder.

"You'll figure it out," he whispered. "But you have to let go of the guilt, or it will leave you no mental space to help Izzy."

That made sense. Not easy to do, but it made sense. "Thank you."

"You're welcome."

Drew's thumb hadn't stopped soothing my fears one smooth

swipe at a time. In the cool night air, frogs croaked around the lake and insects fluttered under the lights. Otherwise, camp was silent, as though waiting for something.

Maybe my heart waited, too.

Although I knew Josh and I were over, he'd hung out there, on the periphery of my life, not entirely gone, but definitely not present.

In the moonlight, Drew's face was inches from mine. His eyes opened wide as if waiting for a question or better yet, an answer. He looked at my lips.

Leaned toward me.

His eyes closed.

And my heart exploded in my chest more intensely than when I'd run through the mud or climbed the fence, or even when I'd found Izzy in the laundry room.

I leaned my head to the side. The tips of our noses touched.

And…

And…

The front door of the lodge squealed open. Drew and I jumped off the swing so fast it clattered against the wooden railing.

I'd been wrong about my heart. It definitely had the capability to pound faster.

"Oh good," Robert said. "You're both here. Let's talk about what happened."

***

THE LIONESSES WOKE UP TO AN EMPTY BED IN THE cabin, and all the logical reactions followed. Wide eyes. Whispers. Questions. I'd briefed Lake the night before on where and how we'd found Izzy. Robert hadn't gotten much more detail out of her before she passed out under the supervision of the camp nurse. The plan had been to let her sleep it off and follow up with her today.

"Izzy's okay," I said. "She's just not here. I know you'll understand when I say I can't tell you any more than that."

But they didn't understand. On the way to the cafeteria, they speculated loudly enough for Lake and me to hear, watching our reactions to guess if they'd gotten warmer. Lake and I found a corner table with

Kate and lowered our heads over our breakfast.

"You two look rough," Kate said.

Lake rubbed her eyes. "It was a long night."

"I bet. I'm sorry."

"Really long," I added, especially when you include the hours I stayed up afterwards wishing Drew and I had kissed while also cringing at the fact we'd almost kissed. I took a bite of my cereal and lifted my head to find Lake and Kate staring at me.

"Oh yeah," Kate said. "She's my best friend, and I can assure you something is going on."

I paused mid-chew.

"Spill," she said, and I was pretty sure she didn't mean my cereal.

"How did you...?"

She waved my question away and nodded with wide eyes.

"Drew and I almost kissed last night."

They both gasped so loudly that the Lionesses and Rock Stars stared.

"Can we be a little less obvious please?"

"Like anyone in this camp doesn't see you two are totally into each other," Lake said. "We need details."

"All of them," Kate added. "Where were his hands? Where were your hands? Did you touch his pecs? Please tell me you touched his pecs."

I covered my face with my hands but couldn't help smiling at my best friend. She was good for that. Before I answered, I searched the room to make sure Drew hadn't come in for his breakfast, too. Then I explained the almost kiss on the porch, including the whereabouts of everyone's hands.

"And now?" Kate asked. "How's the morning after?"

I lowered my head. "I still want to kiss him. Like a lot."

"Yeah you do."

They both laughed, but I groaned. The fears I'd had about not being fully over Josh and that not being fair to Drew if we had kissed muddled my thinking.

"First of all," Kate said. "You're too nice."

"That's not true."

"It is. And that's one of the things I love about you. You're genuinely kind. Look. You want to explore things with Drew, but if you can't commit your entire being to him, you feel you're not being fair. But that's not reality. He knows where your heart is. He knows you and Josh broke up like weeks ago. With all of that, he likes you, and he wants you."

"Yeah, he does," Lake said, and we laughed again.

"You're not doing anything wrong by Drew. If you want, even tell him you're not entirely over Josh yet. Give him a choice to back off or hang out. You're not agreeing to marry him."

"I know that," I said.

"And Josh is great, but he's gone. And he didn't have a graceful exit. It doesn't add up to me, but he did what he did. He doesn't deserve anything from you anymore."

Kate's speech lingered in my mind as we finished breakfast and headed for group therapy. Then, it was time to focus on my girls. Robert greeted us in the same room where we'd first met for counselor training. The circle of chairs was smaller, more intimate.

"Come in. Sit anywhere," Robert said. He smiled widely and pointed to open seats. He showed no signs of a man who had been up all night because an underage girl had snuck alcohol in to camp.

"Thanks for coming, everyone," he said when we were settled.

"Is Izzy coming?" Ann asked.

Robert deflected the question. "Why do you ask?"

The girls glanced at each other.

Robert waited.

Finally, Ann said, "We're worried about her. Her dad is really hard on her. A couple months ago, she got caught skipping lunch to walk to the gas station for a slushie. The next day, she...her dad didn't take it well."

Was she saying Izzy's father physically abused her? The father Robert had attempted to call the night before to report Izzy's drinking? The father who still hadn't returned the call? My stomach tightened at the thought of Izzy being sent home to someone like that.

"Thank you for your concern about your friend," Robert said with a smile. "I appreciate your kind hearts. We need friends that will ask the tough questions for us as we heal. I hope you keep that in mind when you return home and decide which friends to surround yourself with. But let's think about all of this a little more. When we lose someone that is really the foundation of our everyday life, like a parent, or maybe if we live with them, a grandparent, that death shakes the foundation, leaving cracks. When we feel those cracks, we can become afraid or anxious. We may feel powerless, not knowing how we're going to live or how our lives will ever be safe again. When we think we've conquered those fears, they can creep up again, when we least expect them, with triggers that we didn't know existed."

Robert paused and allowed his words to settle with the girls. Savannah and Bridget nodded. Ann cried openly. Jordan remained stoic.

"When we know our friends are feeling these fears and anxieties, our best action is to be there for them, to hear them, and to let them know their feelings are valid." Robert retrieved a stack of notebooks from under his chair. "I know we're all thinking about Izzy right now. It might be difficult to discuss much else. Why don't you all write a note to her? I'll get it to her right after our session. I'm sure she'll appreciate hearing from you."

One by one, the girls took a pen and paper, dispersed to various tables around the room, and wrote. My chest filled with pride. Even amidst their grief, these girls were able to think of someone beyond themselves. A girl who'd barely spoken to them, who'd spent most of her time silent.

"I'll take one, too, please," I said to Robert. "If you have enough."

"Plenty."

"Thanks. And I'd really like to be the one to deliver the notes to Izzy, if you don't mind."

CHAPTER 14

"YOU MIGHT NOT BELIEVE THIS, BUT I'M KIND OF GLAD to see you," Izzy said when I sat next to her in the nurse's office. She looked sideways at the seventy-something nurse working her crossword puzzle. "She doesn't speak."

"Did you try to get her fired, too?" I asked with a smile to make sure she knew I was joking.

Izzy cringed. "My bad."

Remembering Robert's urging to be a good listener, I asked, "Is there anything you want to talk about?"

"Is there anything you want to talk about?" she answered.

"You're good at that."

"What?"

"Deflecting. But I'm here to listen…if you want to talk."

Izzy crossed her arms.

"Okay. I don't want to impose. I can leave you here with the chatty nurse." I raised my eyebrows at her in a way that I hoped showed her I wanted to hear what she was locking up within herself.

She scowled at me. "Fine. Last night was immature, irresponsible, fill-in-the-blank."

"Izzy, what's going on with you?" I waited in silence.

And waited.

"I don't get it," Izzy started. Robert and his silent technique? Total genius. "My dad can blow off the entire planet and get lit every afternoon, but I can't have a tiny drink."

"Wanna tell me about your dad?"

She cracked open another a bottle of fruit punch sports drink and sipped slowly. "He drinks. So does my mom. They're really good at it."

More silence. Not that I planned it. Her candor had startled me.

"Robert hasn't been able to reach him. Probably because he's been drunk longer than I have."

I thought back to her phone calls. "Do you have some place to go when you leave camp?"

"I knew you heard me." She scowled but let go of it easily.

"What about your mom?"

"Locked up down south, and if she gets out, she'll find her way right back in."

"That's why you've been staying with your dad?"

"He told me he isn't made for parenting. It's why he'd dropped me off on my grandma's doorstep in the first place."

Her voice hiccupped when she mentioned her grandma.

"Do you want to talk about her?" I asked.

Tears filled her eyes. "She was feisty. The best cook. She folded laundry with too much attention to creases and edges. No joke. The shirts, shorts—everything, perfectly flattened." She quieted for a minute before adding one detail that chiseled another crack in my heart. "She loved me."

Like Robert had during training, I refused to hide the tears on my cheeks. "I'm sorry she passed, Izzy."

"Me, too."

"Have you ever written about any of this? About your parents? Camp?"

She grinned. "You mean all the activities I passed on?"

I smiled back at her. "Yeah. Those."

"I knew my dad was gonna bail. Maybe I should give him credit for coming at all. Being here, I guess I figured it was pointless to work through my grief from losing my gram. Grief is all I have left of her."

I squeezed her hand. "She raised you. Everything you choose to be every day is a reflection of your Gram."

"I never thought of it like that," Izzy said and lowered her head. "What would she think of last night?"

"That you made a mistake, and that you can and will do better."

"You sound like her."

"She and my mom must have been cut from the same cloth." I retrieved a stack of cards, drawings, and letters from my bag and slid them cross the table to Izzy. "The Lionesses are thinking of you."

She scanned the pages, laughing and tearing up at some of the messages. "I'll read them later." With a glance toward the nurse, she added, "I'll have time. But thanks. This is kind of cool."

"You're welcome."

"I expected this place to be cheesy. With a name like Camp Good Grief, how could it not be?"

I could give her that.

"But the truth is," Izzy said, "I kind of wish I didn't have to leave."

***

I TAPPED GENTLY ON ROBERT'S DOOR.

"Elle, come in. How's Izzy?"

"Feeling remorseful. Talking more than she ever has before."

"That's a start." He gestured for me to sit and passed me a piece of chocolate. One of his secret tricks was to ply people with sugar, so they would feel more comfortable talking. I accepted the chocolate, even though I didn't really need it.

"Thanks. Have you had any luck reaching her father?"

"Unfortunately not. We'll keep trying."

"I have an idea about that. What if she were to stay here as an assistant counselor?"

"What?"

"I could teach her archery. We could use some help down there, and she'd be great. She doesn't want to go home, and quite honestly, she might not have anywhere to go."

"We're not a foster care system, Elle. There are procedures and—"

"He signed her into this camp, right? We have to keep her here until he comes to pick her up, for her own safety."

"You make a good point." He tapped a pencil against his notebook. "We definitely need the help."

"Robert, I'm worried about her. There's a reason her grandmother was the one raising her, and she can't even process that grief when she doesn't have the safety of a home to go back to."

He rubbed his hands over his face. "I may have taught you too well."

"I'll take that as a compliment."

"Do that. I'll see what I can do, but I can't make any promises."

***

ON THE WAY OUT OF ROBERT'S OFFICE, I BUMPED INTO Drew. Again. And knocked papers out of his hands, again.

"I'm sorry!"

"You have to stop doing this," he said with a laugh. "Although I never mind bumping into you."

I handed him a few pages that he'd dropped, afraid to meet his eyes. Fearful of what I might see in them and what that might stir up inside me, too. When I finally gained the courage, he smiled back at me.

"Hey," he said.

"Hey."

"Are you okay? You look a mess this morning."

Ouch. Definitely not flirting. I swatted his shoulder.

"What?" he said.

"Thanks for the compliment."

"It was a rough night," he clarified. "I thought maybe you didn't get a lot of sleep."

"I didn't." I thought of you and your lips for hours. Thank you, brain, for not saying that out loud. "I'll manage. I have a master plan for Izzy that I've to put in motion."

"I have no doubt it will be a success. Need any help?"

"No, thanks. I got it."

He nodded. I nodded. We laughed.

"Sorry," he said. "I don't know if I should say the thing we might both be thinking or ignore the thing that we might both be trying to ignore."

"While you decide, you should know we're at least on the same page."

He lowered his head and grinned, and the combination of that when he looked back up at me? I wanted to fan myself with his papers.

"Elle, I…"

I waited.

"You have a lot going on, and I want to respect that. But if you ever feel like…you don't have so much going on, then I'm here."

Huh?

"That came out wrong," Drew said with a laugh.

"Let me summarize," I said, and he nodded gratefully.

"If I want to talk to you or see you in the future, you might be willing to talk to me and see me?"

He mentally calculated what I'd said. "I think that's about right."

In other words, we both liked each other, but we had no idea if liking each other was the right thing to do right now for too many reasons.

"I have some stuff going on with Izzy today, but I think I'd like to see you and talk to you when the time is right."

He smiled slowly, never breaking eye contact with me. "The time is always right for me."

My cheeks warmed. "Okay. I'll let you know."

"Good. And can I say how very impressive this conversation was?"

We walked in opposite directions down the hall and laughed when we both turned around in a classic movie moment.

He left me with a wave and a flutter of butterflies that told me I was in the best kind of trouble.

CHAPTER 15

ARMED WITH A STASH OF HATE'S MOST COLORFUL balloons she'd planned to use for water battles, I broke Izzy free from her nurse guard and led her on a hike to the archery range in the sweltering heat.

"Can we slow down already?" she said, bent double with her hands on her knees. "I mean seriously, how hot is it out here? And what's with the balloons? Are you going to torture me by making me a clown at some snotty kid's birthday party or something?"

"I see you're back to your old self," I muttered.

She recovered and slogged ahead. Fortunately, the morning heat and sun had already dried a lot of the path from the storm the night before. When the targets were in view, I bounced on my toes.

Izzy collapsed onto one of the hay bales. "Can we take a rest here?"

"Knock yourself out. Well, not literally."

She scrunched her face into a fake grin and rolled her eyes.

I unlocked the shed and propped open the door. Inside, I located exactly what I needed and brought it to Izzy's hay bale. Balloons rained down from my hand to her lap. "Blow them up."

She stretched a pink balloon and put it to her lips. "This is torture."

I blew into an orange balloon until it was about the size of a cantaloupe. Then a yellow one, and green. I worked at a pace twice as fast as Izzy's. Eventually, we had a pile of balloons attempting to escape the trash bag I'd collected them in. When the bag was full, I led her across the range to the targets. There were two side by side. With a green balloon in one hand and a black sharpie marker in the other, I began what I hoped would be the activity that would finally help Izzy.

"Am I allowed to pass?"

"No," I said.

"Robert said—"

"Robert isn't here," I answered. "This is my time, and I believe—in my expert opinion—that you need my time."

"What kind of expert?"

"Someone who's known you for more than a week."

She gave me the side-eye. "Fine. Are we graffitiing the targets?"

"You're so edgy."

She actually laughed.

I raised my marker in one hand and held a balloon in the other. "I had this boyfriend—"

"Counselor Drew?"

I gasped.

Izzy lounged in the grass. "Don't look so shocked. It's totally obvious you're into each other. I don't blame you for a second."

I stood open-mouthed.

"You may continue," Izzy said.

I composed myself. "No. Not Drew." I wrote Josh's name on the balloon. "Tons of fun. Really sweet."

"What happened?"

"He dumped me."

"Oh."

"Yep. On prom night of all nights."

"Jerk."

"By Express mail."

"People mail stuff nowadays?"

"Exactly," I said. With a push pin, I secured the green balloon to the target.

Izzy stood and examined my work. "Josh, huh?"

"Yep." I grabbed a second balloon, wrote "Target Panic," and attached it to the target. The next balloon read "Boy Drama."

I pointed to Izzy. "Your turn."

She looked back and forth between the bales of hay and the targets. "We're going to shoot these?"

I grinned.

She smirked and took the marker. My turn to lounge. I gave her space, so she was confident I couldn't read her words. Turns out the gesture wasn't necessary.

"Alcohol," she wrote and pinned the balloon in place. "I'm done with it. The last people on the planet I want to be like are my parents. I get that they have their own issues, but I want to learn from them how not to live, if that's what you can even call it." She built a rhythm pulling balloons from the bag, writing on them and attaching them to the target. "Headaches. Vomiting. Why the hell do people drink anyway? Bruises. Running. I don't want to run anymore. Weakness. Fear." Her list continued. Good thing we blew up a bag full of balloons.

Before long, we had a multi-colored representation of everything Izzy and I wanted to rise above fluttering against the target. We traipsed back through the high grass to the closest shooting line where I demonstrated the technique for a recurve bow. My balloons disappeared in seconds. I hit the green balloon with Josh's name on it last. The exercise had been for show, mostly for Izzy, but I couldn't deny the heartstrings it pulled for me. Watching my Josh balloon shred into slivers of green tempted me to run through the grass, retrieve each piece and put them back together.

The fact my feet stayed straddled over the shooting line proved that even if I wasn't ready to embrace my new reality, the one without Josh in it, I was closer than I'd been before.

I handed the bow to Izzy.

"Awesome," she said and glided her fingers along the wood. "I've never shot a bow and arrow before. What if I'm terrible?"

"Then we keep practicing."

She took a deep breath, raised the bow, and squinted against the sun. I gently advised her on small adjustments in her hand placement and aim. "You don't squeeze the bow. You sort of gently rest your hand on it. In fact, you're pushing it away from you." I showed her. "A friend of mine that competes has the motto, push, pull, pray."

"I like that," Izzy said. She pushed the bow away from her and pulled the string back. Her arms shook from holding the tension, but when she released, the arrow sailed through the air, landing in the grass a few yards in front of the target.

"Give it a little arc."

Izzy nodded and nocked another arrow. The arrow landed only a few feet from the target, but it still dropped in the dirt.

"Make sure you keep the arrow pointed at the target until the arrow lands. If you let it fall, too quickly, the arrow can be misdirected."

Without a word, Izzy loaded again. Her third arrow caught a balloon along the edge of the target. At the loud popping sound, she jumped up and down.

"Whoa! Deadly weapon in your hands," I scolded.

She took a deep breath. "This is seriously cool."

"Agreed."

"Let's keep going," Izzy said. "I have balloons to destroy."

One by one, the balloons disappeared. Izzy was impressively skilled in shooting. I decided that before she left camp, I'd get her in touch with my old competition league. Shooting could be enough to keep her engaged and away from alcohol. When all the balloons were popped, Izzy set down the bow and stretched her arms above her head.

"How did you get so good at shooting?" she asked.

"I've been competing for years."

"Seriously?"

"I shoot compound bow."

"What's that?"

I retrieved my bow from the shed and added the sight and stabilizer.

"That's intense," Izzy said.

"You get used to it." I explained the different parts of the bow and how it worked. She followed along with more interest and intensity than she'd shown for any other sport or activity at camp.

"Can you show me?"

"Sure." I backed up from the ten yards we'd been shooting from to thirty yards and launched five arrows into the target. Three bullseyes, and two nines.

"That's pretty badass," Izzy said, offering me a slow clap.

"Thanks," I said. "You can shoot down here with me more often if you want."

"Definitely," she said.

"Actually." I took a deep breath, hoping this yielded the outcome I'd wanted but knowing that whatever Izzy decided was what I had to respect. "I was wondering if you'd be interested in staying at camp longer than this session?"

Her faced squished into a face that said probably not.

"Hear me out," I said. "You could be considered for an assistant counselor position and help me with archery lessons."

"A counselor? After what I did last night, Robert is going to give me responsibility?"

I pointed to the broken balloons. "Everyone deserves a second chance. Robert understands the process of grief better than anyone. Nothing is done yet, but it's pointless for Robert to consider it if you don't even want to do it."

"I'd get to work with you?"

My heart swelled at the fact she wanted to. "That's my hope, yes. And, you'll get paid."

She rubbed her hands together. "That seals it."

"Yeah?"

"You know I don't have anything to go back to, and that terrifies me, but Elle…" She pointed to the targets. "This is the first thing I've been excited about in so long. Thank you."

Her enthusiasm—finally—about something made me smile. I'd done it. I'd found a way to connect with this incredible girl. She hugged me, and I squeezed her back.

"Can we shoot some more?" she asked.

"Sure."

"And then what?"

I pointed to the colorful remnants of our frustrations and fears on the grass. "We pick up the pieces."

CHAPTER 16

IZZY APPARENTLY WOULDN'T STOP TALKING ABOUT
our afternoon adventure to Robert, who pulled me aside at dinner
and offered me the opportunity to plan the balloon activity for the
next session. It represented perfect symbolism to face some of the
challenges in their lives, he'd said.

An entirely new activity based on a whim of mine? Wow.

I was still in awe of Robert's reaction when I caught up with Lake
and the rest of our campers at the basketball courts. The girls lounged
under the shade of a tree, fanning themselves with their daily agendas.
Izzy wasn't with them.

"She's on the court," Lake said from behind me.

"She didn't pass?" I asked.

"Nope," Lake said with a smile.

"Even in this heat?"

"I know, right!"

Wow again.

The camp horn blared. Cheering erupted across the athletic fields,
the lake, the pool, and everywhere in between. It was our last full day
of camp. That meant field games and later, after the sun went down,
and the cool evening settled in, a dance in the main lodge.

I rested my hand on Lake's shoulder. "Assistant Counselor Lake?"

"Counselor Elle?" she said, matching my playful tone.

"It's time for the Lionesses to kick some butt."

I led my girls to the lake, roaring, "Lionesses! Lionesses! Lionesses!"

When I saw Drew standing by the water, watching me with an intense stare, I kind of choked on my roar.

"Hey there, Counselor Elle," Neil called out from in front of his pride of Lions—interestingly the name his campers chose for their cabin. Some of the girls from my cabin giggled. Ann, on the other hand, blushed something fierce. During their flirting at camp-wide Red Rover games in the last two weeks, several of the Lionesses and Rock Stars had formed crushes on the Lions. A few more formed crushes on Neil, who looped his arm loosely around my shoulders and looked at my campers. "What do you say, you girls win the girl's race, my cabin wins the boys' race, and then we celebrate later with s'mores by the campfire?"

There were more giggles and cheers.

From the corner of my eye, I noticed Drew still watching me. I wondered if he made any assumption about Neil's arm around me or if he realized Neil and I were only friends.

As we waited for all the other cabins and counselors to arrive, the Lions and Lionesses sat in the shade, a mix of boys and girls, laughing, teasing, and flirting. Even Izzy was talking to a boy.

"I've never seen her do that!" I said.

Neil dramatically bowed to me. "You did a good thing."

I hoped he was right. Robert still hadn't gotten in touch with her father to gain permission for her to stay at camp or to tell him about the incident. In the meantime, he'd talked to a case worker he knew for advice, but time wasn't on our side.

"You're being watched," Neil whispered. He nodded toward the water where Santino and Drew stood side by side. Drew nodded at me this time. I waved, doing my best to ignore my heart palpitations.

"Drew's a good guy," Neil said.

I laughed. "Is that some sort of permission or something?"

"Elle, Josh was my best friend, but he kind of dumped all of us. It makes no sense to me. Maybe it was too hard for him to be so far away when we were all still here together." He shrugged. "I'm trying to respect that's what he wants and hope we'll catch up in a few months when he comes back for school."

"That's all I could think about for months."

"The point is," Neil continued, "he's shown no signs of changing his mind for weeks. It's fair for you to like someone else."

"Who says I like Drew?"

Neil laughed. "Your face."

I swatted his arm as the races started, cuing so much screaming I couldn't hear myself think—probably a gift. The last thing I wanted to do was mull over Izzy and Neil's comments about how I'd obviously been into Drew. I joined the cheering crowd, shouting for Izzy and Ann as they rowed their kayak out into the lake, around the center dock and back. We came in second place and scored our first points in the games. Bridget and Savannah crushed the two-on-two basketball tournament. Lake swam the individual medley in the pool, and on it went. My little Lionesses scored us a spot in the top five cabins at camp, but barely.

"Tradition has it that the counselors for each of the cabins take it from here," Drew announced, and my girls gathered around me with bright eyes and dimpled smiles.

"You got this, Counselor Elle," Ann encouraged.

The other girls nodded, but I wasn't so sure. I could swim, but not fast enough to compete. I had some free throwing skills, but basketball wasn't my strong suit. I could hold my own in volleyball with a sister like Melanie. I felt pretty average at almost everything, but I would give my everything for these girls.

Drew lifted a cloth bag with the Camp Good Grief logo on it. "Every camp activity we could fathom a competition in is written on a piece of paper in this bag. The first place team gets to choose."

Neil flexed, and his Lions roared. Kate and I rolled our eyes at each other, but couldn't help laughing. My prom date reached his hand deep into the bag and dramatically swirled the contents around before retrieving a folded, white paper. All the campers and counselors quieted, holding hands, waiting for the news.

Drew unfolded the paper.

Read it.

His eyes darted toward me, and a smile crossed his lips.

"Archery," he called.

My Lionesses tackled me. Nothing could be heard over their screams.

The other four counselors in the running, including Neil, moped the whole way to the archery range. Drew shut them up by saying if the activities or sports they'd supervised had been randomly chosen, there'd be no complaints from them then.

I'd gotten lucky, but the competition wasn't an absolute. We all retrieved recurve bows from the shed, our crowd of cheering fans standing by. The Lions and Lionesses roared back and forth at each other until even the ever-patient Drew quieted the crowd to explain the rules. We'd each shoot five arrows, but only the best three shots would count. Fifth place—that would be me—would shoot first, and we'd continue in descending order. Based on the calculations, to win it all, I'd need to secure first place in the event. The group of counselors—me, Kate, Neil, Red, and Archer—collected arrows. They all watched me select mine, and I couldn't hide my grin.

"What's the secret?" Neil pleaded.

I selected a group of arrows with strong tips and then bent them gently to gauge how weak or stiff they were. They were as alike as possible to minimize that variable and hopefully get a good grouping.

Kate grinned at me and did the same. She'd been paying attention at our Ladies Night shooting at the club.

"Not fair," Neil complained.

"You're in first place, pretty boy," Kate said. "Suck it up."

Kate's Rock Stars had managed two more points than the Lionesses in the games. She would shoot after me. I couldn't count her out. A Ladies Night veteran, she could at least follow the basics. Warming up, she released her arrow and landed a five. Not bad at all. Then a six. I warmed up with a couple eights and nines. Not bad either.

Drew blew the whistle. "Elle's turn."

Neil pretended to swap his arrows with mine when we retrieved them from the target, and we headed back to the shooting line, which was only at ten yards.

I took a deep breath, nocked my arrow, and pulled the string.

"Push, pull, pray," Izzy yelled.

I laughed before I regrouped and anchored the string against my mouth and nose. When I hit the exact angle I wanted, I released, and the Lionesses howled.

"Ten," Drew called.

I blew my Lionesses a kiss.

The Rock Stars cheered for Kate who hit a respectable nine.

"Yes!" I hugged her.

Red and Archer took pride in hitting threes, something that would definitely not suffice for Neil's competitive spirit.

"I can't believe it all comes down to this," he grumbled. "Elle, take pity on me. Give me something."

"Anchor the string at two points on your face. Push the bow, don't grip it. Gently release."

He followed my instructions, anchoring the string against his nose and mouth. He released and landed a five. "I might need a few more pointers the next round."

I hugged him and ruffled his hair.

"Round two!" Drew called.

Technically, it was an end, not a round, but I forgave his ignorance. Our campers cheered us on.

I nocked my arrow, pulled the string back, and worked through the simple pattern of movements to start my grouping, hopefully in the bullseye. I relaxed my fingers, letting the string slip free and launch the arrow to the target.

"Ten!" Drew yelled.

"Can we put a blindfold on her or something?" Archer shouted.

Kate positioned herself to shoot. When she pulled back, her arm was a little high. I whispered for her to lower it. She released and hit an eight.

We hugged and performed a little victory dance, although the victory wasn't quite ours yet. The Lionesses and Rock Stars didn't seem to mind that.

"Blindfold me," Red said. "Probably won't matter."

I rolled my eyes at Kate.

"Go ahead," she said.

I coached Red on his stance and gave him some pointers about anchoring the string, a gentle release, and a solid follow-through. His score improved to a five.

"Okay. I see the appeal," he said. "Thanks for the tips."

And on it went. I helped Archer boost his score to a seven and Neil even shot a nine.

"Now we're talking," he said. "I'm coming for you."

In response, I shot another ten in the third end, putting the pressure on. Anyone who wanted to tie me would have to shoot straight tens to finish the competition. They didn't, but they took my instruction to improve until everyone was shooting seven or better.

After I shot another ten in end four, my competitors shifted from teasing to cheering me on.

"Perfect score, coming up," Neil shouted when I stepped up to my last shot. They clapped in unison until I took a deep breath and drew my bow. Then they quieted.

I hadn't felt so much pressure in my life to hit a shot at ten yards, but archery was simple if you let it be. Simple steps. Simple repetition. Great results. I repeated the same motions I had for the first four shots and gently relaxed my fingers.

"Ten!" Drew shouted, and the Lionesses tackled me again.

They chanted my name and, "Give us the trophy! Give us the trophy!"

I quieted them down, standing with my arms around them to watch the other counselors hit their last shots. Kate scored a nine. Archer and Red scored eights, and Neil fell to the ground in shock and awe when Drew shouted, "Ten!"

When Neil found his feet, he lifted me into a hug and kissed my cheek. "That was impressive as hell."

"You should see me shoot from thirty yards then," I laughed.

"Name the place. I'm there."

He lifted me onto his shoulders and marched me around the range. Drew rounded us up for the trophy ceremony, which couldn't have been better. Neil's Lions took third. Kate's Rock Stars were second, and the lovely Lionesses, after a very rough few days, screamed until their throats were raw at their first place victory.

When Drew handed me the trophy, he had to press his lips against my ear to be heard. "Congratulations, Elle."

I swallowed hard at his closeness and how it elevated every feeling in my body, even when my adrenaline was already explosive from shooting.

"Thanks," I managed.

Even with all that—the perfect score, helping my co-counselors fall in love with archery, and the most minuscule but remarkable moment with Drew—nothing could touch the pride of watching the Lionesses carry the Good Grief Games trophy back to Cabin 12.

CHAPTER 17

BEFORE THE DANCE, WE HAD A CAMPFIRE PICNIC
planned. Once the girls were settled, Robert pulled me aside and
gave me an update on Izzy, which wasn't much of an update. Only
that he was still trying to reach her dad to get permission for her to
stay on as an assistant counselor.

The girls danced around the campfire with Neil's Lions. We had
gold medals around our necks. Watching them laugh and smile, the
cracks in my heart healed or at least temporarily sealed, allowing
genuine happiness to break through all of the sadness I'd known for
too long. I hoped it was the same for them, too. In a way, I knew
the innermost imprints of their hearts, despite having only met them
two weeks earlier.

"Hey."

I jumped at the sound and put a hand to my chest.

"Sorry," Drew said. He smiled at me and my insides twisted into
knots.

A throat cleared behind me.

"Is this a bad time?" Lake asked.

"What's up?" I asked her.

"Call it confidence from their winning streak, but the girls challenged Neil's cabin to a hot dog and s'mores eating contest."

"That can't be good." Vomit cleanup did not sound appealing. "Let's round them up to get ready for the dance. Maybe that will distract them."

Lake pointed at me. "Good thinking."

"I'll be right behind you." I redirected my attention to Drew. "Sorry about that. What's up?"

He shrugged and laughed but didn't say anything.

"You okay?" I asked.

"Yeah. Congratulations."

"Thanks. I can't believe the first session is almost over. I can't imagine loving anyone like I love these girls, and yet I'm going to have a new cabin of girls to love in a few days."

"Lake will keep an eye on them when you go home for graduation."

"I can't believe that's almost here either. School is your whole life, and then suddenly you're free."

"I'm not," he said with a sigh.

"Next year."

Our small talk didn't match the mood, but I wasn't sure I wanted to talk about what would. As much as I wanted to do right by Drew and his feelings, being around him was like standing in the vicinity of the biggest magnet on the earth covered in a steel outfit. Every second I spent nearby, moving away from him became more impossible.

"I have to get the girls ready."

"For the dance?"

"Yep. You going?"

"I have some work to do, getting the cabin lists and registration packets ready for the next session."

"Right." I tried to hide my disappointment.

"Okay…"

He nodded. "I'll see you later."

On the way back to the cabin, I stopped. I sat on a bench, watching Drew chat with Robert before disappearing into the main lodge. I should have said something. No. We had all summer.

I walked the rest of the way to the cabin without looking back.

With seven girls needing one shower, our five campers had packed up to shower in the pool locker room, leaving the cabin for Lake and me. While she washed up, I pulled out the Josh box. I hadn't looked at it the whole session, and that had to mean something.

I told myself it was the last time, that after today I'd have closure from our relationship. One final glance at the movie stubs, the photos, and a few dried rose petals, memories between my fingers. The collage covered the bed. Once the box was empty, I wrapped my arms around my legs and rested my chin on my knees. One last look at the last year of my life.

At Josh.

I might never see him again. My brain still couldn't understand how someone could be nearly everything to you for so long and then they disappear from your life.

It didn't compute.

The four-by-six photo could barely contain his huge smile. That had always been his nature with everyone until the surprising end. I thought part of me would always miss him, not only because of the romantic relationship between us, but because he had been a good friend. We'd laughed and gone on adventures. He'd cheered for me at competitions and learned about archery. I'd cheered for him and learned about football. Until he'd had to leave, he'd been entirely perfect as a friend and a boyfriend.

If I'd learned anything about myself when I'd started dating Josh, it was that it didn't take me long to love. Josh. Kate. Neil. Even Lake and my Lionesses.

A knock at the screen door caught my attention. From where he was standing, Drew could see everything in front of me.

"Come in," I said, not sure what other option I had.

He did and approached the bed slowly. We both held our breath while he scanned the pieces of my past spread across my bed.

"It's like a shrine," he finally said.

"No, it's not," I said, picking up the mementos and stuffing them back into the box and then into the closet. "It's…memories. I'll likely never even see him again, and that's fine with me."

"You don't mean that."

"I wish him well and all that, but…" I sighed, "it's over. What did you need?"

"Huh?"

"You came to my cabin and knocked on the door."

"Right. Um…" He looked back at the bed, cleared of my Josh memorabilia.

After I'd left the picnic, I'd considered backtracking to find Drew. Had he done the same? But then saw all of the Josh relationship remnants and clammed up again. "Drew, what is it?"

He stood tall and took a deep breath. "I was wondering if…if…"

"If?"

"I feel like I'm in seventh grade."

"Do you want me to ask her out for you?" Lake said from the doorway to the bathroom with a very entertained look on her face.

Drew closed his eyes and groaned before regaining his composure. "If I can get there tonight, would you save me a dance?"

"Awwwwwwww," Lake said.

"Lake," I warned, and she shut herself back in the bathroom.

"You want to dance with me?"

"You are not going to make me say it again," he joked.

"No," I said.

"Oh. Okay," he said. "I'll stay in my office then."

"No, Drew. I meant, no, I wasn't going to make you say it again." He laughed and covered his face. "I am so bad at this."

"You're adorable, actually. Yes. I would love to dance with you."

He pumped his fist, and said, "Yes—to continue with the seventh-grade boy thing."

"Nailed it."

We both laughed, but his gaze caught mine, and it was like an open path existed between his soul and mine. He'd wanted to fall in love, and knowing myself and how amazing he was and how I felt in moments like these between us, I could fall in love with him easily.

Maybe too easily.

"See you at the dance," he said.

"See you there."

He bumped into the Lionesses on his way out, and they suggestively greeted him.

"He's so cute, Elle," Izzy said.

"Tell us everything," Savannah said.

"Stop! There's nothing to tell."

Lake finally exited the bathroom. "He asked her to dance."

The girls cheered, and the cabin rocked. I covered my face and felt myself blushing as badly as Ann turned pink in the sunshine.

"Elle and Drew! Elle and Drew! Elle and Drew!"

There was one hundred percent no way he did not hear that wherever he was.

With blushing cheeks, I rounded up my clothes and hid myself in the bathroom for the lukewarm shower Lake had left me. By the time I finished and dressed, the girls had moved on to new things. Kate and her Rock Stars had crashed the cabin with their makeup bags and brushes, curling irons and straighteners. We rocked out with everyone's favorite music. The mounds of makeup I'd brought with me proved to be quite an asset. For the first time, I regretted not going to the salon with Kate to get ready for prom. I'd also skipped out on the last couple weeks of senior year to come to camp. I'd take being with my Lionesses over watching movies in classes while teachers submitted end-of-the-year grades, but I'd missed yearbook signings, field trips, and other traditions, too.

"Miss Elle," Ann said, rushing toward me in a short pink dress with sparkles. "Which earrings?" She held faux diamond dangles up to her right ear and a pink hoop to her left.

"Are you going for glam or cute?" Stupid question. What fourteen-year-old was going for cute?

"Glam, definitely."

I pointed to the dangles, and she gushed appreciation before running back to the rest of the girls. I took a final look in the mirror at my simple black mini-dress, strappy heels, and silver necklace hanging in three loops, the bottom practically touching my waist. I nodded at myself in the mirror, committing to not missing anything else. I'd push the fog away, somehow. I'd go back home for break, spend time with my sisters, and celebrate graduation like a person should.

I'd live in the moment every chance I had.

"How do I look?" Lake asked.

"Gorgeous," I said, and the Lionesses and Rock Stars agreed.

Lake was long and lanky, but her tight, white tank dress showed curves I'd never noticed before—even in a swimsuit.

"This dress hugs all the right places." She expertly twisted my hair until it was loosely piled on the top of my head. A few strands dangled from the sides, and my own silver icicle earrings were much more noticeable.

"I love it!"

"Good," she said. "Izzy grab those bobby pins on my bed, please."

Izzy ran across the room and returned with the pins. She stood patiently, handing Lake pin after pin. I smiled at her adorable face in the mirror. She was smiling, too. Couldn't beat that.

Once Lake was satisfied, we rounded up the girls for a chat.

"Girls, brace yourselves. It's time to get cheesy." I took a deep breath. "You mean so much to me. You'll always be my first class of campers. I've had such a great time these last two weeks. You're all talented and beautiful, but what I'm most impressed by is how good you are to each other. When we were getting ready tonight, you shared jewelry, makeup, and clothes. You didn't compete with each other. You wanted everyone to look their best. You wanted everyone to do their best on the tennis and basketball courts. You wanted everyone to make the best art projects they could. Competition is good, but you should never let it spoil your friendships. I'm proud to be your counselor, and I've learned so much from you. Specific instances in your lives, tragedies from your past brought you here, but there will be more tough days to come. You all know that. You'll make good decisions, and you'll make bad decisions. But you have to keep doing your best no matter what. I love you."

"That's beautiful," Kate said with tears in her eyes. "Rock Stars, what she said!"

The girls crowded around us in a group hug.

"No tears!" I shouted. "And be careful not to smudge your makeup on the girl next to you."

They all laughed.

"Now, let's go and have some fun."

CHAPTER 18

THE LIONESSES AND ROCK STARS DANCED UNDER THE
spinning disco ball. A few of them scored slow dances with the Lions
or boys from other cabins. Kate, Lake, and I watched, wondering if
this is what it was like to chaperone the prom.

"You know the chaperones are taking bets on who's hooking up
after prom," Kate said.

Lake nodded, but I shook my head. "They're probably trying to
make sure nobody does it on their watch."

"Or drinks too much," Kate said.

"Or at all, maybe?" Lake suggested, and that sounded more accurate.

We all made a cringe face thinking of our own drinking incident.

"That won't happen again," Lake said.

I didn't think so either. Izzy had been hurting, more than I could
imagine. Losing her gram had meant losing everything. Her home,
her safety, her foundation, and especially the one person who had
shown her unconditional love her whole life. I hoped the love she felt
from the Lionesses had helped her realize that a new life might never
be the same, but it could still give her some happiness.

"I want her to be able to stay all summer."

"Still no word?" Kate asked.

"Not that I know of, but chances are her dad won't show to pick her up. Not sure what Robert plans to do about that."

The song changed to a slow number, and the campers shuffled around the room, grabbing their designated partners in the cutest, most awkward way possible.

"Where's your dance partner?" Lake asked.

I shrugged.

"Should we be placing bets on you two hooking up?"

Yes. The answer came to mind instantly, but I revised it by adding the word, "eventually." Not that I said any of that aloud.

"Your face is telling me yes, but you don't want to admit it," Kate said. "Don't forget how well I know you."

"Don't applaud yourself," Lake said. "I didn't have to look at her face to know that."

Kate nudged her with her hip, and she fell into one of the male counselors passing by.

"Sorry," Lake mumbled.

"It's okay," he answered. "Want to dance?"

Kate and I both went wide-eyed, and Lake disappeared onto the dance floor.

"Do you think Drew will even come?" I asked.

"He's obviously into you, Elle."

"Yes, but he saw everything from my Josh box."

"The shrine?" Kate asked.

"It's not a shrine."

Kate raised an eyebrow.

"Fine. It's kind of a shrine." I did a head count of the Lionesses. "I'm gonna get some air. Do you mind keeping an eye on my girls?"

"Sure," Kate said.

I took the exterior stairs to the patio below carefully but quickly, then decided to lose my shoes altogether. I wanted to get further away from the dance as though the distance would offer me some clarity. Josh had been everything to me, but since I'd been at camp, learning about life and myself and these girls—and being around Drew—I hadn't felt the loss as intensely as I'd had at home. In a way, that scared me. That I could love someone that much, but be okay, or almost okay, weeks after breaking up. Could I be the opposite of okay and not know it?

I worked my way down the hill to the dock, feeling the cool grass between my toes, watching the lights reflect off the surface of the water. I didn't know what it was about that view, but it calmed me. I stood there, alone, taking deep, yoga-like breaths, hearing the muffled music in the distance.

"You look beautiful," Drew said.

I spun to face him. "Hi."

"I looked for you at the dance. Kate said you were out here." He wore grey dress pants and a black polo that hugged his shoulders and biceps.

"Hi," I said again, and he laughed.

"It took me a while to get here."

"From your office?" I asked, glancing at the main lodge right up the hill.

"No. Not physically. I mean with you. Josh—I don't want to talk about him, but he was my friend. Still is, and there are things I have to respect about him. Being with your—or wanting to be with you—didn't feel right."

I nodded. "For me either."

"There's a lot we don't know about Josh."

"What do you mean?"

"Nothing," Drew stumbled over his words. "I mean, he changed. And why, you know? Why?"

"I asked myself that a lot, but I'm not anymore. I'm living my life. That's what he wanted me to do, and I'm doing it. Not because he wanted me to, but because I should."

"And I have this fear that if you and I—if we—" He took a deep breath. "That you'll want to get back together with him if you have the chance."

"I'm not sure I could ever trust him with my heart again." I took a deep breath and revealed the most honest part of my soul. "But in some ways, he still has it."

Drew looked away from me and at the lake instead, disappointment etching across his face.

"I'm sorry."

"We're here all summer together, right?"

"I hope so," I said.

"We have time."

"Are you the patient type?" I asked with a laugh.

A few strands of hair Lake had pulled out of my updo blew into my eyes, but Drew gently pushed them back. His hands on my cheeks exploded warmth through every crevice of my body. I leaned into him.

"I've had a crush on you for three years," Drew whispered, and pressed his lips against my cheek. "Would you call that patient?"

In that moment, everything became more clear. Like the steps of shooting, I knew my next steps involved Drew, not Josh. My chest swelled, and I wanted nothing more than to press my mouth against his and show him everything I'd felt toward him, too, but he'd been right.

We had time.

***

NEIL AND I DANCED THE NIGHT AWAY ALONGSIDE OUR campers, being silly and having fun. There were budding romances between his boys and a few of my girls and disappointment on everyone's faces when the lights came on and the music stopped. A group of boys led the way back to the cabins, pushing each other over tree roots and jumping on each other's backs. A string of girls held hands, swinging them front to back and singing their favorite tunes from the night, sometimes in key, sometimes not. Behind us, Ann walked close to one of Neil's campers. They cherished a few yards of privacy, not holding hands. That would have led to way too much teasing, but it wasn't hard to guess they wanted to.

"So cute," I mumbled to Neil, tilting my head back towards them.

He smiled. "Franco. The whole cabin has been riding him for liking Ann, but I think they're jealous. She's a cutie, and she only has eyes for him."

"Summer camp is so cute."

Neil tipped his head toward the front porch of my cabin, to a dark silhouette standing there. I recognized the shape immediately. Drew and I had danced to one slow song, but we'd separated after that, each focusing on our assigned camp duties, and probably even more likely, creating distance because when we'd been close, self-control had been more of a challenge than holding a bow in my hands but not being able to shoot it.

I raised my voice to make an announcement. "Cabin 12 girls, roll call in 15 minutes. Be back in the cabin by then, please."

"Same goes for my cabin," Neil said. But he didn't turn up the hill toward his cabin. Instead, he kept walking with me toward mine. Toward Drew. When we reached the porch, Neil picked me up and spun me until I laughed. "I had fun tonight, Elle."

"Me, too. I'll see you at breakfast."

He waved to Drew and hiked up the hill.

Some of the girls scooted into the cabin while others dispersed for one final walk around camp before lights out on their last night. Although Drew and I had nothing to hide, I waited for them to disappear before I talked to him.

"What's up?"

He bit his lip and handed me a package. "This came for you today." It was too dark to read the return address, and I had no idea who could have sent it. I would see my family the next day at my shooting competition, and I'd be going home the day after that for graduation.

"It's from Lily. I figured I'd bring it by."

"Couldn't wait 'til tomorrow?"

"I guess it could have."

His honesty put me at a loss for words. He'd basically admitted that he'd wanted to come and see me tonight. He hadn't wanted to wait until tomorrow, although he knew he could have. Maybe even should have.

Summer camp was so cute.

I smiled at him. "Thanks."

"You're welcome."

I took a deep breath and kissed his cheek, letting my lips linger there a little longer than lips should for a cheek kiss.

He leaned into me and exhaled. "Elle." My name came out gruff, almost a groan and a whisper at the same time. "I have to talk to you about something."

His voice had shifted to his official head counselor tone.

I pulled away and straightened, too.

"When you go home for graduation next week, how long are you staying?"

"Two days."

Drew looked around the yard and at the ground, up at the cabin and at my toes, pretty much everywhere but my eyes.

"It's been approved since before I signed on as a counselor. Has something changed?"

"Yeah. Something has."

"I'm supposed to miss my high school graduation? Robert can't expect me to do that?"

"He doesn't. It's the opposite. Maybe you should take some time off. Lake's been doing great, and I think she can handle the next session. Enjoy your graduation. Spend time with your family. Hang out by the pool with your sisters. You know, have fun."

An hour earlier, Drew had told me we had all summer to spend time together. He'd wanted to be around me. What had changed? "I'm confused. You don't want me to come back?"

"No. Of course I want you to come back, but I thought some time with your family would be good."

"I need the money for school, Drew."

"I thought maybe the winnings from the shooting competition tomorrow could make up the difference."

Okay, even more confused. "I haven't won anything yet. And there's no guarantee I will. And that was supposed to be a bonus. This is my summer job." I thought back to the dance. Had I done or said something to make him uncomfortable? We'd agreed to take time. Maybe I shouldn't have kissed his cheek like that. "I don't understand what's going on."

"I thought maybe you'd like a little time off to celebrate. I know how your sisters were when you decided to come." He raised his hands in surrender. "It was an idea. I promise, I'm not trying to get rid of you."

Maybe it was the word, "promise," but it reminded me I'd heard promises before that had been broken.

"You sure?"

"Definitely. Totally your call."

Before I could sort through everything he'd said and figure out what was irking me about it all, Ann and Izzy came around the corner, giggling.

"Elle," Izzy said. "Ann got her first kiss tonight!" She makes an ooooh-ooooh sound, and Ann pushed her toward the cabin.

"I should go. Your campers need you." Drew told them goodnight and headed down the path.

If I even began to analyze the last ten minutes, I might have had an aneurysm. A couple of my other campers trickled out of the darkness, and I followed them inside, shaking the box from Lily next to my ear.

CHAPTER 19

"WHAT'S THAT?" ANN POINTED TO THE PACKAGE IN MY
hands, clearly eager to detract attention from all of the teasing about
her and Franco's obvious flirtation.

"Don't know." I grabbed a pair of scissors from my armoire
and cut into the box. Inside was one of my mother's kitchen towels
wrapped around something hard. I unraveled the towel, revealing a
crown.

"Is that a tiara?" Izzy asked.

"It's my crown from prom." I lifted it out of the box and placed it
on Ann's head. She indulged in the moment, blowing the girls kisses
and giving a stiff, queen-like wave. Everyone laughed, and the other
girls asked to see, too.

Ann placed it on Izzy's head and said, "I didn't know you were
prom queen. That's cool."

"Franco would have loved if Ann wore that to the dance," Savannah teased, and it was clear Ann and Franco would be the talk of the
cabin a bit longer.

"It was supposed to arrive earlier," Lake said as she plopped down
on my bed and fluffed my pillow to collapse into it. "Kate called Lily
and asked her to send it, so you'd have it for the dance."

Ah, that was why she'd asked me if my outfit was missing anything.

"Anything else in the box? Maybe some chocolates or something?"

"You know we're not allowed food in the cabin," I told her. "And when I'm gone next week, don't bring any food in here. I finally got the spider infestation under control. I don't want a new colony."

"Yeah, yeah. I'm off to use your toothpaste. Make sure you bring some more back after your super-duper graduation day."

I looked in the box to be sure there wasn't any food before I slid it under my bed. Wouldn't that be awful? Sleeping with bait like that under your head? I shuddered. But there wasn't food. Only a letter on Lily's stationary.

> *Elle,*
>
> *I hope you get this in time. Kate was all "Send it right away." I have no idea how you deal with that person. Things are good here. I took my last test today. I'm so excited to be done with school so I can enjoy some summer reading. Oh, one more thing. Josh called. I didn't know what you wanted me to tell him. I said you were out of town for the weekend. But he said he really misses you and wants to talk whenever you can. I told him I'd pass on the message. Now I have.*
>
> *P.S. You should turn your phone on like a normal human being.*
>
> *Love, Lil*

I read the note three more times before shoving it in the box and under my bed. Long after the cabin fell silent, I stared at the ceiling. Josh had called. He'd called.

And told Lily he missed me.

Drew had said we had time.

Josh had called.

The air in the cabin warmed until it became difficult to breathe. I threw on shoes and slipped out into the cool night. My phone in hand, I climbed as far up the hill as I could while keeping the cabin in view. I turned the phone over in my hands and closed my eyes. Josh had moved away five months ago. Even though we talked as much as we could, I'd lived an everyday existence without him. I'd been adjusting to a new reality the whole time without realizing it.

But if I turned on my phone and had a message from Josh, would I be strong enough to walk away, once and for all? I swallowed. Only one way to know for sure.

I pressed the power button.

The screen lit the dark night. After a few seconds, all of my apps appeared. I tapped my text messages and found two from Josh. My heart raced as if I were still climbing the hillside.

Josh: How's it going, Elle?

My hopes deflated. That was it? No declaration of love? I tapped the second message.

Josh: I get if you don't want to talk to me. I've been thinking of you, and just wanted to say hi.

He'd been thinking of me. Like what? Friends? Missing me more than friends should miss each other? I pressed my fingers against my temples. I would not spiral into a sea of questions. Not again.

My voicemail icon had a number one next to it. The message was from Josh. Reading the texts was one thing, but hearing his voice? I took a deep breath, exhaling as much negative emotion as I could.

I remembered the green Josh balloon from my archery exercise with Izzy. I'd wanted to piece the shreds back together. Was that what I'd want to do with our relationship if I heard his voice again?

I'd spent enough time in the counseling sessions with the Lionesses to know that talking about our experiences, not hiding from them, was part of the process.

I pressed the play button and lifted the phone to my ear.

"Hey, Elle."

My breath caught at the sound of his voice—quieter than usual, maybe a little hoarse like he'd had a summer cold, but nostalgic enough to ignite a fire I'd worked so hard to extinguish.

"I…" He laughed. "I thought talking to you would be awkward, but talking to your voicemail is even worse. Look, I miss you. I don't know how you're feeling about us and breaking up, but I do know I miss talking to you. I miss your laugh. I miss hearing about your competitions and watching you shoot with that intensity you get in your eyes. I miss everything about you, really."

His voice was so low, he could barely speak the last sentence.

"I don't know what the future holds or whatever, but I wanted you to know that. I thought you deserved to know." He took a deep breath. "I hope you'll call me back. You don't have to, I know, but I hope you do."

The message ended, and I started breathing again.

I played the message two more times.

I'd wanted to hear him say those things for weeks—weeks that had felt more like months. I'd gone through grief training and met girls who were struggling with intense loss. I'd nearly lost my confidence because of target panic. I'd spent time with Drew and felt things I couldn't change—that I didn't want to change.

Josh missed a version of Elle Corwin that didn't exist anymore.

The irony was I only discovered the new version because Josh had broken up with me. For almost a year, I had been Josh Brighton's girlfriend. Our lives, our goals, our decisions had been intertwined. Now, my decisions were my own.

I liked this version of myself.

The time on my phone read 11:14 p.m. Josh would probably be up late, watching videos on his phone. If I tapped his name, he'd get a notification on his phone, interrupting the video. He'd answer and say hello. I would say hello. Who knows what would be said after that?

Or, I could follow Robert's advice and accept my new reality, one that didn't include Josh. I could turn my phone back off, follow the trail to Cabin 12, tuck myself in, and fall asleep.

I pressed the button and watched the screen compute my choice.

After a few seconds, the colorful icons faded, and the screen went dark. On my way back to the cabin, I whispered, "Goodbye, Josh."

***

THE NEXT MORNING, THE LIONESSES PACKED THEIR bags and loaded them into their family's cars before heading to the main lodge to finalize their quilt squares. Izzy packed up, but she didn't have a car to take her things to.

"What's going to happen to me?" she asked.

I hugged her. "I don't know about tomorrow, but today, do you want to come to my shooting competition?"

"Really?"

"Please! I need a cheering section. You can hang with my parents and sisters."

"Sounds great."

We cleared permission through Robert, and tearfully said goodbye to the rest of the Lionesses. After too many pictures to count, Izzy and I piled into Kate's car. Seconds before we pulled out of the parking lot, Izzy grabbed my arm.

"Wait!"

"What did you forget?"

Izzy pointed across the lot to where Drew chatted with Robert on the porch of the main lodge.

"You want to say goodbye to Robert?" I guessed.

"No. You should invite Drew to the shoot."

"Oh. No. I, um…" Got a message from my ex-boyfriend last night that I chose to ignore, but also told Drew said ex-boyfriend still has a piece of my heart because he kind of does. In the meantime, I was trying to decide if Drew had managed to steal a bigger piece himself.

Izzy rolled her eyes. "You two are obvious. So what if it's complicated."

"It's more complicated than you realize, Izzy. Last competition, I totally tanked. Like worst of my life."

"Couldn't have been that bad."

"Yeah? It's called target panic because you panic."

"You've been shooting nothing but tens here, right?"

"Not exactly." But close. "But it's different. The stakes are low. Yeah, I want tens, especially in the last few training sessions right before competition, but…" I didn't know how I would react under the pressure of the shooting line with shooters all around me.

"You'll get tens," Izzy insisted. "Don't you want Drew there to see it?"

"You make it sound simple," I said.

"It can be."

I rubbed my face and imagined myself on the range, shooting in the sunshine. Did I want to see Drew watching me?

I sighed and opened the door. Drew saw me coming and waved,

finishing his conversation with Robert.

"Good morning," he said.

"Good morning."

He smiled, and we both laughed at the awkward silence.

I took a deep breath. "I know you're busy. Like always busy, but I was wondering if you wanted to, maybe, come to my shoot today?"

His smile widened. "I'm honored."

"Don't be too honored. It's going to be a tough field, and the last competition didn't go so hot."

"I remember," he said with a kind smile. "You'll be great."

I blushed. Why was talking to a guy so hard, even when you knew they liked you back?

"I got everything prepped for registration tomorrow. Let me clear it with Robert."

My chest swelled with the fresh, camp air and something else I couldn't explain. "I'll be in the car."

He nodded.

When I got back in the driver's seat, Izzy fell into a fit of giggles.

"Stop! He probably won't even be able to come."

"Is that why he's running out of the building now and chasing down the car?" she responded.

With Izzy already in the front, Drew climbed into the backseat. Before things got weird with that unfortunately common awkward silence, Izzy asked what the tournament would be like, and my shoulders relaxed as I poured myself into a world that I loved for its relative simplicity.

"It's a different structure than most of the other shoots I'll be in this summer. The top fifteen finishers earn cash prizes. We'll shoot a 450 round and then a shoot down with three ends of five arrows each."

The car went completely silent.

"Right. Sorry," I said. "We'll shoot 45 arrows, each worth ten points, max. The top fifteen archers will make it into the shoot down, which is like the final, and then we'll each shoot three ends of five arrows in each end."

"Oh," they both said.

"That's a lot of shooting," Drew said, but I thought it sounded like the perfect way to spend the day.

"It will be hot, but thankfully not a lot of wind. That can be tricky."

"I don't know how you do it, but I want to," Izzy said with a laugh.

We got to the outdoor range the local archery shop had set up for the competition. My parents and sisters met us at the entrance. They hugged me like they hadn't seen me for months. I introduced Izzy and Drew.

Melanie raised an eyebrow at me and mouthed Drew's name. I scowled at her, and she suppressed laughter.

Lily slid her sunglasses down her nose, squinted at Drew, and said, "You're cute."

"Uh, thanks."

Lily shrugged. "All I'm saying is I get it."

Drew grinned at me, and I shook my head. "Beyond embarrassing."

"She's adorable. I see where she gets her candor."

"If you can withstand Lily's questioning, then you're worth having around," my dad said, shaking Drew's hand.

Oh my gosh. My family was humiliating. Drew had come to watch me compete, he hadn't asked for my hand in marriage.

"I'm going to check in," I said. "Mom, Dad, can you keep an eye on Izzy?"

My mom kissed my cheek. "Of course, sweetie. Shoot straight."

I kissed her back and rolled my eyes. My mom knew that arrows did not shoot straight but instead wobbled like floppy noodles, but she'd been telling me to shoot straight since before I stood as tall as her waist. Why stop now?

"We'll get the tent set up and ready to go," Dad said.

With the sun, we'd need it.

My dad touched my forearm. "You have the new release, and you've been shooting well?"

I nodded.

"Today will be great."

"Thanks, Dad."

Izzy hugged me. "Good luck!"

In the fishbowl of my home life, Drew stood in a circle of my family members. I could see his mental calculation of whether he should hug me, too. I put him out of his misery and wrapped my arms around his neck. "Thank you for being here," I whispered.

"I'm excited," he answered. "Good luck."

***

WE FOUND OUR WAY THROUGH THE CROWDS TO MY assigned shooting lane, and I worked through my warmups, which went as well as I could hope. I'd be shooting in the first line at the forty-meter distance. Three other top ten shooters were in my group, but all I had to do to advance was place in the top fifty percent. I could do that.

I could step up to the shooting line, take a deep breath of summer air, ignore the sweat building under the brim of my hat and all the complexity of my life to simplify and shoot. My family, Izzy, and Drew watched from about ten yards behind me. My dad coached me along.

"Keep your composure out there," he said. "Think about what you want your follow-through to feel like."

I nodded.

"You got this."

"Thanks, Dad."

"Let's go, Elle" my sisters shouted and clapped.

In the middle of the field on the A line, the four archers shooting at the same target introduced ourselves. I'd known two of the girls from years of shooting together—sisters Aubrey and Audrey.

"Elle Corwin."

"Yes, Audrey?"

"How did I not know you had a brother?"

She waved to Drew, and I groaned. "He's not my brother."

"Oooh," Aubrey said. "What happened to that other fine boyfriend of yours?"

"Also not my boyfriend."

"Didn't answer her question," Audrey said.

"Long story."

The judges called for us to start shooting. Aubrey and I stepped up to the shooting line, ready for our first shot. My body and brain knew the steps, and after a few cleansing breaths and a focus on the prize money I stood to win, I found my center.

The first shot was always the scariest and crucial to start a good grouping, especially in the wind, which thankfully was at bay. I hoped it stayed like that the whole day.

I closed my eyes and let the image of my target panic in the last competition settle over me. Then with a deep breath, I pushed it away.

It was time.

CHAPTER 20

I NOCKED THE ARROW, FOUND MY ANCHOR, AND looked through my peep and sight to the target. Confident I'd set myself up for the best shot, I released.

And hit a ten with the biggest exhale ever.

I could imagine my dad with his binoculars reporting the score to everyone under the tent. I nocked another arrow and pulled to full draw. Release.

Ten.

"Okay, Corwin. I see you crushing it," Audrey said as I reached into my quiver for another arrow.

Third shot—ten.

I could imagine Izzy and Drew remembering the shooting competition at camp. That had been a recurve bow, so much harder, but also at ten yards. Forty looked a lot more impressive to anyone not familiar with the sport. Wait until we got to sixty.

I pulled back for my fourth shot. Ten!

As impressive as it looked to outsiders, it was what I needed to shoot to make the top ten. I went through the actions for my last shot. The pin wobbled, but I trusted my form and released.

Ten!

Aubrey had already finished shooting. She fist bumped me.

"Looking good."

"Thanks," I said. "What did you shoot?"

"Forty-six."

"Congrats."

We stepped back to let the B line shoot.

I glanced at my dad, who was smiling and nodding at me. I nodded back. When the B line finished, we retrieved our arrows and confirmed my fifty-point score. On our way back to the shooting line, I caught Drew's eye, and my heart tripped up. Usually, it would be Josh standing with my parents. I wasn't sure how I felt about Drew being there, but I knew that it was okay Josh wasn't there. A step in the right direction.

"You good?" Aubrey asked.

"Yep."

With prize money and sponsorships on the line, I had no other choice than to be.

I shot another fifty in the second end, and forty-nine in the third. I bid the other competitors good luck and headed for my family.

"Great shooting, honey," my mom said. Dad kissed my forehead.

Izzy clapped. "That was even better than at camp."

"How's the wind out there?" my dad asked.

"Nothing yet."

"They're calling for a little later. I hope they move through these ends before it comes."

"It will hit when I'm lined up to shoot sixty."

"Let's hope not," Dad said.

Drew nudged me with his hip. "Impressive."

"Thanks. You good here, in the tent, with all of this?"

"Definitely," he answered. "You?"

Maybe. Probably. Hopefully. My shooting tradition was to sip a blue sports drink during breaks, but I hadn't had time to pick one up, and my parents forgot to bring one from home. My dad was nervous the change would send me into another episode of target panic.

"Oh honey," Mom said. "You can drink anything and do well."

"Mom, you clearly don't get the superstition of sports," Melanie said, shaking her head.

"I'll find you something," Drew said, and everyone stared at him.

"What?"

"Nothing," I said. "You don't have to."

"I saw a stand selling drinks when we came in," he said. "No trouble. Besides, it'll give you some time to catch up with your sisters. Anyone else need anything?"

Drew took orders and headed off, leaving my dad to mutter. "I like that kid."

How could you not?

My parents watched the shooting and chatted with friends, giving Melanie the perfect opportunity to yank me away from them and demand answers.

"I want to know, too," Lily said. "He's good to look at and all, but didn't you get my message from Josh?"

Izzy's eyes went wide. "Josh called you?"

"You know Josh?" Melanie asked.

"Everyone stop."

They all took a deep breath.

"Lily, I got your message. Yes, Izzy. Josh called me, and Drew wanted to come today. That's all." I didn't mention he wanted to come because I asked him.

Melanie crossed her arms. "That is not all. I see him looking at you. And you're not looking at him all neutral either. He's Drew Peters, Elle. Everyone loves Drew. He's nice, and as Lily pointed out, even nicer to look at."

"What's the thing with the balloon?" Lily asked.

"I love you all," I said raising my hands in surrender. "But I literally feel like I'm having three different conversations at once. Here's the breakdown. I decided not to call Josh back. I popped a balloon with his name on it as an official goodbye. Drew and I like each other, but it hasn't progressed to anything. Now can I please focus on shooting my next end, so I don't freeze again?"

They all nodded. Good timing, too, because Drew returned with a huge blue bottle.

"Thank you," I said. "You've saved my entire competition. Seriously."

"Happy to help."

I took a few sips in time for the scores to come in and confirm I was in the top fifteen. When I stepped up to the shooting line at fifty yards, I urged my brain to focus on the shot and not Drew, but it didn't work. Because it didn't need to. Despite how scattered I'd felt when my sisters and Izzy pelted me with questions, knowing Drew watched me didn't cause any nerves at all.

It kind of inspired me.

With a smile, I pulled back to full draw on my first shot. Here's to starting another strong group. I released and through the quiet of the crowd could hear my dad's voice, "Ten!" I scored another ten before feeling my third arrow catch a slight breeze and land eight points. Sheesh. If the wind was coming, I wanted to finish before it got worse. I moved as quickly as I could and landed a ten. No wind. At full draw for my last shot, I felt a breeze again, but nothing heavy. I held my position a few seconds longer than usual and released for another ten. Forty-eight with wind from fifty yards? I'd take that with a smile on my blue lips. We rolled through the shooting with occasional wind popping up. I scored forty-nine points in both the second and third ends.

"Need another blue drink?" Drew asked with a grin, and I slipped my arm around his waist. His arm naturally fell onto my shoulder.

"I'm really happy with my shots so far."

"You should be," Dad said. "This is impressive. To be in eighth place after the first two rounds—great work. But you know the field's tight. And the wind's coming. Make every shot count."

I nodded, fearing what the wind could do. Every shooter knew it could strike at any time. It was inconsistent, and for that reason, could be totally unfair. I'd already dropped two points on a windy shot. And that had been from fifty yards. I still had to shoot from sixty.

In the sixty-meter set, Aubrey lined up next to me again.

"Where's Audrey?" I asked.

"She's down at the end."

I leaned forward and waved. She waved back. Aubrey and I wished each other luck and got to work. Three more ends. That's it, and I'd earn a spot in the shoot down. I pulled back to full draw. Push, pull, and pray, I told myself.

Release.

Ten! Yes. Phew.

Again. The simple movements all leading to another relaxed release. Ten. I closed my eyes and smiled to myself. I don't know if I'd ever shot this well. But I wasn't done. Arrow nocked. Push. Pull. Anchor. Release. Ten!

I landed two more tens to close out the end, and my tent cheered wildly.

Aubrey shot close to me with a forty-eight. "You're on fire today."

"Thank you," I said. "You're looking pretty good, too."

"I know," she said. "I thought the wind was going to catch us—"

"Don't say it!" I warned.

She held up her hand. "You're right. Forget I mentioned it."

But I couldn't. I mentally urged the judges to hurry up and hustled back to the line with my arrows as if I had any control of how fast the other twenty-nine archers shot.

"You got this, Elle," Melanie shouted.

I agreed with my little sis and shot another forty-nine. If I kept that up, I was on par to shoot an absolutely epic score. Aubrey and I stepped up again. I landed three straight tens, my arms shaking from the nerves and excitement. I didn't know where that would place me in the shoot down, but it would be high enough. Still two shots. I had to focus and land them with high scores before places could be set.

I followed my process to the detail, pulling back to full draw, and sure enough as soon as I released the arrow, a gust of wind caught it, and I landed a seven. I rested my bow on the ground and lowered my head. I barely gave up that many points in a full end let alone one shot. And I still had another shot. If wind caught it again, who knows if I'd even place?

Down the line, other shooters had similar reactions. At least I wasn't the only one caught by the burst.

With a deep breath, I pulled back to full draw and took an extra second to ensure my alignment was as accurate as possible.

And hit the x in the middle of the target for another ten and a tiebreaker if I needed it.

Oh yeah.

CHAPTER 21

I SCORED A SPOT AS A TOP FIVE SEED! THE BAD NEWS?
Because of our scores, I'd compete against Audrey in the shoot down.

"Sorry, Corwin," she said when we stepped up to shoot.

"You're that confident, huh?"

"Confident you're going to crush me?" She grinned. "Yes. I'm sorry you're going to have to eliminate your friend."

"Don't go using that psychology degree on me," I teased.

"You mean my Psych 101 class I got a C in?"

We both laughed and wished each other luck. The shoot down worked differently than the qualifying rounds. Audrey was the thirteenth seed, so she shot first. We'd each shoot three ends of five shots each. On her first shot, Audrey landed an eight. I followed with a ten. She grinned and shook her head. We both hit two tens, and in the last shot, she hit another eight, and I landed a ten, bringing me out of the first end with a four-point lead.

"That cutie back there your good luck charm?" she asked.

"Is that your way of asking what's going on between us?"

"Maybe," she teased.

"I don't understand it enough to explain it."

"Those are usually the best kind. I've never seen you hit so many tens."

"Did you see me catch wind and hit a seven?"

"Highlight of my day," she joked.

We laughed and lined up again, regaining our focus and competitiveness. The end proved closer with her hitting two tens and three nines and me doing the same. With a possibility of pulling herself back into it, especially if one of my arrows caught wind again, Audrey didn't joke on this break. Instead, she kept her eyes on the target. I didn't blame her. She was shooting great, and I hoped she kept doing it.

She hit a ten. I followed with the same. She hit another one. I pulled my arrow back to full draw, appreciating the push she gave me. Release. Ten! She took a deep breath and nocked another arrow, hitting a nine. I took my shot, matching her nine and vowing to finish out the match on my terms, with two more tens. I didn't even watch her shots. I waited for the thunk of the arrow landing and, at the beep that followed, took my own turn. Ten.

Thunk.

Push. Pull. Release.

Ten.

I covered my face and smiled into my hands. Wow! Audrey was right, I was crushing it. We hugged and congratulated each other.

"Seriously," she said. "You pushed me big time."

"Thanks. You did the same for me with all those tens over there."

We hugged again, and I headed for my slosh pit of supporters. They wrapped me in a group hug. After the other shootdowns, the judges' calculations matched me with the sixth seed. I expected a tough matchup since we were seeded close together, but instead, I focused my way to a clear victory by seven points.

"Top four!" my dad shouted, scooping me into a hug. He'd never be able to do that with Melanie who practically towered over him. Both eliminated, Aubrey and Audrey had joined my family, making the tent feel even smaller. They congratulated me and went back to their obvious interrogation of Drew.

I waited for the news of my next match up on the practice range. A competitor himself, Drew seemed to know what I needed and kept his distance. The crowds had cleared significantly, making the potential sponsors more obvious. They wore their company shirts and held binoculars and notebooks in their hands.

If I won my next shoot down, I'd be on the podium. That meant prize money and hopefully gaining the attention of the sponsors.

"How you feeling?" Drew asked.

"Nervous, but excited."

"If you need space, I can go back to the tent and answer any other questions your friends have about my background and intentions." He looked at the tent as if it would breathe fire at him. "I can't imagine a question they haven't already asked though.

I laughed. "Sorry about that. I've known Audrey and Aubrey for years. They're likely being protective. That or curiosity is getting the better of them."

"Second seed," my dad said, interrupting us. "You'll face Shannon Cass from Ohio. They just announced it."

She was good, but I'd been the fifth seed. The difference of a couple of arrows or a gust of wind is all that separated us.

"Good luck," Drew said.

I headed back to the shooting line and checked my equipment. I'd seen Shannon around the indoor circuit, but we'd never shot head-to-head before. If I remembered correctly, she was going into her sophomore year at a university in Michigan.

Now the challenger, I shot first.

When the beep sounded, I nocked my arrow, pulled to full draw, and anchored the kisser button against the corner of my mouth.

Just like shooting at camp, I thought, and released.

Ten!

Shannon shot a ten. I matched it and pulled another arrow from my quiver. She hit another ten. Refusing to drop a point to her, I landed another arrow in the center of the target. We continued like that until she landed her last arrow of the first end in the ten ring, too.

We'd both shot perfect scores.

We shook hands and hugged while the crowd cheered.

"Impressive," I told her.

"You, too," she said. "This isn't even the championship match. Why are you making me work so hard?"

"Back at you."

The runners brought us our arrows, and we readied ourselves for the second end. I shot first again, scoring another ten. Shannon hit the line between the nine and ten rings, earning her the higher score. I followed suit, but on her next shot, Shannon dropped a point, hitting a nine. I finally had the advantage.

Refusing to do anything differently, I shot my shot. My arrow sunk into the center of the target. I didn't even watch Shannon's turn. It was me, my bow, and the target. I pulled to full draw and landed a nine.

One more. I landed a ten. Worst case? We'd tied.

When the runner delivered my arrows, the announcement came. Shannon had hit three nines to my one. I was up by two points going into the final end.

Shannon nodded to me. "Good luck."

"Same to you."

After five more shots, I felt luck on my side. I'd scored another perfect score. When I made my way to the tent, my dad was crying.

"Dad!"

"You've never shot that good before," he managed.

Everyone laughed.

I cried a little, too. "Lowest I can get now is second place."

The ground shook from their stomping and cheering. Drew slid his arm around my waist, and I leaned into him. My chest was a balloon, filled with every good emotion of humankind. Weeks earlier, I hadn't been able to focus on anything but the space where Josh should have been standing, and I'd had the worst competition of my life.

Now, I was having the best.

"Shoot your heart out, honey," Mom said. "Have fun. We're proud of you."

I hugged my fan club and headed back for the line to face off against the ninth seed, who had managed to knock off both the third and first seeds. Her grin showed off her confidence. Didn't matter.

I'd shoot my best. I'd stand on the podium and collect no less than a thousand dollars. I snuck a quick look at the group of sponsors. One of them nodded to me. I nodded back and turned away to hide my smile.

I was so crushing this.

***

BEFORE WE WERE CALLED TO THE SHOOTING LINE FOR the gold medal match, my family dropped their best advice in rapid fire fashion.

"Think about what you want your follow-through to feel like," my dad said.

"Focus on your process," Mel said, giving me a side hug.

Lily pushed her glasses up on her nose. "Statistically speaking, you're going to do well, so embrace it."

Aubrey and Audrey pulled me into a group hug.

"She knocked me out of the winter indoor championship," Audrey said of my opponent, Ophelia Bruno. "Kick her ass."

"Girls," my mom scolded, ushering them away from me to plant a kiss on my cheek. "Shoot straight, honey."

I rolled my eyes at her usual go to. "Thanks, Mom."

Drew stood at the end of the line with a smirk that made me want to kiss him. I shook the thought away. Our first kiss in front of my parents? No thank you. Instead, we hugged, and he whispered in my ear, "Trust yourself."

"Thanks."

The gold medal match differed from the others in the shoot down. The tournament staff had replaced the traditional targets with a bonus twelve-ring option—a white circle, nestled between the seven and eight rings, meaning if you missed, you'd likely end up with a seven or an eight. Shooters had to call out the twelve ring before they attempted the bonus, and they could only attempt once per end.

I had no intention of attempting it.

"Elle Corwin, we meet again," Ophelia said at the shooting line.

I smiled, though I had no recollection of our first meeting. "Good luck."

"Thanks, but I won't need it."

"You might need some manners." The words flew out of my mouth before I could consider filtering them. Oh well. Fifteen shots, and I'd be on the verge of everything I'd worked toward for months.

CHAPTER 22

WITH ONE LAST GLANCE AT MY TENT OF SUPPORTERS,
I straddled the shooting line. As the lower place seed, Ophelia had
the first shot. She hit a ten. Maybe she didn't need that luck after all.

I imagined my follow-through like my dad had said and honored
every step of my process like Mel had suggested and hit a ten, too.
The beep sounded cueing Ophelia's shot, and I readied my arrow.
Nine. I waited for the beep to sound, nocked the arrow, and pulled
back to full draw. I released with ease and scored a nine, too.

Ophelia dropped an eight. I responded to her shot with another
nine. Being down by only a point, she'd be stupid to shoot for the bonus, but she clearly had the confidence, or at least the ego, to go for it.

At the beep, she pulled back to full draw, holding for a longer shot.
When she finally released, she landed another nine. She glanced at
me, and I tried to hide my smile. Maybe didn't do so well with it. It
wasn't about her. Each shot was between me, my bow, and the target.
If I shot my shot, she didn't matter.

I pulled back to full draw and felt the pressure of the string against
the corner of my mouth. Release. Ten! Ophelia rebounded on her
last shot, hitting another ten. I followed, hitting every mark of my
process perfectly until it was time to release. I triggered the release,
but it didn't go. I blinked, keeping the pin on the center of the target

and pulled the trigger again. And again.

Finally, it released, and the arrow wobbled through the air. I knew before it hit the target. I dropped my bow to the rest and ripped the velcro of the release from my wrist. I asked the judge for equipment time out and marched to my tent with my eyes on the ground.

My dad met me halfway. "What happened?"

"The release malfunctioned."

"Oh, Elle."

"The only other release I have is from my last competition."

Neither of us said what we were thinking—the release from when I'd had target panic.

Audrey and Aubrey surrounded us. "Is something wrong?"

"My release…" is all I said, and their hands were digging in their own bags.

"You girls are amazing," I said, pushing the tear from my eye. "I can't believe I blew that shot."

"You landed a six," Mel said. "If you keep up your shots, she could still drop enough points in the next two ends."

I strapped Aubrey's release to my wrist, choosing hers because it was the closest style to mine. I refused to make eye contact with Ophelia on the way back. She hadn't beaten me in the first end. My equipment had.

With her in the lead, I'd shoot first in this end. I blocked out everything around me, and focused on my shot. I'd never used this particular release before, but I didn't have another choice. I extended my arm to full draw, lined the pin in my sight, and—deep breath— released. Nine! Not perfect, but definitely better than a six.

Problem was Ophelia hit a ten. I was down three points.

S*hoot your shot*, I told myself. And I did, this time landing a ten. Ophelia matched it. We took on a mirror routine: I hit a nine; she hit a nine. I hit a ten; she hit a ten. If she matched my shots in the third end, she'd win. I had three points to make up. I could call for the twelve-point ring and go for it, possibly losing the match with a failed shot, or I could ride out the competition and hope she made a mistake.

The answer was clear.

I raised my arm and called, "Twelve ring."

The crowd gasped. I nocked my arrow and pulled back to full

draw. My shots that had landed in the nine ring had fallen low the whole day. I didn't need to correct too much—let this shot fall a little lower to that tiny white circle between the eight and the seven. Finding the best position for the pin, I exhaled and released.

The arrow pierced the white circle, and I leaned forward with my weight on my knees. Un-freaking-believable. I'd hit the twelve.

Ophelia had one more shot. A ten gave her the lead. I didn't even watch.

***

THE RUNNERS DELIVERED OUR ARROWS FOR THE LAST end. Ophelia had landed a ten on her last shot, taking the lead by one point. The beep sounded for the start of the third and final end. I nocked my arrow, pulled to full draw, and triggered Audrey's release. My arrow cut through the target in the center. I exhaled. The next few shots went smoothly. Each of us landed two more tens. When Ophelia pulled back to full draw on her third shot, a gust of wind brushed my face. I held my breath.

Ophelia dropped two points on an eight.

I closed my eyes. With two shots left, I was in the lead, but the wind had found us.

At the signal, I nocked my arrow and vowed to shoot my shot no matter what. I wouldn't wait to feel wind. I wouldn't rush to beat a possible gust in the future. I released. Nine.

Please match me. Please match me. Ophelia worked through her process, holding the shot longer than her usual motion and hit another nine.

Oh my gosh. One shot to go, and I held the point advantage. My body felt like it was growing from the inside out. My throat nearly closed up. My chest expanded and fluttered. My breath came shorter and faster.

Beep!

I normalized my breathing while I nocked my final arrow. Just another shot. Like any other. With my hand pressed against my jaw and the string against my mouth, I got the pin right where I wanted in my sight. Released. And exhaled.

Ten!

I rested my bow on its stand and waited for Ophelia to take her final shot. Without much of a choice, she raised her arm and called the twelve ring.

I stole a glance toward my tent. My dad's hands were on his head, and my mom's practically covered her eyes. Melanie and Lily held hands. Aubrey and Audrey were locked in on Ophelia. Only Drew looked at me.

I smiled at him and gave a subtle wave. He nodded, not a simple acknowledgment of my greeting, but total approval of my shooting.

Ophelia held her shot even longer this time while I did my best to wait with at least the appearance of patience. When she let her arrow fly, the crowd held their breath. When it connected to the target solidly in the eight ring, my little part of the crowd swarmed me.

They lifted me and laughed in a cloud of excitement. The cloud followed me through the award ceremony when Shannon took the podium for the third place prize and Ophelia stepped up for second.

I took first.

***

BOTH AUBREY AND AUDREY HAD PLACED IN THE TOP
fifteen, earning them prize money, too. We hugged and congratulated each other, taking pictures with our medals.

I handed Audrey her release.

"No way. You won a gold medal with it. It's yours."

"I can't keep your release!"

"You can. I have another one at home still in the package." She kept talking over my protests. "For real. I'm not taking it."

Funny. With the prize money I'd won, I could finally buy a new release, and I'd ended up with one for free. I hugged her again. "Thank you. I owe you."

"You beat Ophelia in the gold medal match with flair. That's thanks enough."

"Elle," my dad called.

"Have to go. Love you girls."

"Love you!"

My breath caught when I found my dad talking to a sponsor from Captain Archery. He extended his hand to me. "I'm Bill. That was an impressive victory."

"Thank you."

"I don't think I've ever seen anyone hit the twelve ring."

Not sure how to respond, I thanked him again.

"If you don't mind my asking, did you have an equipment failure?"

"Unfortunately," I said.

"Her release malfunctioned," my dad added.

Bill pressed his lips together and nodded. "It happens to everyone. You were able to rise above that adversity in impressive fashion. Here's the thing. We're looking for a collegiate athlete to sponsor in the store. I'd like to recommend you."

CHAPTER 23

WITH THE SUN LOW IN THE SKY, I SPREAD THE RECURVE bows and arrows across a table in the storage shed for the inventory, next to the medal I'd won that day. I wasn't exactly ready to put it in a box. The award brightened the space, which was cleaner than I'd ever seen it. I might have been going home the next day for graduation, but I wanted to make sure everything was accounted for and ready for our first archery session when I got back to camp.

"Everything there?" Drew asked from the doorway, making my heart flip in my chest.

I paused, my pen hovering above the spreadsheet. "So far, so good."

Drew leaned casually against the door frame wearing athletic shorts and a slightly undersized shirt. "Can I come in?"

"Sure."

He approached the shelving unit I'd spent the last hour organizing. "Good work in here. It might be cleaner than the lodge."

"Thank you. And thanks for coming to my competition today."

"I'm glad I was there. I've never seen anything like that. You were amazing."

"I had one of the best shoots of my life, which is a nice surprise considering my last tournament was probably my worst."

"When was that?"

"The day after Josh...the day after prom."

Understanding flashed in his eyes.

"You have a sponsor on the horizon and won some prize money. Are you going to leave us now that you're rich and famous?"

I held the clipboard to my chest and scowled at him. "I am not rich and famous." But the truth was I'd earned enough to buy the equipment I needed and cover expenses for the fall semester. If a sponsor provided me with some equipment, I might even be set for the full year. With three more summer tournaments offering prize money, I could feasibly quit my counselor gig, hang by the pool during the day, and shoot in the evenings.

Or spend time in Philadelphia.

I ran my fingers over the smooth wood of one of the bows in the shed. "I'm not going anywhere."

"Good," he said. "In that case, you interested in taking on a new student?"

I lowered my clipboard. "You want to learn to shoot?"

With a twinkle of a challenge in his eye, he said, "I think it's sexy."

My throat closed completely.

"Will you teach me?"

The way he watched me with those eyes and wore those tight shirts and bit his lip while he waited for my response, I didn't think I had to teach him anything about being sexy.

"Grab one," I finally managed.

I walked Drew through the process of determining which of his eyes was dominant, and he selected his bow while I retrieved a quiver of arrows. In silence, we walked the length of the range side by side, electricity sizzling between us. I explained the basics about standing perpendicular to the target and offered some pointers about drawing the bow back.

"Recurve bows are easier to pull from the start, but you're holding a lot of pressure to shoot," I said. "Compound bows are the opposite. Once you're at full draw, the weight is light."

With the sun dropping low in the sky behind him, Drew loaded the bow like I'd shown him. Watching him brought my mind back to the time I'd taught Josh how to shoot, but I pushed the memory away.

I still hadn't felt the urge to call Josh back. Instead, I found myself wanting to be close to Drew. That told me everything I needed to know.

He pulled the arrow back.

"This is when you anchor the string in two places. The tip of your nose and the corner of your mouth work."

He looked sideways at me and licked his lips. Despite the setting sun, the temperature increased about seventy-five degrees.

"Next?" he asked.

"You don't have some of the tools I have on the compound bow. You have to line up the arrow to the target, give a little lift for the distance, and release. Try not to rock the bow, and make sure you hold your position until the arrow lands. Otherwise, you could move too soon and send it off course."

He nodded and eyed the target, his arm muscles taut as he held the string. He fired. "C'mon!" he shouted when the arrow missed the target completely.

"Give it time. You can adjust the next shot."

"Your turn," he said.

"Okay." I took a shot. Bullseye. I'd gotten a lot better at shooting a recurve during my time at camp.

"How do you do that?"

I couldn't help but laugh. "How do you do anything in sports?"

"Please don't say practice." He loaded again.

"Slacker," I teased.

He fired. Missed. With slumped shoulders, he explained, "I thought I'd catch on, um, you know, sooner."

"You thought it would be easy," I translated.

He closed his eyes and bowed his head. "Guilty."

"I could move the target closer," I suggested. "It is a whole ten yards away."

He glared at me.

"Okay, okay," I suppressed laughter. "You've been here for how many summers, and you've never learned to shoot?"

Drew loaded again. "I was always busy with basketball. And football." Another miss. "Seriously?!"

Statistically, he really should have hit at least one shot by then.

One more shot that soared high and to the right, and he said, "I'm screwed." He looked at me again, and inched closer. "What other secrets do I need to know?"

Everything around me faded.

"Come on. You have to have some shooting secrets. What have you learned over the years?" He brushed the backs of his fingers against my cheek.

"Um, focus." Yes, that was it. "You have to focus on the target in front of you. Block out everything else."

"Can you do that?" he asked. My cheek still tingled from his touch.

He'd seen me shoot an arrow into the bullseye enough for me to realize he was talking about something else. Someone else. I remembered his expression when he saw all of the Josh memorabilia on my bed.

"Because here's the thing," he said. "I thought that I was a patient guy. I thought since I'd liked this girl for a long time, a few more days or even weeks wouldn't make a difference. But I realized something had changed."

"Really," I managed. "What's that?"

"I wasn't only seeing her in the halls anymore. She wasn't this beautiful person that I admired from a distance. I saw her every day. I got to know her laugh and this quizzical look she gets on her face when she's working out something new. I saw her shoot a bow and arrow in a way that was seriously hot." He pressed his forehead against mine. "She became real to me, and my feelings became real, too."

"Wow," I said. "That's a, wow, really good story."

"There's more."

"More?"

He nodded. "Sometimes, she looks at me, and I swear, I mean without a doubt, she's feeling the same chaotic, uncontrollable emotions I am."

I pressed one of my hands against Drew's chest and slid my other one up around his neck. "You're leaving me speechless here."

He grinned. "That'll work for me."

I took a deep breath and let my gaze fall into Drew's.

"Elle. Can I kiss you?"

I bit my lip. Drew would be the type of guy to ask first.

"Yes," I whispered.

He grinned and pressed his cheek against mine to whisper in my ear, "I was hoping you'd say that."

His lips brushed my cheek, trailing a line from my ear to my mouth. My heart rate had never soared like it did in that moment, not even at full draw aiming for the twelve ring. His fingertips tickled my bare arms, and I leaned into him.

He tipped my chin up and smiled the most adorable, ridiculously cute Drew smile I had ever seen on his adorable, ridiculously cute face. The moment his lips met mine, it was the Fourth of July in my insides. His mouth moved with full confidence, showing me how much he'd wanted this. His hand slid down my back, and mine followed the curves of his arms. His mouth found its way down my chin to my neck.

As if washing away everything that had held us back, the skies opened and poured a wicked rain down without any warning.

"The rain loves us apparently," Drew joked, reluctantly removing his lips from my neck.

We collected the bows and arrows and ran for the shed, giving way to a wave of déjà vu. But this time, we gave in to our chaotic, uncontrollable emotions and had no interest in the rain stopping any time soon.

CHAPTER 24

DREW AND I NEVER FOUND OUR WAY BACK TO THE
shooting lesson. When the evening faded to darkness, the rain slowed
to a drizzle for a few minutes. We headed back to the cabins. Holding
hands with our fingers intertwined, our steps were slow. Something
had finally happened between us. I had the sense neither of us were
eager to rush back to the responsibilities of life. When the cabins
were in view, Drew released my hand.

"I wish I didn't have to," he said.

I smiled at him. "I get it. We have an example to set."

Despite the conversation, he leaned forward to kiss me in front of
Cabin 12 that read cabin two since my sweet Lionesses had knocked
the number one on the building off with a baseball bat.

"I'll walk you in," he said.

When we stepped inside, I was glad he had. The place was dark
and empty. "Where is everyone?"

"This feels like a scary movie," he teased.

"Don't! Seriously!"

"Everyone's missing. We come back and—"

"Stop!"

He laughed but held up his hands in surrender. I flicked on the
main light to find a piece of paper on my bed.

"It's a note from Lake. She and Izzy are sleeping in Kate's cabin."

Thunder crackled, and the lights flickered. We stood in complete darkness again.

"I think the note said I should go sleep there, too."

Lightning lit the room before allowing the night to reclaim it.

"Maybe you should stay here, at least until it lets up."

"What about you?"

"I was hoping to wait it out with you."

"And violate the rule about being in a girl's cabin?"

"For a good reason, all rules can be broken."

"Is that so, head counselor?"

He groaned. "Don't say it like that. This is entirely legitimate."

I kissed him. "Is it?"

He kissed me back. "There might be a good reason."

We laughed and kissed and laughed some more while the lightning sporadically lit our world.

"I have to change," I whispered suddenly, frustrated with the way my wet clothes pulled at my skin.

"Okay."

I used my phone as a flashlight to find clothes in the armoire. Since Lake was taller than me, I found a pair of her athletic shorts and a t-shirt, hoping they would fit Drew.

"Lake's clothes? Seriously?"

"You have a better idea?" I didn't need a flash of lightning to know that the look on his face communicated a very different idea. I threw the clothes to him. "You can change out here." I took my clothes into the bathroom and leaned against the sink. I couldn't stop smiling, but at the same time, my mind raced through all the scenarios that could go wrong. Drew could find out Josh had called me. Josh could come home and find out about Drew, which wouldn't be any kind of violation on my part, but would be totally awkward.

I could fall in love with Drew.

And get my heart broken.

Again.

I shook the thoughts away and changed into the dry clothes. The lightning and thunder hung around like an annoying party guest you desperately wanted to leave. An unexpected bonus was seeing Drew in Lake's clothes. I doubled over in laughter and couldn't even hear his pleas for me to stop. If I'd thought Drew's shirts had been tight, putting him in one of Lake's? No laughing emoji could quite cover it.

Drew tickled me, probably to deflect his own embarrassment, and we landed on my bed.

He picked up my medal from the shooting competition on my nightstand. "It has been a good day."

The shooting competition felt like it had been days earlier, not hours. "It was nice having you there."

"Are you kidding? I was in awe."

"Stop," I said.

"I'm serious. You're amazing. And meeting your family was pretty cool. I know Melanie from school and stuff, but everyone else... And your dad loves me."

"He might love you a little less if he knew you were on my bed right now."

"Ooh. Tough one. I definitely want to be cool with your dad, but there's a special something about being on your bed."

"Shocker," I teased.

Drew tickled me again and kissed me until I was breathless and agreed with him about being in my bed. Entirely.

"Can I ask you something?" he said.

"Sure."

"It might sound totally corny, but..." He took a deep breath. "Does what's happening between us mean that you're my girlfriend?"

My body stilled. Did it? I guess it could.

"No response is bad, right?" Drew asked.

"I'm surprised by the question I guess, and not sure to be honest. It means it's heading in that direction."

"Okay." He frowned and broke eye contact.

"Can I think about it?"

Drew kissed the back of my hand. "Of course."

"Thanks," I said. The cool night air blew in through the screen door. Either that, or the space between us had turned icy. "Drew?"

"Yeah?"

"I don't have to be your girlfriend to not get back together with Josh if that's what you're worried about."

"No. I mean maybe. I'm not trying to lock you down off the market or anything. I guess I want to know that you're at least feeling some of the things I'm feeling. Mostly out of sheer terror."

I kissed his cheek. "If you can be here with me and have no sense of what I'm feeling, then I'm not doing it right."

A lightning flash revealed a smile on his face.

"Maybe you're not." I swatted him, but he raised his hands to defend himself. "No seriously. I think you need some practice."

"I see where this is going."

He nuzzled my neck. "You're the archery teacher, right? Practice is important."

That was true, and I wasn't a quitter. With the thunder rolling in the night sky and the rain pelting the cabin roof, I did my best to prove to Drew practice made perfect.

***

EVEN WITH A SPACE HEATER, THE CABIN COULD HAVE made even the most warm-blooded camper shiver that night. Good thing Drew and I were pressed against each other under multiple blankets. But sleeping on a guy's chest?—not as romantic as I'd expected. My neck was tighter than the string of my bow the next morning. I woke up…oh my God…with my head…on his bare chest. When had he taken his—I mean Lake's—shirt off? A glance at the clock told me we didn't have much time before the first campers arrived. We'd have to get dressed and head down to the main lodge, hopefully without Robert learning we'd stayed together in my cabin and firing us both.

I watched Drew sleep, like I had when we first came to camp, but now it was different. Before, he had been just the hot guy in charge. Now, I was beyond any hope of controlling my feelings for him. I suppressed the fearful thoughts that revelation conjured and enjoyed the view.

Looking fulfilled my interest for a few minutes before my fingers got antsy and wanted to touch. I traced the cuts in his abs, which weren't as defined when he was asleep. Still there, though. Definitely. The tracing stopped when his hand clasped around mine. I looked up, and his eyes were open wide.

"Whatcha doing?"

"Admiring," I said with a smile.

He smirked. "I'm not a sculpture."

"Only chiseled like one."

He laughed and flipped me onto my back, the blanket wrapped tightly around us. "I might keep you around. You're good for a guy's ego."

"Like that's the only reason." When his face lowered toward mine, I put my fingers on his lips and shook my head.

"Rejected? Not good for the ego after all. Probably for the best. I should get out of here before all of camp wakes up."

"Not so fast," I teased.

I reached for my pack of spearmint gum on the night stand, popped a piece, and chewed. He held out a hand, palms up, and I dropped a piece into it. While we chewed, I figured, why stop there? I found my lip gloss and slathered it on before falling back into the pillow and looking up at Drew.

"Ready now?"

In response, I gave him the best good morning kiss I could muster. His body pressed against mine, and I was pretty sure separating us would be a job for the jaws of life.

Or a stray camper.

She brought a gust of cold air with her through the open door. When Drew created some space between us, her shocked expression had to be mirrored by my own. Recognition hit me the same moment it pummeled her.

I was staring into the eyes of Josh's sister.

CHAPTER 25

"ALEXIS BRIGHTON IS A CAMPER THIS SESSION?" I SAID
aloud after she ran away from the cabin.

Drew ran his fingers through his hair as if any amount of rubbing
could scrub out this memory. "Yes."

"And she saw us in bed together."

"She's not in your cabin," Drew said. "I don't know how she
ended up here."

"Is she assigned to Cabin 2?"

Drew closed his eyes and groaned.

"This is a nightmare! I asked you to fix that number on the door."

"The work order is in. I thought—it should have been fixed. I'm
sorry." His eyes were dark, and his lips pursed.

"What she saw…" I took a deep breath. "From her view, you
know what it looked like."

He finally turned to face me. "I know, but it wasn't."

"I know it wasn't, but she doesn't."

He crossed his arms. "How much of this has to do with the fact
that she's Josh's sister?"

"Meaning?"

"If it was any other camper, would you be this concerned by what she thinks? Or is it the fact you think she's going to tell Josh you were with me and that ends your chances at getting back together with him?"

"How can you even ask me that? I'm here with you because I want to be. I told you that. It would be nice if you'd believe me." I slid the box from home out from under my bed and retrieved the letter from Lily. "Read this."

He did.

"Josh called to talk to me," I said when he didn't speak. "I didn't call him back. It's over between us."

"Maybe you should call him," Drew mumbled.

"I don't want to! I don't want to be with him."

"What if you change your mind?"

I didn't get why Drew was pushing me so hard on this. "Is this why you wanted me to stay home after graduation? You knew Alexis was coming."

He shrugged, and a voice in my head screamed that there was more to it than that. But what?

"Is Josh here?"

"What?"

It all made sense. Why he'd tried to get me to agree to be his girlfriend the night before. His fear about me wanting to be with Josh if I'd get the chance. "You said new counselors were coming for this session. You tried to get me out of here, to send me home. Alexis is here as a camper, but she and Josh do everything together. Admit it. He's here."

Drew sighed and shook his head.

"He's not?"

"No," Drew said.

"Then why…" My voice trailed off.

"I knew Alexis was coming," Drew finally said. "I thought, maybe, having her around, it would make you miss Josh."

Before I could respond, Lake catapulted herself through the door and dropped her overnight bag on the floor. She looked unsurprised to see Drew there. "Good morning, Drew."

I pressed my fingertips into the corners of my eyes. "Lake, this isn't a good time."

"Not for you it isn't," Lake said softly. "Robert sent a message for you to see him in his office."

***

TEN MINUTES LATER, WE STOOD OUTSIDE OF ROBERT'S closed office door. Side by side, we waited for the hammer. I knew what it likely meant for me—a summer of filing at my dad's office. Drew was the head counselor; they needed him more than they needed me. But he'd violated a major rule, and a camper had witnessed it.

The door opened, and Alexis appeared. She pointed to Drew and said, "That's him."

Robert shook her hand. "Thanks for coming in, Alexis. We'll get to the bottom of this. You go get settled in at Cabin 2."

Alexis worked her way down the hallway with her head down, not looking back.

"Elle, why don't you have a seat in my office? I need more coffee." He brushed passed us and mumbled, "Lots more coffee."

I collapsed into one of Robert's chairs and waited for him to finish telling someone in the hallway to take over registration since Drew would be unavailable. Robert and Drew appeared in the doorway. Drew sat next to me, and Robert closed the door behind them.

He sank into his chair, the cushion letting out a whoosh of air with his weight.

"Let me say this. Our chat here today is going to go much better if you two are honest with me. I'm sure Drew already knows that."

Drew nodded.

"Let's talk about these allegations. Not a comfortable subject, but necessary."

Drew squirmed in his seat before opening his mouth to speak. "It's not what it sounds like. We were freezing. We were short blankets. We slept in the same bed."

Robert leaned forward and placed his hands, palms down, on the desk. "Short on believable explanations, too. In the spirit of honesty, you expect me to believe that's all there was to it? I've heard the rumors about you two. I've seen it for myself."

"There was a little more to it than that," I admitted. "We woke up right before Alexis came in. We were kissing. That's what she saw."

Robert glared at Drew.

"I know," Drew said. "But I promise, the storm was bad last night when we fell asleep. The power was out."

"You said that when you called me," Robert said.

"You called him?" I asked.

Drew nodded. "I used a radio I'd left in Cabin 11 earlier in the day. I had been there fixing the sink, or at least trying to. After you fell asleep, I remembered it was there and grabbed it. I didn't want to end up in trouble for being in another counselor's cabin overnight without permission."

"Yes, there were extenuating circumstances, and you informed me, but…"

I'd never seen Robert speechless.

"Robert, I don't want to go home," I said. "If that's your decision, I'll go. But I love it here."

"I know you do. You've done great work here, especially with Izzy. Alexis says she has no interest in telling anyone about what she saw in your cabin."

I wondered why she had even bothered to report us to Robert. It didn't make sense.

Thankfully, Drew asked the question I wanted answered. "Did she give you a reason?"

Robert made eye contact with me. "She doesn't want anyone to know her brother's girlfriend is cheating on him."

Huh?

The accusations written all over Robert's face told me he'd believed her. He thought I was two-timing Josh. And Drew.

I could see Drew questioning the possibility of it. That I'd lied about us breaking up, that I'd led him on all this time. I wanted to explain, but this wasn't the time or place for all that.

The real question was why would Alexis lie?

The answer came to me quickly. She wouldn't. Which meant she didn't know we'd broken up.

It didn't make sense. She and Josh had always been close, telling each other everything. Why would he not tell her we broke up more than a month earlier?

"You two get started on your day. We'll talk about this more later. In the meantime, no more time in each other's cabins, and be respectful of your roles here. No PDA or whatever they call it, in front of the campers."

"Thanks, Uncle Rob."

Uncle? I hadn't known Robert was Drew's uncle. Maybe that was why he'd given me such a dirty look for potentially two-timing his nephew. This was such a mess. How could it possibly get worse?

Unless.

It was drop-off day. Family day. Alexis had been alone at the cabin, but was she alone at camp?

Only one way to find out. Drew and I left his uncle's office, but I pulled him into another empty one.

"Who was scheduled to drop Alexis off?" I asked Drew.

"We're back to this?"

"I need to know if I'm going to bump into him around the next corner."

He crossed his arms and took a defensive stance that I don't think I'd ever seen on him. "What if Josh were here?"

"Then the next two hours would be awkward."

He was silent, but his darting eyes and hand twitches told me he was full of questions. I tried to answer them. "You saw the letter from Lily. You saw me at prom when I was a wreck. You know we broke up."

"Yeah. I know that."

"What's with the doomsday façade then?"

"I…" Drew swallowed. "I want to tell you something."

"Okay." I waited, but he didn't say anything else. "Drew?"

"I don't know how or if I should. Maybe I shouldn't." He crossed his arms, creating more distance between us than there had been since the first day we met. After a minute, he shook his head. "I shouldn't."

"Okay," I said, not able to hide my irritation. "I have to finish packing," I said. "My parents will be here soon to pick me up."

Drew took my hand. "I'll walk you back."

I looked around for Alexis, but we were alone. Drew dropped

my hand. "Sorry."

"I don't understand why she would think I was cheating on Josh. Why hasn't he told her that he broke up with me?"

"I don't know, but you'll be home and able to avoid running into her again."

"Yeah," I said, but part of me wanted to talk to her.

Robert called Drew on the radio before we left the main lodge. He needed help with a situation, so I was on my own. Feeling nostalgic, I wandered the building one last time, saying a sort of goodbye to the quilt squares and the place overall. I'd miss it. Izzy waved to me from the registration table, and I smiled. She'd be safe and happy—at least for another two weeks. Then we'd figure something else out. We'd have to.

I passed a classroom with an active group therapy session and heard Alexis's voice.

"Technically, I'm here because my grandmother died last year, but it's not what's on my mind now. My family wanted me out of the way, I think. My parents have been doing everything they can to take care of him."

Who did Alexis mean by "him"? Whoever it was, maybe Josh couldn't come back for prom because he was helping take care of him, too. But why wouldn't Josh tell me that?

"We moved away from our home, all my friends—everything—to be near a cancer center in Philadelphia. I know it's selfish, that I'm selfish. I couldn't tell anyone. He wanted it to be a secret, to maintain some control. I guess that's what people who are sick do. They control whatever they can, even if it's whether they get cherry Jell-O or chocolate pudding in their hospital lunches.

"I've been locking it up for months," she continued, "this anger and resentment, the fear I'm going to lose him. I have nobody to talk to. Poor me, right? There's my brother, lying in a bed, fighting cancer, and I'm angry I had to leave my friends behind."

Her brother. Mason? Or could it be …

No.

I couldn't move. Or breathe. I leaned against the wall, my weight pulling me to the floor. All at once, the pieces inside of me I'd worked for the last month to heal shattered into the tiniest shards with the sharpest edges. Everything made sense. Josh's sudden move. Him not being able to come and visit. Why he'd stopped video calling. Why he'd broken up with me. The reason he'd gone dark on social media. He'd wanted privacy.

From me. From everyone.

And there was the hoarseness in his voice on that message. Not from a summer cold. From cancer.

And I decided not to call him back.

I closed my eyes and let the dagger that thought brandished slice through my heart. I huddled in a doorway down the hall while the class dispersed. I didn't want Alexis to see me. Clearly she and her family had done everything to hide Josh's secret.

Was he dying?

No.

Josh sprinted around football fields, soaring into the air, extending his arms for the perfect catch. He wrestled with Neil until they laughed too hard to go on. He played volleyball in the backyard with Melanie and tinkered with science experiments with Lily. His eyes twinkled with humor and passion and…life.

The break up—how and when he'd done it—didn't matter anymore. Before Josh had moved to Philadelphia, he'd said, "I'll see you again. And I'll think about you every day. I promise."

"I'll think about you every day, all day," I'd told him, my bottom lip puffing out. Then he'd kissed me goodbye.

Months had passed.

I'd moved on, like he'd told me to do, finally reaching a place where I didn't think of him every day.

But had he kept his promise?

Was he lying in a hospital bed, fighting for his life, thinking about me?

CHAPTER 26

I WASN'T SURE HOW MUCH TIME PASSED WITH ME sitting alone. At some point, I willed my legs to move. When I opened the door to Cabin 12, which could obviously be confused for Cabin 2, I found Alexis Brighton throwing armfuls of my clothing out of the armoire.

"Hey!"

She glared and dumped the rest of the clothes into my suitcase, which was open wide on the floor. She reached for the Josh box, the last item on the shelf.

"Don't touch that! What are you doing?"

"What am I doing? You should talk."

"Alexis, I—"

"Heard you were being exiled. I thought I'd help you pack." She sat on the suitcase to shut it and began zipping.

I tugged the Josh box from her grasp before she could direct her wrath to it. "We need to get a few things straight."

Her eyes were dark, her lips pressed together tightly. I wanted to hug her. Instead, I sat on the bed and rubbed my temples. "Alexis, I'm sorry. You might be surprised to hear me say this, but it's good to see you."

"I wish I could say the same. I mean it would be if I didn't walk in to find you on top of one of my brother's friends."

Technically, he'd been on top of me. But I wasn't about to correct her.

"Alexis, sit down."

She crossed her arms. "No."

"Your brother broke up with me."

She backpedaled a few steps and fell onto an empty bed.

"Yeah. I had the same reaction. He sent me a letter on prom night."

"My brother dumped you by letter?" She shook her head, pointing at me. "You're lying."

I dug to the bottom of my Josh box and passed her the letter he had written. "Why would I lie about this?"

She read it, and although I could tell she believed me, she still shook her head. "Why would he lie? He needs you more than ever."

"You were there, Alexis. You saw us together. I was crazy about him. I'd never cheat on Josh. If he hadn't broken up with me, we'd still be together." I nearly choked on the words. I'd admitted Drew's exact fear. Vowing to deal with that another time, I went on, "He pushed me away, probably to hide the fact he was sick."

She covered her face with her hands. "He's made us all keep it quiet. He's so depressed. My parents are afraid he won't get better because he doesn't want to."

"What happened, Alexis? Is he gonna be okay?"

"He's really sick."

I urged my body to stay upright, using every ounce of energy I had. "What is it?"

She hesitated. "Non-Hodgkin's Lymphoma."

I'd heard of it. It was like one of those words people said that elicited sad nods and creased brows. A disease I'd never had to know anything about because it had been distant, unreal even. Not this time. This time, it had caused my insides to twist into a knot that I wasn't sure would ever be smoothed over.

Alexis' arms were around me, too. I wasn't sure how that had happened. Or when. Josh was on my mind. Josh burying me in snow. Josh chasing Lily with a handful of icing from the cut-out cookies we'd made for our family movie night. Josh holding his stomach and laughing when he caught her and smeared icing on her cheek and then she did the same to him. Josh brushing my cheek with his fingertips. Josh kissing me.

I wrapped my arms around his little sister and let her cry. "I'm sorry, Alexis. I'm so sorry he's sick."

"Me, too," she whispered through sobs.

Alexis sat upright and swiped the backs of her hands across her cheeks until the tears were gone.

"You don't have to be embarrassed about crying here," I say. "They encourage that sort of thing."

"I've heard," she said, her lips quivering into the slightest smile. "He didn't want anyone to know. He's been in and out of the hospital so much. I wondered how he was hiding it from you, why you hadn't been to visit him. He didn't tell us that you broke up."

"I figured when you told Robert that I was your brother's girlfriend."

"But now you're with Drew? Just like that?" Her voice was accusatory.

"Drew and I got together...recently. What you saw, Alexis, I'm sorry for that."

"It wasn't anything major. Boys and girls kiss, right? I thought you were cheating on my brother."

"I know."

"He's so sick, and he talks about you every day. He misses you, Elle. When I saw you and Drew..." She shook her head and squeezed her fists into tight balls.

"You wanted to completely destroy my cabin?"

For the first time since I'd seen her there, she laughed.

When she sobered, I said, "He's not good?"

She looked away. "No."

Neither of us spoke. I'd been okay with living a life without Josh, but not with him not being alive to live his. I ran my fingers along the edges of my Josh box and carefully lifted the lid. Josh's face smiled back at me from all of our memories. The movies, the snowball battles, the kisses snapped by holding the camera a foot away from our faces and hoping for the best outcome. Sifting through our history meant more and hurt deeper than any other trip I'd taken through this box in the past.

"What's that?" Alexis asked.

"Mementos of your brother."

We looked through them in silence, each touching the photographs with the same deference.

"He doesn't look like that anymore. Don't tell him I said that. He lost his hair and a lot of weight about a month ago. I mean he's still my brother, but it's different. We all know it."

"A month ago?"

Alexis nods.

When he'd broken up with me. When he'd decided he didn't want to see me anymore.

Suddenly, the pictures and memories in my hands weren't enough. "You said he talks about me?"

She smiled wide. "All the time. He's been waiting to beat this cancer for months, so he can come back to Pittsburgh and see you." Her smile faded. "The kicker is you're not going to be alone when he arrives."

Her words were a knife in my already broken heart.

***

MY PARENTS WERE INFORMED THEY DIDN'T NEED TO pick me up, and Lake had begrudgingly agreed to let me drive her car. Now, it was time to inform Drew that I wasn't going straight home. I bit my lip on that one.

Our relationship was still new, fragile, and despite his general confidence, when it came to Josh, Drew was beyond insecure.

No. He'd get it. Once I told him Josh was sick, he'd understand. Of course he would. Josh was his friend, too.

Drew said he'd stop by the cabin, but I was too anxious to sit around. The door to his office was open, but he wasn't inside. I poked around the other rooms, but they were all empty. I heard voices coming from Robert's office. I found Drew there.

I knocked and said, "I'm on my way out. Came to say goodbye."

Robert raised an eyebrow at his nephew and cleared the office. "I'm going to let you two talk."

Drew refused to meet my gaze.

"Oh my gosh. Am I fired?"

"No," Drew said. "We haven't talked more about that. We've been busy with check in."

I sat in the chair next to Drew. "Then what's going on?"

"How do you know something's going on?"

My mind raced through possibilities, trying to put together some puzzle pieces I didn't know existed. If it wasn't about me being in trouble with Robert, then what? Alexis? Wait. Did she already tell Robert about Josh being sick this morning?

"Drew. Do you know about Josh?"

He lowered his head to my shoulder. I hugged him, knowing how much he must be hurting for his friend. "It's okay. I was shocked, too. Did Alexis tell Robert?"

Drew took a deep breath. "No."

"She told you?"

"I knew."

As in: past tense?

Drew had known Josh was sick. And he didn't tell me.

CHAPTER 27

"HOW LONG HAVE YOU KNOWN?"

He slouched in his seat and looked away from me.

"Drew. How. Long?"

"I've known from the beginning. When he first got sick."

I swallowed, unable to speak.

Drew paced around Robert's desk. "His family came to mine because we'd had a similar experience with me being sick when I was younger. They wanted help and support, but Josh was adamant that people didn't know. He wanted to fight this off, get better, and then be back to his normal life without everyone pitying him."

My chest twisted the same way it had when I'd read that letter from Josh before prom. "I don't believe this."

"We all knew he was underestimating what it would take to beat the cancer. We wanted him to tell his friends and to build a network of people who loved and supported him, but he didn't want the attention."

"You've known all along… All this time we've been spending together, you…"

"Yes," he said quietly.

"You came into this having knowledge I didn't have. Do you think for a second I would have dismissed Josh being sick if I'd known?"

All of the times that Drew had suggested I'd want to get back together with Josh—it all made sense now. "You knew that if I knew he was sick, I'd feel differently about him breaking up with me."

"Do you?"

My instinct was to shout "of course," but that would hurt Drew and despite everything, my conscience stopped me from doing that.

"Elle, you have no idea what it's like."

"No. I don't," I said. "Because I've been kept in the dark."

"You get so much attention when you have a sick kid. It helps in a lot of ways. Blood drives, collections, fundraisers. But it's also the nonstop phone calls, the looks of pity, the impositions when all you want to do is take care of the person you love, and if you're the sick one, breathe without puking every five minutes."

Drew's intensity pushed me to silence.

"Josh was larger than life. It's cliché, I know, but that's the only way to explain it. An epic athlete and the life of every party. He had a perfect girlfriend, a pending graduation with honors, and a college scholarship—everything in front of him. The life people dream of, and in a split second, it all crumbled. He wanted privacy to face it, and his family wanted to give him anything they could. They didn't have control of much else."

"I get that," I said, barely above a whisper. "But what if Josh doesn't come home? And I never knew? Never got to say goodbye? Then what? You know enough about grief to realize how wrong that is." The thought of Josh dying sparked too much anger to slow down my emotions. Or my mouth.

"Elle—"

"You can't protect people from grief. And if I know that, you know that. You also knew I'd want to be there for Josh. You figured if I didn't know he was sick, I couldn't go running to him."

"I wanted to tell you, but I promised him, Elle."

"I have to go…"

"Please don't leave like this, Elle. We were in a good place."

Keyword—were. I hustled outside to meet Lake and get her car keys, running the facts of my new reality through my mind. Josh had called my house more than a week ago. He'd asked me to call him, and I hadn't. He needed me. Alexis had said it herself. Lake threw my duffle bag in the trunk of her car. I hugged her. "You have no idea how much this means to me."

She handed me the keys.

Drew jogged toward us. "Elle, please. I'm sorry I didn't tell you."

"I have to go."

"Don't drive like this when you're upset. Lake, tell her not to drive like this. Iron Valley is too far."

"I'm not going to Iron Valley."

He stepped back, his face creased with worry. "Where are you going?"

"It doesn't concern you."

***

BY THE TIME THE CAR CRUNCHED THE GRAVEL DRIVE past the archery fields, I had to take deep breaths to suppress the heat of anger flushing through me. Every moment I'd spent with Drew, every quiet, perfect moment, he'd known Josh was sick. He'd let me open my heart to him, knowing what he knew.

I had accepted my new reality, a life without Josh in it, but knowing he was sick…? I didn't know what to think.

Instead, I drove.

And drove.

I drove through the winding hills of the Pennsylvania turnpike and the tunnels of the Appalachian Mountains, worrying about Josh every minute. Part of me feared he'd be gone by the time I arrived, but realistically, his family wouldn't send Alexis away if he was that sick.

I'd only known Josh was sick for a few hours, and already, how many irrational thoughts and fears had I had?

Too many.

After a few hours of suppressing guilt and contemplating what I was going to say when I saw him, a green sign on the side of the road revealed I was nearly there. I'd saved for a trip to Philadelphia for weeks, but there wasn't time for exploration. I was graduating from high school in fewer than forty-eight hours. I called ahead to the hospital Alexis had said her brother was in, and they'd told me I had thirty more minutes of visiting hours. In seven minutes, I'd parked in the garage of the hospital. In twelve, I'd maneuvered the maze of hallways to a set of hidden elevators for the oncology wing. Even after hours of driving, I still wasn't ready to walk into Josh's hospital room.

I didn't know what to expect, but I knew he was not expecting me.

I wandered the hallway until I saw his room, 489. The nameplate read: Brighton, Joshua.

I stepped into the room slowly. The television was off, and the room was quiet except for the hum of medical machinery. I leaned forward to see beyond the curtain and was relieved to find Josh asleep.

I'd wanted to see him for months. I'd dreamed about it, how he would lift me into his arms, spin me around, and kiss me the way he always had. But this reunion was nothing like that. The sun wasn't shining on us. There was no rainbow or music or laughter. Only Josh with pale cheeks and no hair. Josh hidden under a mess of blankets. When I touched his hand, I knew they weren't doing their job in keeping him warm.

His arms weren't as muscular as I remembered.

But his face—with one look, my heart pounded harder. He was still Josh.

I squeezed his hand, daring him to wake up, wondering if that was what I really wanted. All the wires and tubes reminded me of my grandfather's struggle with cancer. Of his utter defeat. I prayed it would not be the same for Josh, for his family, and for me.

But Josh hadn't wanted me to know he was sick, and now I was there, watching him sleep. I wasn't sure where the line between right and wrong was, but I sensed I was flirting with it.

"Excuse me. Can we help you?"

I turned to see Mr. and Mrs. Brighton in the doorway.

"Oh, Elle! How in the world did you get here?" Mrs. Brighton said and rushed to hug me, squeezing tightly. "Thank you for coming."

"Maybe we should step outside," Mr. Brighton said when Josh stirred.

"It's good to see you both." In the hallway, I explained how I'd seen Alexis at camp, leaving out the part about Drew and hoping Alexis was willing to do the same. "I know Josh might not want to see me, but I'd really like to talk to him."

His parents looked at one another as though discussing it with their eyes.

"I think it's a brilliant idea," Mrs. Brighton said. She raised her hands as if in prayer. "Finally, somebody knows about Josh. He didn't want anyone to know, but we've wondered if things would be different if he'd had his friends here."

"Still," Mr. Brighton said to his wife, "you know his wishes. I'll talk to him in the morning. Until he says it's okay, I don't want him to know you've been in to see him."

I could accept that.

"We'll check on him one more time," Mrs. Brighton said. "Then you can follow us back to our house and spend the night there. You'll want to call your parents and tell them you got here safely."

"Thank you," I said. "But I don't want to intrude. I can stay at a hotel."

Mrs. Brighton shook her head.

"Nonsense," her husband said. "You'll stay with us where we know you're safe. There's plenty of room."

"Thank you," I mumbled.

In the grand scheme of things, I got it. Who wanted people to see them sick? I'd had the flu and mono before, and had been a wreck. And when I had my wisdom teeth out, my dad said I looked like the semi-square faced, former Pittsburgh Steeler, Carnell Lake. None of those things were as serious as cancer, but the point was the same. Nobody wanted people to see them at their worst.

But that was also when everyone was capable of caring the most.

Mr. Brighton insisted on driving Lake's car since I'd been driving for hours and needed a rest.

"Do you think Josh will see me?" I asked when he pulled out of the hospital parking lot.

"I'm not sure," he said. "I know he misses you. It's been hard for him to leave all of his friends behind. I'm sure Alexis told you he didn't want anyone to know he was sick. I think he thought he would come here, be cured, and then go back to Pittsburgh like nothing had ever happened."

"And now?"

Mr. Brighton looked down at me and exhaled a deep breath laden with stress. "Now, he might not have a choice. He needs a stem cell transplant."

"Oh," I said, not really sure what that meant.

"Nobody in the family is a match. We're going to have to start looking to friends and even strangers."

"You'll have to tell Josh's friends?"

He nodded. "We're waiting for him to come to terms with everyone knowing he's sick."

"I think a lot of people at school would get tested for Josh. I'll get tested tomorrow."

Mr. Brighton patted my hand. "Thank you, Elle."

"There has to be a match. He has to tell them."

"I completely agree," Mr. Brighton said with a weak smile.

Between us, we left unspoken what could happen if Josh refused.

CHAPTER 28

IT HAD BEEN WEEKS SINCE I'D SLEPT ANYWHERE BUT a non-air-conditioned cabin. Now, I was in the Brighton family's cozy townhouse. Mr. Brighton carried my bag to Alexis's room while his wife pulled some towels from the bathroom Alexis shared with her brothers. Mason was away for the week at a football camp. The Brightons had timed Alexis and Mason's camps this way so that they could focus on Josh, and there I was. Intruding.

"Are you sure you don't want anything to eat?"

"No. Thank you," I insisted. "Some sleep is all I need. Thanks again for letting me stay here."

Mrs. Brighton pulled me into a bear hug. "It's so nice to have you here, sweetie. Get some rest. Help yourself to anything at all."

They disappeared into the hallway and closed the door behind them. I plugged my phone in and saw I had five missed calls. Lake, Lily, and of course, Drew, multiple times. I ignored the messages and punched in a quick text to Lily telling her I was with the Brightons. No need for Mom and Dad to worry. Out of courtesy, I sent Lake a similar text. She responded that she was around the campfire with the group, and she'd passed my message on to Drew, who had been asking about me every ten minutes. I didn't reply.

Alexis's bed was so comfortable I was in danger of falling asleep on top of the covers in my clothes. I talked myself into getting a shower to wash the frustration from the day away. In the bathroom, I poked at my tired face and puffy eyes. I looked to the right at another door. On the other side was Josh's bedroom. I turned the knob and let myself in. The light from the bathroom shone across the dark room, creating shadows on the walls. The room wasn't much different from his old one in Pittsburgh. Same blue plaid sheets and comforter. Same trophies from football, baseball, and wrestling. Same photos on his bulletin board.

Photos of me.

I had the same photos in my Josh box—the snowball battle, us making snow angels, a shot with our Pittsburgh Penguins hats pulled low, the hockey arena behind us. There were even a couple movie stubs. The whole board was composed of remnants from our relationship. In the center was a picture of me at Prom. I recognized it immediately. Kate and I were being silly, laughing after I was announced Prom Queen. She kissed my cheek, and I tossed my head back in laughter. There were two other prom photos next to it. Kate had posted all three online, which must have been how Josh got them.

I wondered if he saw these photos as my reaction to him breaking up with me. That could explain why it had taken him so long to call. Maybe he'd thought I was happy with it, that I was fine.

I wasn't.

I pulled the photos off the board, and an envelope fell from behind it, fluttering to the ground.

In Josh's handwriting, the words on the front read, "If I die…"

My legs gave out. I couldn't take my eyes off his words, written in blue ink. Couldn't—wouldn't—begin to imagine what was inside the thick envelope.

But it was clear. Josh had sat down with a pen and paper and poured himself into whatever was inside of that envelope with the full knowledge—even the belief—that he was going to die and he wanted these things to be said. I pressed it to my heart and made sure the tears puddling around me didn't smudge his writing or soften the paper. All of the moments of the last few weeks—learning about grief, flirting with Drew, meeting my campers, winning the field games, being focused on my shooting competition as if everything in the world could be solved with a sponsor and a few hundred dollars—they gripped me in a net laced with the kind of guilt that rooted me to the floor.

I was angry at Josh for leaving me behind, but I was the one that had left him behind without even knowing it.

***

THE NEXT MORNING, JOSH'S PARENTS DROPPED ME off outside his hospital room with tears in their eyes.

"We'll be right here," they whispered as I walked into Josh's room again. This time, the blinds were open allowing the sun to light the room, and the TV blared Sports Center. I smiled. He might be sick, but he was still Josh, forcing me to watch ESPN.

"Hello?" Josh said tentatively.

Once I was in view, I stopped looking at the floor and made eye contact with him. Terrified he was going to send me away in anger, I waited for a reaction.

He laughed.

"What's funny?"

"I never expected you." He opened his arms wide, tubes and wires hanging from them. "Come here."

I fell into him like no time had passed. He squeezed me to his chest so hard I thought I might hurt him. "I thought your parents told you I was coming."

At the same time, he said, "Elle, I can't believe you're here."

"I can't believe you're here either," I said, pointing to the hospital bed.

He lifted his hand to his bald head. "It's the new look."

"Is it now?" I laughed again. I've forgotten how funny he was. This was going much better than I'd thought it would, it was really good to see him again. "I'm sorry I didn't call you back."

He nodded. "I deserved that."

"It's not that."

"Yes it is."

I couldn't stop my smile. "Maybe a little, but more than that…" I struggled to find the words to explain why it had felt right not to call him at the time.

"Forget it." He patted the chair next to his bed. "When my parents said a friend was here, I never thought it would be you."

"Is that because they think we're more than friends?"

He winced. "Sorry about that."

Not willing to crack that can of worms open any further, I asked, "Who were you expecting?"

"You don't know him. A friend of mine. His name's Drew."

My chest tightened. "Drew?"

"He works at the summer camp Alexis went to." He gestured to the tubes dangling from his nose and arms. "He's the kind of guy who would drop everything and drive out here to check on me."

Yeah, he was.

"How did you hear about me?" Josh asked.

"I work at this summer camp…"

He grinned. "Ah, you must know Drew then."

"Yep." Guilt crept up my throat.

He studied me for a moment. "So you saw Alexis. Who could expect her to keep quiet?"

"You know, it's healthy to talk about things, to express your fears and feelings," I said, but then quickly added, "for people who are comfortable with that sort of thing."

He raised an eyebrow. "You do know Drew."

"And," I ventured, "in the spirit of talking openly, I have to say I'm disappointed you didn't tell me yourself."

He rested his head back against the pillow and looked at the muted television. "I couldn't, Elle."

"You have to know I'd want to be here for you."

"I didn't want you to be," he said quietly. "I was naive, though."

"About what?"

He sighed. "I never met a challenge I couldn't conquer. I thought this would be the same. I could go away, get treatment, work hard, and bam—no more cancer."

"And now?"

"I'm not sure."

I leaned back in the chair, watching the muted television too, but not registering anything happening on the screen. I had to respect Josh's decision, but I didn't have to like it. Navigating that contradiction took a lot of self-control.

"Why did you lie to your family?" I finally asked.

"I guess I didn't want it to be true, us not being together."

I scrubbed my face with my hands in frustration. "Then why did you break up with me?"

"Look at me, Elle. I mean, really look at me. Do you see this wire? I don't know what it's for. Maybe it tells the nurses whether or not I've died yet. Or this tube? I think that one gives me fluids and my medications, lots of medications. I've gone through chemotherapy, and in response my body has pumped out just about every disgusting substance you can think of. I've barely walked down the hall in a week. My parents look at me with hope and fear, knowing there's a chance I might die any day."

"Stop talking like that." But he didn't.

"And now you have to face it, too. I didn't want you to be a part of this because there's nothing good about it. Why would you want to see me sick and helpless? To hear the doctors talk about how long I might live? Or maybe you wanted to sit beside me and hold my hand while I had nightmares, seeing my own funeral? It's painful and fearful and fatal."

That last word hung in the air. It was the third time Josh had mentioned dying. And so cavalierly, too. I imagined his face on one of the quilt squares at camp and had to steady myself against the edge of his bed.

"Elle? You okay?"

Not even close.

"I loved you." I couldn't help but laugh at myself for being blunt, answering a question other than the one he'd asked.

"I know. I loved you, too."

Our admission dangled there in midair. We'd both used the past tense, but did we mean it to be?

I wasn't sure I knew the answer to that, or maybe even that I wanted to know.

"The day before prom, I got some bad news," Josh said. "The treatments hadn't gone as good as my doctors had hoped. I thought that was the end, and I didn't want to take you down with me."

"Take me down? Josh, if something had happened to you, and I'd never known what you were going through or had the chance to say goodbye, it would have destroyed me."

He sat forward and slipped his hand into mine. "I thought it would be easier for you if we weren't together at all. You could move on and be happy. Then when I was gone, you would get the news and be okay."

"Okay that my first real boyfriend died of cancer away from all of his friends? That he died never knowing how much I cared about him?"

We sat quietly, letting our words, fears, and frustrations sink in.

"You're right. I'm sorry." He smiled at me and even with the sickness ravaging him, his grin made my whole body tingle.

"Your dad says they want to plan a donor drive for you."

He shifted in his bed and looked out the window. "I don't know."

"I do," I said, drawing his attention back to me. "You're going to do that drive, Josh."

"Elle, don't."

"Oh, I'm going to. Alexis is a wreck. Mason adores you. I can't assume he's any better. And your parents? They're like walking in this zombie land of trying to save your life when you don't want it saved."

"That's not true. I want to get better."

"Then get better," I said.

"And if it doesn't work? What if I put myself out there and get all this pity and nobody even comes? Or maybe they do, and nobody's a match. And did you know after all of that, even if you find a match and get the transplant, the cancer could come back even more aggressive?"

"That sucks, Josh. No way to sugar coat it. But is the answer to hide an envelope in your room for everyone in case you die? That's supposed to make it better?"

His stare dug into my soul while I replayed the words in my head and realized what I'd said to him.

"Did you open it?"

"No," I said. "I was looking at a picture on the bulletin board, and it fell. I put it right back where I found it."

He lowered his head and sighed.

"This isn't you, Josh. You're not a guy who lies in a bed, waiting to give up. You're the one everyone counts on to win the game. Why don't you see that? Why can't you envision yourself defeating this?"

"Look at me. What do you see?"

"The same person I've always seen."

"Liar." He brushed his fingers against my cheek. "I see a change in you. You're more beautiful than I remember. You're feistier. Stronger."

With his hand against my cheek, I felt weak. Too weak. I'd made a promise to Drew that things were over between Josh and me. And there I was by his side, melting all over again.

I could be stronger. I could tell him the truth about Drew and me. I could tell him it was going to be friendship—and only friendship for us.

Until he said, "I missed you so much, Elle. I still love you."

CHAPTER 29

JOSH'S PARENTS CAME INTO THE ROOM SECONDS LAT-
er. They smiled at us, the happy couple. I excused myself to give them
some family time and made the mistake of checking my messages.
Neil had messaged when he'd heard from Lake about Josh. Kate had
texted when she'd heard from Neil who heard from Lake. Drew had
called and left a voicemail.

*Elle, it's Drew. Please call me. I hate how we left things. Can you
at least text me when you get there, so I know you're okay?*

My fingers hovered over the screen, but I didn't know what I
wanted to say. Instead, I toured the hospital, stretching my legs and
exploring. I missed the wide open spaces of camp. The lobby gift
shop tempted me to find something Josh and I could laugh about, but
the best option felt more nostalgic than silly. I paid for it and headed
back to Josh's room. I found him alone, gazing out the window.

"Where are your parents?" I asked.

"Grabbing lunch."

I shook the paper bag in my hand and said in a sing-song voice,
"I got you a present."

He rolled his eyes, but grinned. "You didn't."

"Oh, I did. It's epic."

"Epic?"

"Astronomical."

"An astronomical gift in that little bag?"

I set it next to him. "See for yourself."

With a laugh, he reached inside and pulled out the stuffed purple star. He pressed his thumb and forefinger against his eyes and held them there for a minute. His lip quivered when he said, "Thank you."

There was a time I might have swallowed my own tears. Instead, I thought of Robert and let them fall. Josh could see them and know that I cared. He deserved that. "The purple is for Iron Valley, obviously. And the star is to give you something to look forward to. When you're better," I choked on my words. "We'll get Harris' telescope out and watch the stars together again."

He nodded, and I got it—it was hard to talk through your tears. Instead, he opened his arms to me like he had the moment I'd walked into his hospital room, and I fell into them, squeezing him so hard the cancer didn't have a place inside him.

If only it were that easy.

"Elle?" he whispered.

"Yeah?"

He waited for me to make eye contact before continuing. "I talked to my parents, and we're going to do the stem cell drive in Pittsburgh. They'll announce at graduation that I'm sick."

"Oh, Josh. You're doing the right thing."

"Doesn't mean it doesn't suck."

"Everything about this sucks." I sat up and held his hand. "How does it work?"

"I've been getting blood and platelet transfusions a lot, so they'll host a collection. People can donate, have a vial of blood taken to be tested for the Match Registry, or both."

"What's Match Registry?"

"It's a national registry, and anyone like me who needs a transplant can benefit from it."

"You'll find a match. I know you will."

Josh squeezed my hand. It seemed like an impossible task, but I refused to live another lie. Josh had lied to me for months. He'd lied to his family. I'd lied about Josh. Drew had lied about Josh. Enough lies.

"Josh, we have to talk."

He released my hand and sank into his pillows again. He knew what was coming. I wasn't sure if that made it easier or harder. "There's someone else?"

"Not officially, but ... possibly. I don't want to lie to you about that."

He nodded. "Thanks, I guess."

"I'm really sorry."

"It's my fault, Elle. Not yours. I made a huge mistake. Lots of them. Lying to you, then breaking up with you."

"I'm here for you, Josh. I'll get tested today before I leave the hospital, and if I'm a match, consider the transplant done. If I'm not a match, I won't flip my tassel at graduation until every single senior signs up to be tested. I'm in your corner." I pulled his hands back into mine. "I'll be a friend to you, but that's all I can give right now. I'm sorry."

Before I left, I fulfilled my promise and got a blood test. It would take a few days—maybe longer—to get the results back. When I hugged Josh goodbye, he insisted he was okay with us being friends.

"For now," he added as an afterthought, grinning. I had little doubt that the second he was better, he'd pursue me like he had a year earlier. He'd be romantic, thoughtful, creative, and ... tough to ignore.

But before any of that, Josh had to survive cancer.

***

I DEBATED THE LOGISTICS OF MY PLAN DURING THE five-hour drive from Philadelphia to Pittsburgh. When I stopped for gas, I called around to find a truck we could get for the ceremony. Thirty miles later, I had three trucks confirmed and clearance from the school's Superintendent to host a blood drive on campus. I called Kate and told her to post details online. She insisted I focus on driving while she called around, asking local businesses and churches to support the drive on short notice. Most people remembered Josh Brighton as a standout on the state championship football team. They promised to be there.

Kate called to say the senior class had been reposting her message all afternoon. She'd started a social media page, A Cure for Josh Brighton. The page already had 300 fans. Someone would be a match for Josh. I knew it.

"That's incredible," I told her.

"There are four-hundred-and-fifty graduates tomorrow. We can do better than that."

I had faith we would. Kate could be persuasive. Scary, even.

By the time I parked Lake's car in my driveway, A Cure for Josh Brighton was more than 1,000 fans strong. All of that in one day. I called Josh's parents to share the news and told them I'd gotten home safely. The sun hung low over the roof of my neighbor's house. Exhausted, I decided to leave my bag in the car and sneak in. Maybe I could have a few minutes of peace before my parents asked questions. The kitchen and living room were empty.

I grabbed a cold drink from the fridge debating something I'd put off for too long. I hadn't spoken to Drew since I'd driven away from camp. He'd called. I hadn't answered. Planning Josh's stem cell drive had been the perfect distraction, but until morning, there wasn't much else I could do.

I tapped a text to Drew: I'm home safely. Thanks for checking on me.

Bubbles appeared instantly.

Drew: So am I.

What did that mean?

My phone rang in my hands with Drew's name on the screen. "Hey, Elle."

"What do you mean you're home?"

"I took a couple days off to come home for graduation. I thought you might need a friend."

I definitely needed that.

"I'm sorry I didn't tell you."

I closed my eyes and leaned my head back against the couch. Part of me had wanted Drew to tell me the truth, but I understood he'd been in a bad position. "It was a lot to take in, but I get you were honoring Josh's wishes."

"Thanks," he said quietly.

"Can you forgive me for running off like that?" I asked. "I did exactly what you were afraid I'd do."

"Did you?"

"You mean did I get back together with Josh?"

Silence filled the connection.

"Josh knows he and I are friends. He's okay with that."

"For now," Drew said with a nervous laugh.

Clearly, Drew knew Josh better than I realized.

CHAPTER 30

HATE, NEIL, DREW, AND I ARRIVED AT IRON VALLEY HIGH
School early the next morning. We debated the campus layout and
came up with a game plan that stationed the three bloodmobiles, as
they were apparently called, at different entrances to the football stadium. Nobody could enter the graduation ceremony without passing
at least one mobile donation center. I put Neil and Drew in charge
of the heavy lifting. Kate and I posted flyers all around the field and
tucked them into the graduation programs.

When I found the guys to check on logistics, a crowd of football
players surrounded them. Owen Malone and Julia Medina joined
Square Weaver at the front of the pack.

Square, the King to my Prom Queen, hugged me, lifting me off
the ground. "Elle, I'm sorry to hear about Josh. We got your back.
Whatever you need."

I swallowed hard, his reaction reminding me that everyone here
thought Josh was still my boyfriend. I made eye contact with Drew.
He had to be making the same mental calculation.

I thanked Square.

"Some of the guys showed up to help," Drew said. "They'll help
distribute juice and cookies to everyone after they're tested and make
sure nobody topples over."

"We got everything under control, Elle," Square said.

"Thank you all. I know it would mean a lot to Josh to see you here."

"He will see everyone," Kate ordered. "Elle, get in the picture with the guys."

I stood in the center while Kate snapped the photo. "I'll upload this to A Cure for Josh Brighton and text it to his parents."

"That's a great idea, Kate. Keep taking pictures throughout the day and updating social. That might get more people down here."

The trucks arrived, and the boys took over setup. They lined up chairs and registration tables for potential donors. They even poured orange juice into glasses. They were seniors and underclassmen, and with the day being all about Josh, it felt like a graduation wasn't even on the agenda. My phone rang. The caller ID said: Mr. Brighton.

I answered pleasantly, happy to share the news with Josh's parents, but it was their son's voice on the other end.

"You're incredible," he laughed. "I delete my substandard social media, and now I have a super star page."

"Technically, Kate did that."

"Don't be so humble. I've seen the pictures. You put this all together for me. I can't thank you enough, Elle. You're really amazing."

"Josh, everyone wants to do this for you. They're all worried about you."

"I wish I could be there with you," he said.

I glanced at the massive screen on the football field. "I have an idea, if you're up for it."

"Anything for you."

***

MOM AND DAD SHOWED UP THE MOMENT THE DRIVE started with Lily and two carloads of her friends. Melanie came with her teammates. Everyone older than eighteen vowed to get tested. Those were the rules. It killed me to think that someone who was seventeen or sixteen passing out cookies or juice could be the match Josh needed, but they couldn't save him because they were too young.

"I wish we could get tested," Lily pouted, echoing my own

thoughts. "For Josh and for Alexis. I couldn't imagine you being sick."

I felt a lump form in my throat. "Lil, that's sweet."

"We have to do something for her," said Lily's friend, Stella.

When Lily's face lit up, I knew she had a plan. "Elle, do you have any flyers left?"

"Sure, but we put them all around the stadium."

"But we could put them up somewhere else, like on all the cars in the mall parking lot."

The rest of the girls agreed.

I hugged her. "That's a great idea!"

"Really?" Lily asked.

"Sure. Why are you surprised?"

"No reason," Lily smiled.

"Lil…?"

"My ideas are never as good as yours. That's all." My little sister shrugged as if she hadn't just paid me the hugest compliment. "Where are the flyers?"

I gave her what we had left from Kate's father's abuse of public resources. "You'll probably have to make more. The trucks will stay as long as there are people here to donate and get tested, so think big."

"We can make copies at my house," Stella said.

"What's taking Mom and Dad so long?" Lily asked. "We need to get going on this."

Yeah, really. I'd thought it would be a quick prick, and then people would be out of there. If that was how long it would take, we could have problems. I told the girls to wait outside, and I climbed into the van to find my parents reclined in chairs, tubes filled with blood extending from their veins to bags beside them.

I hadn't given that much blood to be tested at the hospital in Philly. "What's going on?" I asked the nurse.

"There's a major need for blood right now, and everyone who donates will count toward Josh's account," my mom explained.

"What do you mean Josh's account?"

The worker taking my parents' blood explained that Josh and everyone like him has an account with credits. When people donate, the credit applies to him, so he has enough blood to get through the days and weeks it may take for us to find a match. It wasn't only about testing people for the stem cell match. It was also about making sure Josh had enough blood for his transfusions, so he could survive until the transplant. And through the long recovery process, too.

I got it. I really did, but we were at a heavily populated event with people willing to get tested. If every one of them donated blood, too, we'd never have enough time to test everyone.

"What if people only want to test for the Match Registry?"

"They can do that."

My dad squeezed my hand. "It'll be okay, sweetie."

I nodded, not totally convinced. The nurse collected the pints of blood from my parents, and they sipped their juice. I slumped into the chair between them, all my fears over Josh's condition swirling through my mind.

"I'm proud of you, Elle," Dad said, nudging me. "You're helping girls at camp. You're working hard for the Brighton family. Your kindness is inspiring."

Tears filled my eyes. "Thanks, Dad."

"Your mom and I have been talking, and we want to match every dollar you make this summer."

"Seriously?"

He hugged me. "I'm sorry about Josh. This is our way to support him and you."

I'd spent money on gas and tolls to get to Philadelphia, and I'd miss out on two weeks' wages being home instead of at camp because of the whole Drew and Josh situation. And maybe, hopefully I'd take another trip out east. Even with the gold medal winnings from the last tournament, a match on my bank account would mean everything.

"I love you, Dad," I whispered.

"I love you, too. Now let's find this kid a match."

***

MY PARENTS AND LILY'S CREW PILED INTO OUR CARS and headed for the mall. A few other girls showed up and asked what they could do to help. I gave them Lily's number. My once-annoying, surprisingly resourceful, little sister directed them to another shopping center parking lot and demanded they call friends to cover three other local plazas. Each of the three donor testing trucks had a line, and a few football players were on an excursion to the grocery store for more cookies and juice.

A woman who looked slightly younger than my mom approached me. "Are you Elle?"

I reached out to shake her hand. "Yes, thank you for coming."

"This is incredible. I want you to know what you're doing for these patients is such a gift. If not Josh, some other family waiting for a donor might get positive news from this event. You're saving lives here today."

I'd wanted Josh to get healthy more than anything, but people were out there praying the same for someone they loved, too. Imagining another family huddled around their loved one in a small hospital room, crying from the good news of finding a match had me swiping at my eyes yet again.

"We," she pointed to a man walking toward us, "went through this with our son. It's not easy, but it's worth it."

"That's encouraging. How's your son doing?"

Her face tightened, and she leaned into her husband.

"He didn't make it I'm afraid," he said.

Any composure I had shattered. "Oh my gosh. I'm so sorry."

"We didn't find a match, but we did find donors for two other patients."

I looked around at everyone being tested. What if no one was a match for Josh?

"Elle, our situation was different. Our son had a special case, and finding a match for him was more difficult than usual," the woman tried to reassure me. She hugged me tightly. "I'm sure you'll find a match for Josh."

I forced a smile and made an excuse about needing to check on something. I found a quiet area near one of the trucks and sobbed. Then I searched my social media. The drive had been posted everywhere by so many people. But there had to be something else we could do.

"Elle, watcha doing?" Drew asked as he approached me. He kept his distance. We'd agreed would be best. No need to spark scandal by canoodling with Drew.

"There aren't enough people here."

"Each truck is maxed to capacity with an hour wait."

I replied to a post Square had made online, pleading with people to come get tested. "There's no guarantee someone here is a match."

Drew pulled the phone from my hands.

"What the hell!"

"Elle, stop." His voice was annoyingly calm.

"Give me back my phone."

"Don't do this to yourself."

"Now!"

"Not until you hear me out."

I walked away. "Whatever. I'm sure I can find another phone."

He looped his arm around my waist and pulled me to him. "This isn't something you can control. You have to accept that."

I pushed him away and kept walking.

"You put all of this together, Elle. Hundreds of people are here. You did that."

"And what if it's not enough?"

"You're doing the best you can," he insisted.

I ripped my phone from his grasp.

"If I'm not making phone calls and posting online to get more people here, I'm not doing the best I can."

He raised his hands in surrender and backed away. The parking lot was nearly full. More cars pulled in. The lines were too long. People might not want to wait. Maybe the key wasn't getting more people here but ensuring the ones who were there were tested. I searched online for the number I needed.

CHAPTER 31

HATE WAS A ROCK STAR ORDERING EVERYONE AROUND. Maybe I was too because after a few very persuasive phone conversations and several promises to rally student support for specific community service initiatives the following school year, another crew was on its way. Without a truck, they needed a space to work in.

The principal allowed us to use the gym. It was big enough to accommodate everyone who wanted to test or donate. The new crew arrived as I entered the stadium to meet with the principal and technology director. Immediately, the lines shortened and people moved to their seats for the ceremony more quickly.

"Principal Welch." I extended my hand. "Thank you for everything."

"Anything for one of our own," he said. And the mayor of course. Kate's dad had power around here not only because of his position but because people appreciated him and would do anything for him. "I'm sorry to hear what he and his family have been going through." He tugged at his sleeve to reveal a bandage on the crook of his arm. "I've had my test, and I'll be encouraging everyone else to do the same."

"The Brighton family is going to be so grateful."

"I also got his account information. I donate blood regularly and will start attributing it to him directly."

That was a good idea, too. I could post that on social after the drive for anyone else who regularly donated. "Thank you."

The principal nodded and led me to the staging area behind a massive backdrop on the 50-yard line. "While I want to be helpful today, there is only so much we can do. The ceremony will have to start on time."

"Of course," I said. "Kate and a few other students are talking with people in line. We're asking that anyone who is not here for graduation might allow those who are to go ahead of them. She's tempting them with snacks and entertainment from the dance team."

Principal Welch smiled. "She's quite resourceful, that one."

Without a doubt.

As the seats filled with relatives and friends of my classmates, a couple of seniors in caps and tight, short summer dresses roamed the stands with clipboards getting anyone who hadn't been tested to sign up for a time following the ceremony. I was certain the idea was Kate's. As the ceremony start time neared, the focus shifted from the donor drive in the parking lot to the graduating seniors in the stadium. With two minutes to spare, Kate took her place on stage as the class President. I sat behind her. I held no office. I was a new addition to the stage.

I was there to speak about Josh Brighton.

I didn't have a speech, but I had one hell of a visual aid.

When Principal Welch stepped in front of the microphone to welcome everyone, I scanned the crowd for Drew. Too many faces, and not enough time. Under my gown, I texted him a simple apology and asked where he was. He promised to come inside in a few minutes. He was checking on all of the trucks, which were still busy with people from around town who had no reason to attend graduation. They were there for Josh.

Someone would be a match. Someone had to be.

"Here to talk about this donor drive is a graduating senior who happens to be our Prom Queen, Elle Corwin."

When the polite applause fizzled, I leaned into the microphone. No words came. An image of Josh running down this very field, extending his arms to catch a pass from our quarterback Julia consumed my mind. I closed my eyes and found my breathing.

"Hello, everyone. I want to start by thanking Principal Welch and the Blood Drive Network who provided the trucks for today's donor drive. Our technology director Mr. Tyler has also been great in setting up a sound system in the parking lots, so everyone who is still in line can hear the ceremony. I want to take a brief moment to talk to all of you in the stadium and everyone who is taking the time to get tested at the trucks."

I paused, not really sure how to summarize my feelings, fears, and hopes for today. I wanted to share something amazing, something that made everyone want to get tested. But when it came to Josh, there was no magical tale. The truth was all I needed.

"Many of you know Josh Brighton. Ten minutes with him is all it took for me to be hooked. He is a standout athlete, incredibly funny, and friendly to everyone in this school. He is the apex of popularity, not for any one reason, but for so many reasons. He's a special friend of mine. When I heard he'd been diagnosed with cancer, I was devastated."

I choked on my emotions for a second before recovering.

"Josh didn't tell his friends he was sick. He didn't tell us that when he moved to Philadelphia, it was really to be close to a cancer center for treatments. He wanted us to remember him as the dynamic, popular, fearless classmate he was. But there's a problem with that plan, and this problem provides an important lesson to Josh, to me, and hopefully to all of you. Josh can't fight this disease on his own. He can't take control of his health, placing all the weight on his own shoulders. He can't do this because he needs a stem cell transplant. He needs someone else who is willing to save his life.

"As teenagers, we want to have complete control over our lives. We want to drive instead of letting our parents drive us. We want to work on school projects independently instead of working in a group with partners that may not be dependable. We want autonomy from siblings, bosses, and sometimes even friends. But it's impossible to be in control of everything, all the time. I know that now, and so does Josh.

"We need someone else out there to help. It could be any of you. Someone sitting on these bleachers could be the match the Brighton family is praying for. Josh competed with his whole heart every Friday night in this very stadium. He gave so much of himself on this field. It's fitting that this is where we will give back to him. This is where we'll find someone who can save Josh's life. I know today is a special day. It's a day of celebration for every graduate. But it can also be a day of celebration for Josh Brighton and his family. I'm asking that each of you, before you get back into your cars and go home to your healthy and happy families to celebrate such a momentous occasion, please register with volunteers outside in the parking lot. Get tested to be a donor. Please."

The stadium erupted in applause. As the crowd quieted down, I saw Drew leaning against the fence near the entrance, tears on his cheeks.

"Before we move on, there's one more thing I want to share with you," I told the crowd. The technology director pressed a button on his remote and the screen behind me lit up with Josh's face. He looked like he had when I last saw him. He was in his hospital room. The light from the windows made the room bright. The tubes and machines were still in place.

"Hey, everyone," Josh said and lifted his arm to wave. The crowd screamed as if they were watching a championship football game, not a dark moment in a commencement ceremony. The teachers, administrators and students on the stage around me smiled, their eyes watering. "I want to thank Elle for that amazing speech. You make me sound much better than I deserve credit for." That was Josh, so humble. He thanked everyone else, too. His audience reacted to him immediately—sensing the severity of his illness, howling with laughter at his jokes, succumbing to tears at the power of his story. They were enthralled by him. And so was I.

There was something about Josh Brighton that was attractive on all levels.

In life, if you were lucky, you met people who were like polished gems—rare, stunning, and coveted. In other words, people like Josh Brighton.

***

AFTER THE CEREMONY, JULIA MEDINA INVITED THE SE-niors and everyone who'd volunteered for the drive back to her house, the recreational compound we'd all enjoyed at some point over the years. The last time I'd been there, it had been with Josh.

Julia hugged me too hard when I'd arrived. "Elle! I can't believe the news about Josh. I'm furious at him for not telling us."

"I was, too."

We chatted about Melanie, who was at the party somewhere with the volleyball team and Harris and about the fact we graduated. There was something surreal about going to the same place and seeing the same people for your whole life and then suddenly, you were free to go and do whatever you wanted.

Julia's sand volleyball court transformed into a dance floor. People filled the pool, the pool deck, the hot tub, and the pavilion. Kate had some history with Julia's brother, Jake, so they'd snuck off somewhere together. I ended up sitting around the fire pit listening to graduating seniors reminiscing on the good times.

All I could think about was the hope that Josh would have more good times.

Someone sat on the tree-log-turned-bench next to me. I didn't even have to look to know it was Drew. The guys around the fire greeted him, shaking hands of giving nods. After everyone settled back into their conversations, Drew and I watched the fire together in silence. The day had been long and full and dedicated to one thing, one person. In some ways, it hadn't even felt like graduation.

"Drew?"

"Uh huh?"

"What's up?"

He sighed. "I promised myself I wouldn't bring this up again."

Josh. I got it. Especially considering I'd told thousands of people only a few hours earlier exactly why Josh was so special. "Was it my speech?"

He stiffened. "It was passionate."

Drew had been by my side all day long, working to save Josh's life, fearing I might prefer Josh over him. How could he compete with a guy like Josh? A guy who was sick to boot? A guy that had stolen my heart completely only a year earlier.

I leaned closer to him.

"When I was in Philly," I said slowly, "Josh told me he loves me, that he wants to get back together."

He rested his elbows on his knees and lowered his head. "Doesn't surprise me."

"Drew, Josh means a lot to me. We were close. I'll always care about him, and I certainly want him to get better."

"You don't think I want that?" The light from the flames of the fire pit accentuated the creases of pain on his face.

"Of course you do. Look, you've been friends with Josh forever, right?"

"Yeah."

"I think you're as amazed by him as I am," I said. "And you don't want to be with him, do you?"

He surrendered with a crooked grin. "You've made your point." When he avoided eye contact and looked only at the fire, my heart twisted in my chest. "Here's the thing, Elle. I'm not the kind of guy to swoop in on another guy's girl. At least I don't want to be."

"I'm not an object. I don't belong to anyone," I said.

"I didn't mean it like that. When I first approached you, I thought it was over between you and Josh—or maybe I told myself that, so I didn't have to face how selfish I was being."

"If you were being selfish," I said, "so was I."

"You didn't know he was sick. I did. And I still…" He shook his head. "The point is it's not over for you two. Not by a long shot. He broke up with you for all the wrong reasons, and I'm afraid you're … I'm afraid that we're whatever we are—for the same wrong reasons."

A memory of Drew and me in the rain sparked feelings that felt anything but wrong. On the archery range that day, it was like I'd been shot through the heart with one of my own arrows—or some other stupid cupid analogy. Seeing Josh again triggered a lot in me, but none of it had felt current. Not like my feelings for Drew.

But here Drew was, in front of me, making a choice for me, like Josh had.

"The guilt is destroying me, Elle. Josh is my friend. He's sick. He doesn't deserve to be part of some high school love triangle because he had a bad report from his oncologist. Let's face it, if he wasn't sick, you and I would have never happened."

"But we did happen," I protested. "Drew, don't do what he did. Don't make the decision for me."

He looked at me in that fierce way of his. There was nothing I could say to persuade him. I'd seen him dole out enough discipline and make enough executive decisions at camp. The tightness in his jaw was his tell. "I'm not making this decision for you, Elle. I'm making it for me." He leaned forward to kiss my cheek. "I'm sorry."

And then he was gone.

CHAPTER 32

BACK IN THE ARCHERY SHED AT CAMP, KATE DROPPED her head in her hands. "You got dumped again?"

"Your compassion is overwhelming," I muttered.

Lake didn't do any better. "You might want to see someone about this. My mom knows this great psychic. She could help cleanse your aura or something."

I sorted and stacked arrows for the three of us. Izzy would have been with us, too, but she was going through private training with Robert to improve her assistant counselor skills. Her father had finally called back and given permission for her to stay the summer. None of us knew what came for her after that, but we'd bought her time, and that had to be enough for now.

After the visit with Josh, the excitement of graduation, and the low of being dumped—yet again, all I wanted to do was shoot something. I figured a stuffed plastic target was better than, say, a fickle teenage boy.

"Let me get this straight," Lake said. "Drew has liked you forever. He practically stalks you this summer—in like the most non-creepy way possible—and then when you're finally on the verge of being together, he ends it so you can get back with your ex."

"That's about right," I said.

"Is he up for some martyr award I don't know about?" Lake asked and fumbled with the string of her bow. "How the hell do you do this again?"

Kate groaned. "She showed you like a million times."

But I showed her again, going through the whole process and shooting a bullseye.

"Maybe I should watch." Lake pulled a bottle of nail polish from her pocket and bent to touch up her toes.

"Are you serious right now?" Kate jabbed. "We're here to commiserate with our fallen friend."

I loaded and shot again. "I haven't fallen anywhere." One after the other, I buried the arrows into the center of the target.

"You all right?" Kate asked after I finished shooting all the arrows in my quiver.

My two closest friends at camp were sitting side by side in the grass with fresh nail polish on their fingers and toes, their eyes wide with concern. They were silly and wonderful. And they were here. Josh and Drew had both been a part of me, but they'd chosen to change that. All I could do now was enjoy the people who were in my life. People like Kate and Lake. With them around the next two months, I thought I could manage.

The gentle hum of a golf cart sounded down the path and came into view a few seconds later. Drew was behind the wheel.

"Oh hell," Kate said.

"I told you. I'm fine," I lied.

Drew circled around and parked next to us. He waved to Lake and Kate and headed toward me. I did my best to stand tall but appear nonchalant at the same time.

"Elle."

"What's up?"

He handed me two grocery-sized bags filled with packages of balloons. "Robert asked me to deliver these to you."

For my new archery activity. I peeked inside to find markers, too. "Perfect. Thanks."

We stood in silence, but I couldn't look at him directly. I pretended to study the contents of the bags as if it mattered how many balloons were inside.

"Anything else?" I asked.

"Have you, um, talked to Josh?"

"Seriously, Drew?"

"What?"

"You can't ask me that. You can ask me anything you want about my job or campers or archery, but you can't ask me about Josh. Not after you broke up with me."

"You said you weren't my girlfriend. Technically I couldn't have broken up with you."

I pressed my fingers against my temples. "Is there anything else you need?"

When he didn't answer, I allowed myself to look him in the eye and instantly regretted it. He might have ended things, but his eyes revealed every one of his emotions without any confusion.

"That's all," he said, barely above a whisper.

I managed a nod before he climbed back into the golf cart and drove away.

***

WITH THE CAMPERS FOR THE THIRD TWO-WEEK SES-
sion arriving the next day, Lake, Kate, Izzy, and I went for a swim. It was fine. So were the campfire and songs and s'mores that followed it. And the sleepover when we laughed and read magazines and teased each other. All fine. No mention of Drew or Josh or boys at all, really, which must have been the result of a Herculean effort by Kate. And it really was fine, fun even, but in a way, I felt numb to it all.

Being at camp meant two things—trying to avoid Drew while pretending I wasn't avoiding Drew and waiting for news about Josh's stem cell transplant. If I'd learned anything at Camp Good Grief, I had to find a way to build a life in my new normal. The next morning at breakfast, Drew was at the coffee station, filling his travel mug, which basically meant he was going to be away from the office for the morning. He might be overseeing registration. Or have plans to take one of the golf carts and check on all of the fields and equipment.

Suddenly I got an idea. "I'll be right back."

Kate grabbed my arm, stopping me before I could even push my chair back and stand.

"No," Lake said emphatically. "You do your thing. Let him do his."

"I have to be around Drew for the rest of the summer. It's time to find a way to make that work."

Lake sighed. "She has a point."

"Kate, let me go."

She recoiled. "Fine. But if he makes a move to take his shirt off for any reason, look away. You'll become a puddle of drool."

Good advice.

By the time I threw the remnants of my French toast and eggs in the trash and filed my silverware in the appropriate buckets, Drew had packed an apple and banana into his backpack.

"Hey," I said.

"Oh. Hey."

He was doing that weird nodding thing and looking anywhere but my face. I knew it from my own toolbox of avoidance strategies.

"Are you going on an equipment check, by any chance?"

His shoulders relaxed a bit. "Yeah. Robert thinks a few campers got into mischief in the last session. He found a punctured basketball floating in the lake and thinks there might be more stuff on the bottom."

"Are you going skinny diving to retrieve it?"

"Um…you mean scuba diving?" His face was red—like really red.

"Scuba diving," I repeated. "That's what I said." Right? He was shaking his head. I replayed the line in my mind to check. Are you going skinny… "Oh my gosh. I'm an idiot. I didn't mean…"

I considered crawling into the cupboard next to me and hiding until the humiliation passed. Instead, I sighed a deep, okay-here-goes-nothing sigh. "Obviously that was a Freudian slip or whatever," I confessed with my eyes closed. "Let's get it in the open. I'm attracted to you. We tried something. It didn't work. But now, we have to find a way to coexist in this very small space for the rest of the summer." When I opened my eyes, Drew was nodding.

"Ditto everything you said."

Finally, we agreed on something. Would have been great if we could have agreed on something else, say, being together. Nevertheless…

"Want some company?"

Drew pointed to the cooler. "Grab a bottle of water. I could use some help inventorying all this equipment."

***

TURNED OUT THE EQUIPMENT WAS MOSTLY SAFE AND sound but stored in the wrong place. Drew resolved to lecture the counselors on where things went. I resolved to get through the summer without drooling over Drew. To be successful in my resolution, I threw myself into work. The archery instructors revised the curriculum to include balloons. The campers loved the idea of lining up all of their frustrations and annihilating them one-by-one. We saw a huge increase in archery interest and an impact on how well the campers shot. For the artsy campers, we even added paint. Eventually the grass surrounding the targets, and some of the targets themselves, resemble an abstract painter's dream.

It was a blast, but it also got me thinking about paintball and the last time I'd played it with Josh and his siblings. Alexis and I kept in touch. The hospital was working its way through the samples, but they hadn't found a match for Josh yet. Someone I didn't know matched a transplant candidate from West Virginia and had agreed to go through with the donation.

One life saved.

After the campers packed up and headed to dinner one day, I stayed to shoot, relying on the rhythm of it to diminish at least some of my stress. The doctors said it could take days to weeks to work through all of the samples and learn whether we'd found Josh a match. Lake, Robert, and some of the other counselors and staff from camp had gone to a local hospital to be tested, too, so they had those samples to work through. I'd kept my phone with me and on at all times ever since getting back to camp, although the reception wasn't always the best. I didn't want to miss a call that said I was a match.

"Elle?"

I jumped at the sound of Drew's voice.

"Sorry," he said. "I've been here a few minutes waiting until you finished, but it didn't seem like you were going to see me."

"I was a million miles away, I guess." I sensed heaviness in his demeanor. "What's wrong?"

He handed me a folded piece of paper. "Message for you."

My heart stopped, and I sat on a hay bale. Drew sat with me.

"Do you know what it says?" I asked.

"I do," he said quietly.

I closed my eyes. "I can't look."

He pressed the message into my hands and didn't let go. I held my breath and unfolded the paper.

"Philadelphia hospital called. Ms. Corwin is not a match for the patient."

The word "not" had been underlined.

I slumped against Drew.

"I'm sorry, Elle."

"It's okay. It won't be me, but it will be someone. It has to be." I rested my head on his shoulder, wetting his shirt with my tears.

"Elle?"

"Yeah?"

"We should head back. They're calling for rain."

I laughed and sobbed at the same time. "Of course they are. What else could happen when you and I are at the range by ourselves?"

Drew brushed my tears away. I tilted my head back to look at him. His gaze softened while his eyes held a fire that told me he was remembering the last time we were at the range and rain had come. The paper crinkled in my hand, breaking the spell of me and Drew.

I pushed myself up. "Thanks for bringing it to me. They're making progress. For every person they eliminate, it's on to the next sample to find a match."

Drew hugged me. "We'll find someone."

"Maybe we should schedule another drive. In case."

"Sure. Anything I can do to help."

"Thanks."

"Your next competition is this week, right?"

"Yes. If I shoot well, I might get that sponsor." I shook my head. "It all seems silly now—how focused I was on that when Josh was just trying to survive."

"That feeling is completely normal, but like we tell the campers, you have to keep living and loving your passions. It's what makes you who you are."

"Thanks."

Thunder growled again. We rode side-by-side in the golf cart back to the cabins. I was safe and dry with my campers in Cabin 12 before the rain came.

CHAPTER 33

DAYS PASSED WITH NO OTHER NEWS OF A MATCH.
With only two days left in the third session, Lake, Kate, and I rounded
up our campers—they had stuck with the original cabin names of the
Lionesses and Rock Stars—for dinner.

"We're definitely missing one," Kate said.

Lake flicked her pointer finger up and down, counting all of the
campers from ours and Kate's cabins. "Yep."

"All of mine are here," Kate said.

Process of elimination dictated it wasn't good news for Lake and
me.

"Shalene isn't here," the Lionesses announced at the same time
I realized the quiet artist in my group was missing. She'd been late
for meals before. I'd bet she was still in the art room swirling paints
across a canvas or sketching the view from the window.

"Do you want to head to dinner, and I'll find Shalene?"

Kate and Lake nodded.

The paths were quiet. Only a few campers lingered playing Fris-
bee or eating picnic dinners on the grassy areas around the lake.
The building that housed the art gallery and studios was similarly
abandoned. Save for one person.

"Shalene?"

With ear buds in, she didn't respond. The brush in her left hand swiped and smoothed blue paint across the black canvas on an easel in front of her. A body of water formed in the foreground with already well-defined trees in the background. Although the landscape was similar, the painting represented a lake other than the one here at camp. A clock across the room chimed, announcing only thirty minutes left for dinner.

I tapped Shalene on the shoulder, and she startled.

"Oh, Elle." She removed the ear buds. "I didn't see you there." Slowly, she looked around the room, her gaze falling on one unmanned easel after another. "Where is everyone?"

I stifled a laugh. "Dinner."

She looked at the clock. "Oh gosh. I'm sorry. I'm late again. I just…I was…" She tossed her apron over a hook on the easel and packed up her supplies.

"You're quite the artist," I said. I studied her painting. "Can you tell me about it?"

Her smile was wide. "We have a summer house near Lake Pymatuning. Before my grandpa got sick, we spent every moment we could there."

"Want to tell me about him?"

Shalene wiped a stack of brushes clean and dropped them into an empty cup. "He didn't even know who I was by the time he died. I know it's stupid, but sometimes I felt like if I painted, the pictures would get through the diseased parts of his brain and somehow click, making him remember. One time, I really think it worked. I did a charcoal of the porch swing at the summer house. And he knew it right away! It was like I had him back, you know?"

"There's nothing wrong with wanting to remember special moments or to try and salvage something that people think might be lost."

"Yeah," she whispered.

We both stared at her painting for a minute, and I wondered if she was thinking about lost time like I was. Lost time with Josh. Then with Drew. With Lily, who is suddenly grown up and aware and not the annoying kid I remember. With Melanie, who thankfully would be an assistant counselor in the next session.

"Elle?" Shalene said. "Can I come here and paint some more after dinner?"

I put my arm around her shoulders as we turned for the door. "Sure thing."

***

THE NEXT DAY, I CONVINCED SHALENE TO ABANDON THE art studio and join me at the range. I promised her it would be an artistic experience. We had more campers than ever lined up and ready to shoot.

"Where did all these kids come from?" I asked Neil.

"Word got out about how fun it is."

Okay. That was good. And terrifying.

"Can you help me wrangle them while Lake and Kate fill more balloons?"

"Sure thing."

Together, we put the kids in groups of four. Each group had one bow and five arrows.

"Everyone will get to shoot five times," I called out to them. "If you're not shooting, sit on the hay bales."

Eager to shoot some paint-filled water balloons, the campers listened with no trouble.

"That went better than I thought," Neil said.

"Give it time."

The first shooters lined up. I demonstrated the positioning for them and delivered an arrow into the bullseye. They followed. Only one of them hit a balloon.

"Yes!" he shouted.

"Okay. Second shot. Ready."

And on we went until paint stained the grass, and most of the balloons had been popped.

"I'm going to check on Lake and Kate with the other balloons," I told Neil. I hustled around the other side of the shed to find both of my friends covered in multiple colors of paint.

"What are you doing?"

Kate pointed to Lake. "She started it."

"You are not wasting the balloons on each other. There are twenty kids out there waiting to shoot them."

"She sounds kind of judgy," Lake said.

Kate scowled at me. "We might need to loosen her up."

I held my hands up. "No."

They nodded and grinned, each reaching for a paint-filled balloon. "No!"

I ran toward the range, but not fast enough. A balloon thumped against my back; red paint splattering everywhere.

"I can't believe you did that!"

Lake and Kate kept coming. They hit my thigh with a blue balloon. The kids screamed and descended, each grabbing balloons until it was an all-out battle.

"No faces," I shouted, not sure anyone could even hear me.

Red, blue, green, and yellow paint soared in all directions.

"That's it," I said, swiping four balloons for myself. Kate caught my eye and ran in the opposite direction. I hunted her down and landed a green balloon on her previously clean back. Lake was next. I turned her shoulder red. Neil stood on the edge of the range, his arms crossed, and his clothes completely clean.

"Hey, prom date?"

He widened his eyes. "Elle, you wouldn't."

I launched both at him, landing a red and yellow mix down his front.

"That's it!" He picked me up and carried me to the grass near the targets where he tickled me until I rolled uncontrollably through the mix of colors on the ground.

A whistle sounded through the field.

At once, the campers silenced. At the edge of the range, Drew and Robert stood next to the golf cart. Robert had the whistle in his mouth and an astonished expression on his face. Drew very openly tried to hide his laughter.

"Since you've clearly had your fun," Robert said in a measured tone, "head back to the cabins. Use the hoses to rinse before you go inside."

Knowing how terrible I must look with grass in my hair and being a tie-dyed human, I approached Robert. "Things got out of hand."

"It was my fault," Kate said.

"Nevertheless," Robert said, "we'll be shutting down archery for the next session."

Oh no. "Please, Robert, I can clean this up, and then everything will be fine."

He put his hands up to stop me. "Elle, it's not because of that. We need you with your campers the whole day. Lake won't be with us."

Lake and Drew whispered a few feet away. Her eyes went wide.

"What's wrong?"

Lake hugged me.

"Is everything okay with your parents?" I asked. "What is it?"

"I'm a match, Elle," Lake whispered. "I'm Josh's match."

CHAPTER 34

FOR A MOMENT, I COULDN'T BREATHE. JOSH'S MATCH?
Josh. Had a match. Then I was the balloon, deflating until there wasn't
an ounce of pressure left. I clung to Lake, a girl I'd only known for
a month and who was about to save Josh's life.

"Are you sure?" I whispered, my tears wetting her hair.

"They'll have to run more tests to confirm everything, but it looks
good."

It looked good.

Oh, thank you, world.

"How did you hear?" I asked when we broke apart.

"Josh's doctor called to see if Lake could come in for confirma-
tion," Drew said.

"Do you know what that means?"

"They'll want to confirm everything for safety, but they wouldn't
call her in if they didn't think she would be a match," Robert offered
in his soft voice.

"Why are we still standing here?" Neil asked, and we all laughed
and hugged—even Robert, who came away from the hug also looking
like a tie-dyed human.

***

I WALKED LAKE TO THE MAIN LODGE, HELPING HER
carry her bags. Drew took them from me and loaded them into her car.

"Thanks," I said.

"You're welcome," he answered.

Lake raised an eyebrow at me and pulled me aside. "Please work it out already."

"I don't know that that's going to happen any time soon."

"I've told him a million times he's being an idiot."

"You said that to him?"

She raised her arms in a gesture that meant, don't I always say what I think.

I laughed a little. "Thanks for doing this."

She shushed me with a flick of her hand.

"I mean it," I said, hugging her. "Josh is a special person. It's only fitting another special person is the one to save him."

"It's not me. It's the near perfect matching human leukocyte antigens—according to an explanation of stem cell transplants on the internet."

I squeezed her tighter. "It's going to be okay."

"I hope so," she said.

So did I.

***

ON THE WAY TO DINNER, I COUNTED THE GIRLS, AND
sure enough Shalene was missing again. Kate agreed to keep an eye on the Lionesses. I packed two meals and a couple bottles of water and slipped out of the cafeteria. Shalene was alone in the art room, her ear buds a bit more speckled than the last time I'd found her there. She was working on a new painting. Something abstract. Something very red. Her arm swung elegantly, with such a rhythm that I refused to disturb her. I knew that zone. I felt it when I shot and everything else in the world melted away.

I found my way to an empty easel and stared at the blank canvas. How in the world did she do this? I knew what I wanted the canvas to look like, but I had no idea how to create that image with the globs of color and various brush sizes in front of me. Logic told me to start with the background. Black. Purple. Dark blue. I squirted the paint from the plastic bottles and swiped the colors across the canvas. A little more blue. More purple. When the brush didn't do the trick, I used my fingers and swirled, swirled, swirled the colors until they looked perfect.

I stood back and studied the results.

"Not bad," Shalene said from the table by the door. She bit a French fry. "I didn't know you could paint."

"I can't." I washed as much of the color from my hands as possible. "This is my first attempt."

"Then definitely not bad. But I can give you some pointers if you want."

I looked back at the random swirls of darkness I spent the last hour creating. "I hardly think I'm in the position to refuse."

Shalene and I painted for another hour before rejoining the rest of the cabin around the campfire. The girls sang songs and told ghost stories. Although there was a shortage of counselors, the one great thing about Camp Good Grief was that the counselor-to-camper ratio was already small enough that when one of us had to deal with a situation or work independently with a struggling camper, there were usually other counselors who could pick up the slack. And grouping the cabins together, like Lake, Kate, and I had tended to do, created more opportunities for the campers to connect with each other.

"Well, well, well. Welcome back," Kate said when I squished a melting s'more between two graham crackers and fell onto the bench next to her. "Someone has been nonchalantly looking for you all evening."

She perked her left eyebrow, and when I looked in that direction, I saw Drew laughing with a group of male campers and counselors. Neil waved when he saw me, and I did the same.

"If he's been nonchalant about it, how do you know?" I asked.

She scoffed. "Have you met me, Elle?"

Good point. When it came to guys, the girl had a gift. I couldn't deny the flutter I felt hoping in this case her powers hadn't failed her, but even with that flutter, as I sat around the campfire with my Lionesses and my friends, laughing and telling stories, part of me kept thinking that someday Josh would experience the joy of doing this.

***

I SAID GOODBYE TO SHALENE AND THE OTHER LIONESS-es after an epic field games competition and uneventful dance that Drew didn't show up to. Probably for the best. We had one day off between sessions. The same day Lake was supposed to see a doctor and confirm she was a match for Josh. I grabbed a quick breakfast with Izzy and Kate before heading to the archery range to clean and pack up since we wouldn't have enough people to cover the activity the next session.

My bow called to me the second I unlocked the shed doors. I set up the targets and shot as the sun climbed higher in the sky wondering about the human leuk-whatever Lake had mentioned. Matches were difficult to find. I'd known that when we'd held the drive at graduation, but I'd refused to consider Josh wouldn't find one.

I checked my phone. Still no word from Lake. How long until they knew for certain she was a match? When would they schedule the transplant? Did Josh have that much time? The wait was killing me.

I unloaded my quiver, shooting nines and tens consistently with the occasional eight or seven thrown in. With each exhale, I released the bow, some of my tension and fear fading away. When I retrieved the arrows after what was probably my twentieth round of shooting, I turned to see a single figure standing at the hay bales. I'd know the posture anywhere. He held a bow in his hands.

"Thought I'd shoot a little since we're closing down shop," he called. "If that's okay."

"Sure," I said, traipsing back across the field toward him.

"I didn't know you'd be here."

"It's okay, Drew. We work together. We're good."

"I know, but…"

But—memories. Memories of us here in the rain. Of me teaching him to shoot. Despite the fresh aching in my chest, the memory seemed like it was from a different lifetime.

"I'll take a break, so you can shoot from closer," I said.

"Thanks a lot."

"I didn't mean it like that."

He laughed. "It's the truth. I'm lucky to hit the target at ten yards."

I pointed to the shed. "I have a lot of cleaning up to do."

I refused to look back at him. Inside the shed, I took a deep breath and listened to the thumping of his arrows connecting to the target. I indulged in a few minutes of watching him. He'd gotten better.

Good for him.

***

MELANIE ARRIVED LATER THAT DAY. I HUGGED HER UN-til she made me let go.

"Are you okay here? My gosh."

I took her hand and led her toward the lake, where we'd start our tour. "I love it here, but it's been a summer."

"I know. I'm sorry."

We caught up on her life—her volleyball league, the upcoming camps she'd attend, things with her and Harris, Lily's latest science experiments, the fact my parents were spending the week on a romantic adventure.

"That never happens," I said.

"I know! Dad's been working less since he heard about Josh." She shrugged. "Maybe something good to come out of this."

"Lake hasn't called with an update yet," I said. "Waiting is one of the hardest things on the planet."

"Tell me about it," she said, grinning at the lake. "I've been waiting for this for weeks."

I squeezed her. "Was Harris disappointed?"

"Very much, but you know, he has a big plan to blow stuff up in his backyard to fill the gap, and then he's off to science camp."

I shook my head. "Who would have thought little Harris next door would have grown up to be such a cutie?"

Melanie blushed. "Things are good with him—like so good—it doesn't feel real."

"Enjoy it. You two are great together, and I hope it never changes."

I showed Mel the volleyball courts next and introduced her to some of the other counselors in the main lodge. We walked the loop to the archery range but didn't shoot. By the time we made it back, a crowd had formed around the campfire. The food table had been set up. The sides of fruit and chips had been pulled from the cafeteria. Corn hole games, laughter, and camp stories filled the air.

Melanie smiled. "I can see why you like it here. It's chill."

"Wait until the campers arrive tomorrow."

"Melanie!" Drew greeted my sister with a huge smile and a hug, but our greetings were slightly demurer.

"Hey," I said.

"Hey," he answered.

Melanie raised her eyebrows. "Is it time to eat? I'm starved."

"Food's all there. Cook up whatever you want on the fire."

"Thanks," she said. "Join us."

Drew glanced at me and then back at my sister. "Uh."

"Sure," I said. "Join us."

"Okay."

Okay. Yay!

The older I got, the more sarcasm became my life.

I hung back while Drew and Melanie chatted with ease. Izzy and Kate caught up with us, and I leaned more into their conversation than my sister's.

Eventually, Izzy nudged me. "Is she hitting on your guy?"

"No, it's not like that. She has a boyfriend she adores. I have a feeling she's trying to build a bridge."

"Better be a long bridge," Kate quipped.

Thanks, best friend.

CHAPTER 35

MELANIE WORKED TO PULL ME INTO THE CONVERSA-
tion around the campfire as much as she could. Her favorite move
was, "Elle, tell Drew the story about (fill in the blank)."

I complied. Drew laughed. And my sister tried again.

She'd kept her ace for last. Without a cloud in the sky, the stars
brightened like spinning fractals of light.

"Elle?" Mel turned to me. "Can you and Drew help me with
something?"

Drew stood without a second thought. "Lead the way."

Melanie headed for the parking lot, and hit the button that lifted
the trunk. She unfolded a blanket to reveal the homemade tubes.

"You brought Harris' homemade telescope?" I asked in disbelief.

"Yep." She handed some of the parts to Drew and others to me.

"I can't believe he let you borrow this."

"Please," she said. "The boy loves me. He's got my back in all
things."

"As it should be," Drew said, and I refused to wonder if he thought
I hadn't had his back when we'd tried to be whatever we tried to be.

Instead, I focused on helping Melanie assemble the telescope,
surprised by how much I wanted to experience that rush of zooming
in on the stars, the moon, and if we had the chance, even Saturn,

with its clever little rings. The telescope enthralled the counselors and staff. Melanie pointed out the different stars, and I had nearly everyone download the star gazing app by the time people started fading and heading back to their cabins.

That was the point that my sister reached her arms in the air, stretched and insisted the first day of camp had tired her out. We, of course, should stay and enjoy the telescope while she headed back to the cabin.

Drew raised an eyebrow at me as my sister walked away, and I had no doubt he'd seen through her efforts as easily as I had.

"She's crafty," I joked.

"She is. My personal favorite was all the times she asked you to tell me a story."

"You picked up on that, too?"

"She asked you to tell me eleven stories in one hour."

I laughed. "I didn't realize it was that many."

He took a turn, looking through the lens. After a few seconds, he stood to adjust the knobs and reposition the view. "I'm flattered. The fact she wants us to…"

"She wants what's best for me," I said.

Drew stopped adjusting and stared at me. I refused to look away, making him sit with the reality of what I was saying. That we were good for each other. That we hadn't been whatever we'd been for the wrong reasons. The longer his gaze held mine, the harder my chest thumped. I thought he might kiss me, but he held his ground. For too long.

"Is it my turn?" I said finally.

He nodded.

I stepped closer to him, brushing against his shoulder, but he didn't move away. With my face against the eyepiece, I turned the knobs to search the night sky. Finally, I found Saturn and its rings. It had been mine and Melanie's favorite for years.

"Check it out," I said and moved so Drew could see it.

"Is that Saturn?"

"Yes! This summer, it's not up until late, which means it's pretty much bedtime."

He stepped back from the telescope. "Thanks for showing it to me.

We should get a telescope for the camp. Everyone loved it."

"You should. I'm sure Harris could recommend something or even build it himself."

I bent forward to the eyepiece for one last look at Saturn, spinning away up there in its perfect orbit. When the planet moved out of the view three times, I decided to call it a night.

"Can I help you pack up?" Drew asked.

"I'm good."

He laughed and picked up a few pieces I'd disassembled. "I'm not letting you carry all of this."

"Okay. Thanks."

We walked to my family's car in silence, a silence that angered me more than anything Drew had done before, which said a lot.

"Drew?"

"Yeah?"

"Do you ever think we can get back to being us? Laughing together, talking, having fun?"

"We had fun tonight."

"I know, but my sister had to pry it out of us."

"It's hard for me, Elle. It's not that I don't want to. Sometimes, it's natural, and other times, it's...not."

Like times we were alone together, in the dark, gazing at the stars, trying to avoid the raging romance tingling our insides. Maybe that was the key—avoiding romantic situations. I'd treat Drew like one of the girls or one of the guys. Like Neil. Neil and I got along great.

I organized the pieces of Harris' telescope into the makeshift travel case he'd designed to keep the delicate pieces safe.

"Okay. It was fun." Like I would with Neil, I hugged Drew and patted his back with a thump before releasing him, but he didn't let me go.

"What are you doing?" His fingertips teased the skin above my shorts, sending chills down my arms.

"Thought process—Neil and I are buds. We get along fine, and I hug him goodbye like that. I thought if I hugged you goodbye like that, we'd be good."

"Does it ever feel like this when you hug Neil?"

I shook my head, and he leaned his forehead against mine.

"There are a lot of thoughts going through my mind right now, and none of them are friendly," Drew whispered.

Mine either.

But Drew took a deep breath and stepped backward, dropping his hands from where they'd been around my waist and shoved them into his own pockets. "I guess we still have some work to do."

I wasn't sure "some" quite covered it.

***

I INFORMED MELANIE, WHO HAD BEEN WAITING UP very untired-like that her plan hadn't worked, but she shrugged. "I'll be here two weeks. I'll manage a reconciliation by then."

If anyone could do it, it was my little sister that had carved herself a starting position on a team thick with seniors. She knew how to crush a goal.

With the hope of a new group of campers and two weeks with my sister, I slept through the night and woke up ready for the day.

Drew had said during the first session that the first day was a tearful one, but I cried more than I had any other first day when I checked my phone in the morning and saw a text from Lake. *Match is confirmed. I'm taking a medication to boost stem cell production in my body. Then harvest time! Josh should have the stem cells within a week.*

A week. Josh could be on his way to health in one week.

CHAPTER 36

LAKE WAS BACK AT CAMP LESS THAN A WEEK LATER.
She and Melanie buddied up immediately. The three of us, Kate, and
Izzy had become quite the crew. I couldn't believe we were down to
only three more weeks of camp together. We made the best of it with
evening challenges and games with our cabins, campfire song-writing
competitions that made us laugh until we cried, and anything else we
could fathom. Neil and Kate cheered me on at the next shoot, which
passed in a blur of me wanting to honor the goal I'd set for myself that
summer while also wondering how anything could be more important
than Josh getting better.

After I earned the third place position on the podium with a tiebreaker shoot-off, Bill from Captain Archery said the sponsorship
was mine if I wanted it. The prize money boosted my bank account.
Melanie loved camp so much, she offered to stay through one more
session, which Robert accepted immediately.

The summer was working out exactly how I'd hoped, or how I'd
hoped before I'd met Drew and learned about Josh's illness. Like my
grandmother always said, "Circumstances altered cases."

Circumstances kept Drew from being at my shoot and from me
telling him all about it when I got back to camp, like I'd wanted. He
stuck around the main lodge more and more, and neither of us spoke

about the moment we'd had at the telescope. Or at the car.

All the while, a number ticked down in the back of my mind. Twenty-two.

It would take twenty-two days to hear if the transplant had worked for Josh. My campers in the fourth session had made a calendar for me in art class. Each day, we'd crossed off a box.

When there was one day left, Izzy, Lake, Kate, and Melanie planned a day of adventure to distract me. I saw through it immediately.

"The earliest they're going to call is tomorrow," Melanie finally said.

"You don't know that."

"We do, Elle," Lake insisted. "Let's have fun with the girls and leave the phone behind."

I handed her the device and did my best to invest myself in the pool games and the poolside sunning. At dinner, I bumped into Drew, old-school style, knocking papers out of his hands.

"It's like a rule," I said. "If you're carrying a pile of papers, I have to take them out."

He smiled. "Good to see you."

Hoping he meant it, I said, "Thanks. You, too."

"Are you freaking out?"

"Entirely," I said. "Have your parents heard anything?"

"They won't until tomorrow. I think the Brightons are tweaking, too."

"How could they not? I keep playing in my mind how we got here. When I visited Josh, I had to yell at him to do the drive. It was infuriating."

"You yelled at him? A sick man in a hospital bed?"

"Shut up. I'm serious. He deserved it. Letting his pride get in the way of something that was good for him."

As if we both heard the words and the fact they could apply to someone else, the friendliness in our conversation immediately turned awkward.

"And we were doing so well," Drew joked.

"I didn't mean it like that."

"I know."

I collected an armful of chocolate milks for my campers and nodded to Drew. "Maybe we'll do better next time."

He saluted me. "Next time."

I didn't believe we'd be anything other than awkward around each other, but with Josh's big news on the horizon, everything else seemed small.

The next day, I got Robert's permission to shoot. With bottles of water and sunscreen, I headed for the archery range. I propped my cell phone on one of the hay bales and even built it some shade with the leaves of a mini tree branch. I checked the bars—three—and made sure the sun wasn't breaking through the leaf cover to overheat it. Ringer on. No messages missed.

Ten a.m. Word could come any time.

I shot. Forty yards. Fifty yards. Sixty yards. Compound bow. Recurve bow. Then back to compound. Checked my phone to make sure it was working. Yep.

What if the transplant hadn't worked? All that hope. All that time and waiting. The cancer could come back stronger.

Please, no.

Josh was already missing fall semester for sure. As a transplant recipient, he'd be in isolation for one hundred days. Today was day twenty-two. That meant he couldn't be out and around people until mid-October. Minimally. With a mask.

If the transplant worked. And if it hadn't, then—no. I wouldn't think about that.

I checked my phone again. Nothing.

Spent on shooting, I packed everything into the shed and headed back to camp. I watched the Lionesses and Rock Stars swim from a distance, not able to engage mentally or emotionally. I thought about calling Alexis, but the Brightons were probably getting calls from so many people today. I had to be patient.

Melanie sat on the bench next to me. "You okay?"

"I've mentally repeated the mantra that patience is a virtue about twenty-seven-thousand times today."

"I'm sorry, Elle. Do you want to talk about him?"

"I don't know."

"We could tell stories, laugh." She shrugged. "Just kind of honor him."

"Is that like weird, like something you do when someone's dead?"

"Don't people always say talk about someone while they're alive?"

Despite everything, I laughed. "I don't think that's what they say."

She took my hand. "Well, that's what we're doing today."

She dragged me to the campfire and set up a few tables together. The rest of our Lioness/Rock Star crew rounded up food, drinks, utensils, napkins and surrounded me. Kate told great stories about Josh since they'd been friends forever. Neil caught on to what we were doing and joined in, adding the guy angle we didn't know from football and other boy things. At some point, Drew found his way to the celebration, smiling at me from the other side of the campfire.

Neil had everyone laughing at a locker room bathroom break gone wrong when my phone rang. The group fell into silence.

The caller ID read Mr. Brighton.

"Oh my gosh."

"Answer it," Mel said.

I lifted the phone to my ear. "Hello?"

"Hey, beautiful."

I fell to a squat at the sound of Josh's voice. I was crying before he said anything else.

"Elle, oh my gosh. Don't cry."

"I'm sorry. Hearing your voice…"

"Clearly we need to talk more," he joked.

"Will we be able to talk more?" I said, asking something else entirely.

"I'd talk to you every day of my life if I could."

"Stop torturing me, Josh. Did it work?"

He laughed. "It worked, Elle."

Sobs consumed me. Melanie took the phone and got the news for herself, since I was no good at even speaking. She shouted the update to everyone, and the entire camp erupted in applause. Neil pulled me upright, and we held onto each other as tightly as we would have held Josh if he were with us.

At some point, my phone was to my ear again. I walked away from the group until I could hear.

"Sounds like you're having a party," Josh yelled.

"For you. Everyone here was waiting for the news, Josh. Everyone."

His voice caught. "People have been so good to me. I can't even understand it."

Lake wrapped her arm around my shoulders.

"Oh my gosh," I said, switching to speaker phone. "Lake is here."

"My lifesaver," Josh said.

Lake had tears pouring down her face, too. "I'm glad it worked. Congratulations, Josh."

"I can't wait to meet you," he said. "I'm going to give you the biggest kiss."

We all laughed. And laughed. There was nothing but laughter and its close friends—grins, smiles, giggles.

Josh was going to live.

Seventy-eight more days, and we could see it for ourselves.

CHAPTER 37

WEEKS LATER, AT THE END OF THE SEASON, I STOOD AT the top of the hill, looking down at the cold ashes of the campfire, remembering the way everyone had crowded around it, telling stories about Josh while we'd waited for news. I thought about the moment we'd gotten the word that his life would be a long, beautiful one.

In the distance, the lake sparkled in the sunshine. The pool sat still except for the occasional breeze disrupting the smoothness of its surface. Cars had dwindled from the parking lot, and the sounds of campers marching to and from activities singing their favorite camp songs played in my memory.

I'd have a little more than a week at home before I packed up for Mon Valley to live with a roommate I didn't know and start a college experience so far from the one I'd planned.

Neil, Lake, Kate, Izzy, and I had had a tearful goodbye after breakfast.

Izzy was on her way to Erie to live with an aunt Robert had found. She'd be safe and happy and start shooting archery competitively. I couldn't wait to see her on the circuit.

I'd thanked Robert for the best experience. He offered me a counselor spot for next summer, but I couldn't accept. Not now. There were too many days between now and then, too many things that could happen to change the trajectory of my life.

There was one last person to see.

Drew was supposed to meet me in a half hour, but Melanie had texted she would arrive in ten minutes to pick me up. I found his cabin with little trouble. The door was ajar, and I gingerly pressed it open to see him doing pushups with his shirt off.

The universe had a sense of humor.

At the sound of the creaking door, he looked up at me, laughed, and collapsed against the floor. "What are you doing here?"

"Don't let me stop you," I teased. And flirted. I was definitely flirting.

"I was going to meet you, remember?"

I took my time looking around the cabin. "I've never been in your cabin before."

"That's true. Girls aren't supposed to be in guys cabins."

"And vice versa?" I challenged.

"Exactly."

"And when has that stopped you?"

He grabbed a towel from a rack in the bathroom and wiped his face and neck while I explored the room, so I could imagine him there when I thought of him in the next week. And even the next summer, if I didn't come back.

The space was pretty bare. On the dresser, there was deodorant, a beach towel, an extra box of peppermint toothpaste, and a framed photo of him with his parents. He must have been like ten years old. He'd been skinny, his head a little too big for his body. Definitely not the Drew standing in front of me.

"I think you need some more decoration." I stepped back onto the front porch and retrieved the wrapped canvas. "This is for you."

He tossed the towel over his shoulder and leaned against the wall. "You didn't have to get me anything, but did I ever mention I love presents?"

"No." I laughed.

"I do." He eagerly but also cautiously tore the paper until the dark swirls and bright stars of the night sky were visible. He propped the canvas on the dresser and studied it. "Is that Andromeda?"

I nodded.

"It's beautiful."

"I'm glad you like it. I added Saturn in the corner. I don't know that the perspective is accurate. I studied a lot of charts, but I figured since it was the first miracle we'd looked at in the telescope, I should honor that."

"Wait, you painted this yourself?"

I nodded. "With Shalene's help."

"Elle, I'm speechless. This is incredible."

"It's not."

"I thought you picked it up at a store in town or something. Seriously."

"Stop."

The quiet, tentative tone of his voice reminded me of the more tender moments between us. "Are you sure you want to give it to me?"

I took a deep breath and tried to remember the speech I'd practiced in the shower every day for the last week. "When I bumped into you in the hallway at school the Monday after prom, I had no idea who you were. I was lost, Drew. I was weeks away from graduating high school and going out into the world when people expect you to have answers. I had nothing but questions. I needed a job for the summer, but I only wanted to shoot. You made that a possibility for me. I'm not saying you saved me or anything, but you gave me the opportunity to save myself."

Like his uncle, he let his tears fall openly, and I did, too.

"This has been the best and most challenging summer of my life. Thank you for bringing me here. Thank you for looking out for me and encouraging me. Thank you for making me feel things that I thought I couldn't feel after Josh broke up with me. You're a remarkable person. How can you not be when you've lived through what you have and you spend your summers here?"

"A simple yes would have covered it," Drew joked.

"No," I countered. "It wouldn't have."

He smiled. "Thank you. For everything you said."

My phone buzzed. "Melanie's here. I have to go."

He swiped at his eyes. "This place isn't going to be the same without you."

Knowing I'd regret it if I didn't, I wiped away his tears and reached up onto my toes until my lips pressed against his. He responded instantly, dropping his towel and picking me up. I wrapped my legs around his waist and put every thought and emotion I couldn't say into our kiss, knowing it could be the last time I saw Drew Peters. A few seconds later, my phone buzzed again, and Drew let my feet settle back to the ground. I hugged him and whispered, "I'll miss you."

"You have no idea," he said.

I waved on my way out the door, replaying the perfect kiss in my head all the way back to the parking lot. As much as I hated to admit it, the kiss didn't only say all the things Drew and I had meant to each other that summer.

It had also said goodbye.

CHAPTER 38

TWO MONTHS LATER

THE MOMENT JOSH BRIGHTON AND I LAID EYES ON
each other, we couldn't be separated. We were backstage at the
Homecoming football game. One hundred-and-four days since his
transplant, the event was his first foray into public life. Only a few
people knew he'd be there. He'd called me a few days earlier and
asked if I would join him to share the good news of his recovery.

Um, yes. A million times, yes.

Of course, a football game at Iron Valley meant Drew would be
there, too.

"I can't believe I'm touching you," Josh laughed. "No computer
screen between us."

I'd washed my hands with soap and water for forty seconds before
seeing him, making sure not to touch a single thing since. That's
why I could squeeze his hand and rest my masked face on his shoulder. We'd chatted almost every day online, but a three-dimensional
Josh—even one wearing a mask—beat a two-dimensional one any
day.

"You feeling okay?"

"Great," he said. "They have a reserved section in the bleachers
for us to watch the second half. I'll be far away from everyone and

their germs. You should join us."

"Definitely."

Principal Welch greeted us and explained the lineup. We'd wait behind the stage until the homecoming court was announced. Then we'd step out and wave to everyone.

"It will all move quickly."

I looped my arm in Josh's and held tight, fearful he would fall or get sick or something that would set back his recovery.

"Thanks for being here," he said. "Without you, my mom would have insisted I come out here with my walker." He pointed to the sideline where he'd left it.

"Josh Brighton cannot walk across this field with a walker," I insisted. "I got you."

He pressed his masked lips against my forehead. "My numbers were amazing this week, so the doctors cleared me for this. I still can't believe it. I might go into culture shock."

He'd meant it as a joke, but I couldn't dismiss my fears so easily. My brain had calculated that his doctors wouldn't have released them if there had been danger, but my emotions threatened a downward spiral at any moment.

Principal Welch moved us into position. From our vantage point, we watched the Homecoming Court approach the field. My heart skipped at the sight of a football jersey at the end. Melanie had told me Drew had been elected to the court along with her besties Ashley and Chandra. As the ten candidates got closer, I recognized that Chandra and Drew were partnered up in the last position. Chandra held his arm like I held Josh's. He leaned close to her and said something that made her laugh.

I wanted to know what it was.

Josh connected the dots when he saw them and asked, "You okay?"

"We're here to celebrate your life. Are you kidding?"

"You know that's not what I meant."

In the past two months, I'd come clean about Drew and everything else. Josh and I had never been closer, but without any question, our closeness was friendship.

"Does he know you're here?" Josh asked.

"You know I haven't spoken to him since I left camp."

"Drew is a solid guy. From experience, I can tell you what it means to screw up something good."

I rolled my eyes.

"Don't do that to me."

I laughed, and the sound must have caught Drew's attention. Not more than twenty yards from us, he missed a step when our eyes locked. He shook his head and squinted. Josh and I waved.

"Good luck, man!" Josh shouted, and Drew nodded.

The announcer briefed the crowd on each candidate, and everyone quieted to hear the results of the vote.

"And your Homecoming King is…Drew Peters!"

Josh screamed. I may have, too. With Drew's crown secured on his head, he turned in our direction. I raised my hands above my head to clap.

"Finally, your Homecoming Queen…Chandra Jackson!"

I screamed for my little sister's bestie.

"It's time," Mr. Welch said as the announcer shifted to talking about a very special former student and Viking football player who had entertained the crowd on this very field.

"That's you," I whispered, teasingly.

Still holding my arm, he kissed my cheek. "I wouldn't be here without you, Elle."

"Don't make me cry. I will kill you if you ruin my makeup."

Josh's family and I stepped out from behind the stage and walked to where the fifty-yard line met the sideline. With the Homecoming Court on the field, I could feel Drew's eyes on me and hear Chandra's cheers, an impressive reality considering the crowd was on its feet, stomping and screaming for Josh. Josh released my arm to wave to everyone in all directions. I clapped along with his family, and Alexis tucked herself into my side, wrapping her arms around my waist.

He deserved every second of this victory and so much more.

***

I WAITED OUTSIDE THE STADIUM LOCKER ROOM AFTER the game, hoping one of the Iron Valley High students standing along the wall in their short shorts and painted faces wasn't waiting for Drew, too.

A handful of his teammates left before him. I held my breath when he appeared in the doorway. At first, he didn't see me. One of the girls along the fence called out to him, "Hey, Drew. Congratulations."

"Thanks, Clara." He hugged her, and my heart shattered. Wishing the concrete wall would open and devour me, I stayed as still as possible and hoped they'd walk away without turning back.

As if he could hear my thoughts, Drew perked up and slowly spun towards me. "Elle?"

"Hey," I said.

An epic smile spread across his face. He dropped his bag and rushed toward me, scooping me into a hug. "Elle," he whispered my name again. "I can't believe you're here."

"Good game," I said when he set me back down.

"Thank you."

"And congratulations on your Homecoming victory. You're really racking up the royalty titles."

He blushed. "It's really good to see you. Hey—I've been shooting, you know."

"Seriously?"

"Yeah. JoAnn is teaching me."

"She taught me!"

"I know. She's proud of you. Talks about you all the time."

"That has to be boring," I joked.

"Not really," Drew said, his eyes sparkling under the lights.

My cheeks warmed at his comment. In my peripheral vision, Clara watched us with her arms crossed. "I don't want to get you in trouble."

"What?" Drew looked to Clara and then back at me. "No. She's my buddy's girlfriend."

"Oh. Sorry. I guess I assumed..." Now I was definitely blushing.

"I'm presently unattached."

I prayed I did not grin like an ecstatic child.

"Since we have a history of making assumptions, mind if clear something up?" he said.

"Sure."

Drew took a deep breath and folded his hands behind him. "I saw you and Josh on the field, and then up in the bleachers, away from everyone, kind of close."

"Two old friends catching up," I said. "We stayed away from everyone to minimize his exposure to germs."

Drew fought a grin, too. "I'm glad he's on the mend.

"Me, too. He might even be able to start college in the spring and play football next fall."

"He deserves it."

"He does."

We started this dance of smiling at each other, looking away, and then smiling again. Until we laughed.

"Do you want to go for a walk?" Drew asked.

"Sure."

"I'll put my stuff in my car." He pointed to the small lot where the football players and coaches parked.

"How's senior year?" I asked while we walked.

"Strange," he said. "A weird limbo of still being here but thinking of the fact that next year, everyone will be somewhere else."

"Sounds about right."

"How's college?"

"So far, so good. Archery competitions will start soon, so I'm increasing my training. Classes are good, not too tough, but a challenge at the same time."

"Choose a major yet?"

I laughed at the banality of our conversation.

"What?" Drew threw his bag in the back of his car and watched me, waiting for an answer. I took a deep breath. With Josh, I'd had everything planned. Our relationship. Our college. Our future. I'd tried to control everything until life shook up our world and set us on different paths. If anything, it had taught me that you can plan as much as you want, but the future wasn't guaranteed. The only guarantee was living in the moment.

"We've talked about everything but what I really want to talk about," I admitted.

"What's that?"

"How much I miss you."

Drew stilled.

"I think back on it sometimes and don't even know what happened between us. My emotions were heightened with Josh being sick. Wanting to help campers like Izzy and Shalene and all the others. Taking on their fears and grief. And graduating. Through all of it, I didn't realize that in the chaos, something really remarkable was happening."

Drew nodded toward the path around campus, and we set off.

"It was a lot for me, too," Drew said. "I don't think I've ever been so disappointed in myself."

"Why?"

"I knew Josh loved you. I honestly thought he was getting better, that he was home that weekend I saw his family. Turns out, they were home talking to doctors about a transplant match. He was fighting for his life, and some friend I was. I saw an opportunity with you, and I took advantage of it."

"Josh had broken up with me," I said. "Before you and I even spoke to each other."

"Doesn't make what I did right."

"Doesn't make it wrong either," I argued.

"That's what Josh said."

"You talked to Josh about this?"

"I apologized," Drew said. "I worried that if you and I hadn't started things that you would have gotten back together with him without question."

"Probably," I admitted, and Drew's head drooped. "But that doesn't mean getting back with Josh would have been the right thing to do. Sometimes, no matter how much you don't want it to be true, life changes us. Decisions are made, and you can't go back." It had taken me a long time to understand that.

Drew slipped his hand into mine and turned me toward him. "Is that what happened with us?"

I rested my free hand against his chest, feeling his heart beat fast, and gazed into his intense eyes.

"No," I whispered.

His lips twitched into a smile. "And now? I'm a senior in high school. You're a stunning college girl who lives an hour away."

"I used to obsessively plan things, but they never worked out right," I said. "Now I'm trying to just live in the moment."

A raindrop splatted onto my cheek. Then another. Within seconds, the sky opened and poured on us.

"Of course," Drew said, laughing and pulling me under a nearby tree, still thick with yellow leaves.

"The rain does like us," I joked, squeezing water from my hair.

He grinned and leaned back against the tree trunk. I inched closer to him, my heart racing with possibility. Drew tipped my chin upward and rested his forehead against mine. I closed my eyes.

"The way you kissed me when you left camp …" He sucked in a breath. "I thought about that. A lot."

"Me, too," I said.

"I should have come after you."

"Maybe we needed that time to figure things out."

"Yeah?"

"Depends, I guess," I said. "What have you figured out in the last two months?"

In response, he kissed me. The rain trickled through the leaves and branches, dripping onto us. I shivered in the late fall air, and Drew pulled me into his warmth. He ended the kiss with another peck on my cheek.

"Elle? What did you mean when you said something remarkable was happening this summer?"

"You were there," I teased.

"I was, but that doesn't mean I know what you were thinking."

"I was falling in love with you," I whispered.

Drew squeezed me closer and kissed me so hard I had to hold onto him to keep from falling. When he pulled away, he grinned at me and asked, "Does this mean you're my girlfriend?"

I laughed until he joined me. "You're something else."

He shrugged.

"Do you want me to be your girlfriend?"

"More than I want to hit a ten-point shot from sixty yards, and I want that a lot."

"Archery comparisons? That's how you're wooing me?"

"I'm serious. I've been working on that shot for weeks. And yes, that's exactly how I plan to woo you."

"What if I agreed to be your girlfriend *and* taught you how to hit the shot from sixty yards?"

He smirked. "It'd be my dream come true."

As the rain trickled through the leaves above us, I buried my fingertips into my new boyfriend's hair and kissed him like I'd been dreaming to for months.

Guess it was my time to make dreams come true.

ACKNOWLEDGEMENTS

I can't believe this is the final book in the Iron Valley Vikings series, at least for now. Never say never! Thank you to everyone who has read these books and supported my journey!

I started telling these stories with my alma mater, Valley High School, in mind. Familiar locations, memories, and friends influenced every one of the books. Writing the series was the ultimate nostalgia. Since the publication of Gridiron Girl, the teachers, administrators, parents, and students from the New Kensington-Arnold School District have been incredibly supportive. I can't thank you enough for embracing these stories and me as an alum. To all you Vikings, you were then and always will be my people. Vs up!

Too often, we emphasize the "next step" in sports. Athletes are preparing for middle school, then high school, then college, and then pros. In this book and in all of my sports stories, I aimed to celebrate the moments we might otherwise forget when we're striving for glory. While we love the glory, we can't forget that sports are about maintaining our health, building self-esteem and resilience, learning teamwork and discipline, embracing our passions and establishing life-long friendships. Playing sports and all that entailed saved me at a time of my life when I desperately needed saving. Thank you to the parents, coaches, boosters, and athletic administrators that make youth and high school sports possible.

To the children and teens who play sports—THANK YOU! Keep competing, and enjoy the magic of the moments. You will cherish the memories in years to come :)

Authenticity is paramount to me when I write. Thank you to

Chieftain Archery Club, especially Wendy Booth, for teaching me to shoot! Thank you to archer Dawn Houser for answering research questions quickly and often and for reading the story. Thank you to archers Christi Wilson, Wendy Booth, Teresa Michael, Cara Stoklosa, and Kat Wiles for reading the manuscript and troubleshooting scenes and language with me. Meredith and Isabella Carabin, thank you for graciously sharing your medical knowledge and experience.

Grief is something I've struggled with over the years, and it comes in many forms. I was honored to explore grief in this story and grateful to the Highmark Caring Place in Pittsburgh, and especially to Kevin Sunderman for offering me a tour of the facility and sharing his knowledge about how children navigate grief. Thank you, Kevin, for also reading the manuscript. Your insights enriched my story in powerful ways.

To be in the depth of a story makes it difficult to see its flaws. To my beta readers—thank you! I could not navigate this journey without you: Tara Creel, Megan LaCroix, Caitlin Lennon, and Abigail G. Scheg.

The team at Wise Wolf Books—thank you for believing in me and these sports stories! Publishing four books so quickly has been an experience to say the least. Thank you for pushing me to achieve this feat and for the support along the way. On to the next one!

Thank you to my readers! You are the absolute best. Keep buying or borrowing books, please! Review them and share on social media. You make this world of pretending possible, and writers the world over cannot thank you enough. I hope these stories empower and inspire you.

My family is my why. I love you! Thank you to my natural family and my found family for always lifting me up—my siblings, cousins, aunts, uncles, friends, and in-laws. My children are my biggest fans, and they humble me with their support every day. Thank you for being the best kids ever! To my husband and high school sweetheart, thanks for being there for me then and here for me now.

As Juliet said, "Parting is such sweet sorrow." Writers know how real their characters become; their lives are no longer fiction. Thank you to my Iron Valley Vikings for allowing me to explore your world, your passions, and your ambitions. "I shall say good night till it be morrow."

A LOOK AT:
ABOVE THE FOLD

From the author of the Iron Valley series comes a slow-burn romance in this captivating contemporary novel.

Carnivalesque is the perfect escape—if you can score an invitation and find its secret location.

The carnival boasts exhibits like glow-in-the-dark bumper cars, King's Court speed dating, a pitch-black maze you could get lost in forever, and thousands of teens—dressed up, in costume, and wearing Mardi Gras masks to protect their outward identities. At Carnivalesque, privacy is paramount. No cell phones. No press. No social media, which makes it the perfect scoop for seventeen-year-old journalist, Mackenzie Davis.

Mackenzie needs this story to get her journalism goals on track. She stalks through the forest to find the carnival thinking one night there and she'll have everything she needs to make her dreams come true, but she falls in love with the escapism and extravagance of Carnivalesque—that or Kierk, the guy who can get her backstage and knows the answers to all of her questions. With every exhibit and every flirtation, her pile of lies builds. As she gets closer to the story and to Kierk, she faces a choice she never thought her practical, career-focused self would have to make: her first love or her future? Unless… there is a way she can have both.

AVAILABLE JANUARY 2023

ABOUT THE AUTHOR

Tamara Girardi grew up playing sports with the neighborhood kids. Often the only girl, she loved nothing more than smashing a home run at the opportune moment or stealing the basketball from one of the guys and scoring two on a breakaway. In high school, she fell in love with the quarterback and played football in the back yard with him and his two quarterback brothers. Watching them play, she wondered, "What would it be like if they'd had a baby sister? Would she play quarterback, too?" And just like that, the idea for Gridiron Girl was born.

Also an academic, Tamara is an Associate Professor of English at HACC, Central Pennsylvania's Community College where she teaches creative writing, technical writing, composition, and literature online. She has a PhD in English from Indiana University of Pennsylvania and studied fiction at the University of St. Andrews in Scotland. Tamara also writes picture books.

She lives in a suburb of Pittsburgh, Pennsylvania with her husband and four adorably rambunctious children.

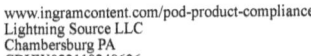